Praise for Carrie Fisher's THE BEST AWFUL

'Hilarious and original. The Best Awful's *account of a Hollywood mental breakdown is funny, perceptive, engaging, touching – without ever veering into sentimentality – and honest (though of course it's all entirely fictional)'*
HELEN FIELDING

'Ms. Fisher's most amusingly snarky book since Postcards from the Edge . . . *tartly funny, inviting readers to tag along on a wild manic ride'*
NEW YORK TIMES

'With her intimacy and insight, Fisher manages to bring that essential sense of me-too to a world of Hollywood excess, starfucking and therapy that none of us is ever likely to experience . . . a fascinating and grotesque insight into fame, from someone who has seen it from most angles. Fisher has earned a name as a clever and witty comic novelist with the ability to bring humour and insight to the grimmest of subjects'*
INDEPENDENT ON SUNDAY

'Fisher's best book since Postcards from the Edge . . . *her fondness for criminal wordplay is allowed to run rampant'*
SCOTSMAN

'Carrie Fisher's take on Hollywood is dark, hilarious and always entertaining'*
HARPER'S BAZAAR

'As in Fisher's debut Postcards from the Edge, *this fizzes with puns and wisecracks'*
MARIE CLAIRE

'A heartbreakingly funny, corrosive, blazingly honest novel'*
DAILY MAIL

'Wickedly funny'*
HEAT

'I'd been looking for a beautifully written, hilarious romp about mental illness for ages, and finally Carrie Fisher has come up trumps'*
GRAHAM NORTON

D1407352

Also by Carrie Fisher

Postcards from the Edge
Surrender the Pink
The Best Awful

Delusions
of Grandma

Carrie Fisher

POCKET
BOOKS

LONDON · SYDNEY · NEW YORK · TORONTO

First published by Simon & Schuster Inc, 1994
First published in Great Britain by Touchstone, 1994
This edition published by Pocket Books, 2005
An imprint of Simon & Schuster UK Ltd
A Viacom Company

1 3 5 7 9 10 8 6 4 2

Simon & Schuster UK Ltd
Africa House
64–78 Kingsway
London WC2B 6AH

www.simonsays.co.uk

Simon & Schuster Australia
Sydney

A CIP catalogue record for this book
is available from the British Library

ISBN 0-6848-5803-7

Typeset in Sabon and Optima by
Palimpsest Book Production Limited,
Polmont, Stirlingshire

Printed and bound in Great Britain by
Cox & Wyman Ltd, Reading, Berkshire

*To Chana and the late, great Jules
and my bona fide Billie Catherine*

Oh, little girl,
my string bean,
how do you grow?
You grow this way.
You are too many to eat.

What I want to say, Linda,
is that there is nothing in your body that lies.
All that is new is telling the truth.
I'm here, that somebody else,
an old tree in the background.

– Anne Sexton,
'Little Girl, My String Bean, My Lovely Woman'

I know that it is all
a matter of hands
Out of the mournful sweetness of touching
comes love
like breakfast

– Anne Sexton, 'The Fury of Abandonment'

*T*he Chinese have a curse, 'May you live in interesting times.' As curses went, Cora felt that this was truly the best she'd ever heard. Not that she was particularly fond of curses, but in her opinion this one was eminently applicable, far superior to the generic 'Go to hell' or the cheery 'Break a leg' or even the medieval 'A pox on your house.' For many years, she had thought that this first, favorite curse had actually gone, 'May you have an interesting life,' and she had liked that version also, but then, an interesting life didn't encompass as large a radius as these interesting times. A single interesting life didn't necessarily include drive-by shootings and carjackings and riots. Such were the times that Cora lived her interesting life in – times with unpopular verdicts and cults and cinders floating down from the sky. Cora's life was a much smaller affair, surrounded on all sides by these ever-darkening, incomprehensible nights and days.

And then there was the thing where the Chinese character for 'crisis' was also the character for 'opportunity.' The way Cora understood it, you didn't even have to turn it upside down for it to fly. What doesn't kill you makes you stronger. Or as her friend Noel, the dermatologist, liked to say, 'What doesn't kill you makes you look really, really bad.' Breakfast cereal for the nuclear age – if you survived, you would not only glow in the dark, but a fun sort of fierceness would protect you, even from yourself.

In any event, if she'd understood the night she saw

Arsenio interviewing Sally Jessy Raphael – if she'd been able to interpret that as some kind of omen – perhaps she would have done things differently. Talk show hosts interviewing other talk show hosts. Many held this to be one of the twelve signs that the world is ending – ending or interesting, Cora couldn't determine which. She remembered thinking at the time that when talk show hosts begin interviewing one another, someone or something somewhere is being rendered obsolete. The audience, say.

But by then she was pregnant and it was becoming increasingly complicated to pursue a line of thought – much less to catch an optimistic fish on the end of it. She felt that her brain had, in effect, melted and slid into her swelling neck. 'The trouble with getting introspective when you're pregnant,' she said to her friend Bud, 'is that you never know who you might run into.' This was one of her meager attempts to transmute her pregnancy into some form of entertainment. For Cora, gestation was threatening to become a frightening, humorless, ill-prepared romp toward what would most likely turn out to be a lifelong bout with a kind of maturity that wouldn't exactly lend itself to her brand of joy. But that didn't stop her from attempting to fashion for others a cheap laugh from what was conventionally an intimate experience.

Cora was beginning to experience the gnawing apprehension that somehow, and soon, she, too, would be rendered obsolete. The beast of her beauty, which she had formerly led around by the leash, would break free of her grasp and bound away, leaving her attempting to be interesting as hell. Already so many things seemed so very beside the point that even if she were able to determine how and why she'd gotten here, the here where she'd arrived was long past the point of no

2

return, just outside of wedlock, straight past help, and precariously near death. Things had taken root beside the point, things with ugly, leering faces.

It was important not to focus on these disquieting details. Cora forced her mind back to the poem she'd been doodling:

The writing on the uterine wall
Was a childish, albeit musical scrawl,
It kept time and company with a dividing double-
    timing cell
Quick crocheting a creature I would come to
    know well.

She frowned, dissatisfied, then returned to her more pressing tasks.

She packed her suitcase carefully, then stood for a moment and rested. She passed her hand over the slow, warm curve of her abdomen, where Ray's baby lay. The curve was as yet very slight indeed – most likely it had already existed before pregnancy. But already Cora saw herself as infinitely, incredibly larger, unbearably more exhausted and irritable and miserably ill-suited and ill-prepared for the role she was about to undertake.

Even though it was generally accepted that you pressed your genitals together with someone and after a stretch of time and considerable discomfort a tiny human was born, in her heart she could not believe it was so. That babies were a result of sex. It was simply too strange to be true. Like tornadoes and tide pools and pearls found in oysters, it must have to do with some inexplicable deep-sea magic, the way waves curled or stars fell or the haunting faraway music of the spheres – there was simply no earthly way that fetuses could be formed from intercourse. No intercourse she'd had, anyway.

Cora sighed and closed the suitcase, pausing briefly to look around the hotel room. A wave of nausea swept over her. She stared at the ceiling to steady herself and began to compose another poem:

> Someone summered in my stomach,
> Someone's fallen through my legs.
> To make an infant omelet
> Simply scramble sperm and eggs.

She lifted her bag and stepped into the living room. She paused at the bedroom door opposite and knocked.

'Hello?' a male voice called hesitantly.

'It's me,' announced Cora. 'The expectant mother. I'm ready to roll.'

Dear Esme,

I suppose I ought to mention at the outset that the reason I chose the name Esme was . . . well, the fact is, I don't have a good reason. It's just that what you come to discover about babies' names is that everyone has incredibly strong ideas about virtually every one you come up with. I mean, it's either the name of the gym teacher they hated or some despicable criminal (Jeffrey or Adolf or Ted, for example). Everyone gives you these books of names, which explain the origins of the proposed handles – English, Greek, Indian, etc., and then, infuriatingly, tell you what they mean. Though the only ones I can remember at this point are Penny (bobbin maker), Carol (little man), and Brendan (stinky hair). That one really kills me – I mean, who's gonna name a child after an extremely awkward characteristic that might even, God forbid, turn out not to be temporary? I guess

4

it's better than going all out and actually naming the poor kid Stinky Hair. What about Vomitsalot or Weird-Looking Ass? I think your father's name means 'twig' or 'clearing in the meadow.' Some sad, picturesque Welsh thing.

Anyway, I always liked the name Esme. My friend Cliff says it sounds like a noise your nose makes – so I suggested naming you simply Sounds Like a Noise Your Nose Makes. I guess it is a little embarrassing that the main way people remember it is the Salinger story, and that there isn't really a nickname for it. The whole name that I picked for you was Esme Bing Beaudrilleaux. The Bing part because bing in Chinese means double happiness (and, as it turns out, is also a popular firecracker). Besides, it just seemed to rhythm out right. Of course you never know. At the last minute, I could just up and name you Little Nancy – Little Nancy Girl for short.

I hope to write you all sorts of pithy, succinct advice to help you to move through the world easily – not without a care in the world, but a care so far away in the world, perhaps, that it has another area and dress code. (By the way, I never used the word perhaps before I was pregnant. Perhaps it's a hormonal thing.)

I am resigned to the fact that you will like your father better than you'll like me. Hell, for a long time I liked him better than me – and that was after living with him the better part of a year, which doesn't exactly endear people to you as a rule (ask around). I'm childish enough for this to be an issue for me, but stoic enough to plan on accepting it over time. My two dogs, Stella and Jim, whom I've had for over ten years, came to prefer him to me. He just has this – I don't know how best to express it – this 'way with people,' as they say. All I can say is that dogs and infants rarely lie. Of course, this could also be because they can't speak.

In any event, should I turn out to be one of the few First World women to die in childbirth, as my mother has predicted – my friend Bud likes to say she suffers from delusions of grandma – I thought I ought to (A) point out that I was the parent to spare and (B) leave some notes for your father and his compliant new wife to give you when you come of age (i.e., when you begin to find things amusing and quirky and not numbing and alien as I did, particularly toward what turned out to be the end). Things I meant to have mentioned to you well before you were five. Be that as it may – and it looks as though it might – I remain, as long as possible,

Your ever-lovin' mama,
Cora

E veryone out in Los Angeles huddled around the film industry as though it were a fire, stoking it with screenplays and starlets and deals. And the fire made you hot, depending on how close you could get to its center, how consistently you could string out your name or image with a recent hit. People behaved like heat-seeking missiles, and they would attach themselves to you as long as you were warm and glowing, as long as your name was the right size to fit over a marquee or at the bottom of a contract. They would walk by your side and bask in your recognition as long as you were recognized. As long as you were in your glory, they were in it, too. It was a strange sort of criterion for choosing your intimates – the idea being that if you knew enough people who were the right kind of upwardly mobile, you would be slimed by their success, would slither rapidly upward with them. Soliciting success, making yourself somehow necessary to those whom, for one reason or another, people wanted to see – it was a higher order of opportunism, true, but what was wrong with wanting to do well? Or wanting those around you to do well – so that you could distort yourself up to their size. Success was regarded as infectious, just as failure would surely contaminate you. You needed fires lit under you and stoked.

Cora had grown up in a large, square house just outside Beverly Hills. Both of her parents worked in service to the film industry – some might even say they thrived. Her father was an art director and her mother a

7

costume designer. Neither smiled much in photographs, but both loved to have them taken.

Cora was aware of the more shallow, sinister aspects of what outsiders called Hollywood, its stereotypes, loathsome and alluring. In L.A., people were known instead of knowing, incendiary as opposed to insightful or incisive. Or, worst of all, incognito. For all of that, this transient place was home. The corner drugstore Morley's was gone, and Newberry's, the five-and-dime, had been replaced by an art gallery and a stationery store. But she was most aware of the constants, the topography. The parks she had driven by all her life but never strolled through. 'Downtown,' a place of violence and poverty – forbidden, remote, other. The sunny, smoggy, green place where she resided.

Cora rewrote films. She was brought in at the eleventh hour to 'polish' the dialogue or 'punch up' the scenes. If you thought of it as polishing, it seemed more genteel, having to do with taking the existing silvery scenes of speak and increasing their shine. Or, on the coarser hand was a glove – and it was no kid glove, it was there to attempt to knock a little more sense into the script. Bring out the characters, make them more defined, insightful, funny, compelling – in a word, make their conflict worth attending to for up to, but God forbid not beyond, two big-budget hours.

Cora found that writing suited her temperament, or rather kept her tempo. She lived with the sense of having to keep up with a quicker beat, able neither to slow nor stop, simply to crash without much warning, and in her own quiet way, burn. A captive of her own captivating quality, she stood behind it all stunned, a slave to commotion. She had long ago determined that since she was fated to play loud, she would work below a whisper; Cora would write.

8

First, tentatively, stories. Then, surer, plays, and finally a screenplay.

Unfortunately, she had gotten off to an extremely good start. That is to say, it filled her with unreasonable expectations. Or unfollowable expectations.

She had written a film for a very good director. It was based on a short story of hers that had run in *Interview*. The story was about an obsessive love affair, and the funny thing was that the obsessive love affair had been between her and the director, whose name was Vincent DiBiase. They had met and become lovers after he hired her to redecorate his house in the Hollywood Hills. So on a certain level she hadn't taken it seriously at all when he had gotten a studio to buy the story. Of course, the fact that Vincent was fairly well respected – he'd won an Oscar early in his career and had since been nominated for another – didn't entirely slip her mind, but she kept it rather away. After all, most of the time these things came to nothing. Someone wrote a book or a story and it was snapped up by a well-known director or producer, even perhaps one who had been nominated for an Oscar. Or, God forbid, someone who knew the formula for achieving commercial, if mixed-reviewed, success. A script would be written, a buzz would be sounded, followed by very little fury. Sometimes a star got attached for a couple of months while a script doctor attempted to nurse the thing toward passable, green-lit health – but alas, in the end, it was all just scripts passing in the night.

But strangely, in Cora's case, this scenario was not spun. Her story was purchased by a studio when she was twenty-seven and still working part-time in interior design. She was hired as the screenwriter, paid scale, and given a deadline. In the bargain, she also got an agent and joined the Writers Guild. Vincent gave her a copy of Syd Field's *How to Write a Screenplay*.

'I can't write a screenplay,' she had moaned to him at the onset of these overwhelming intangibles.

'Listen, you couldn't be any worse at this than you were at decorating my living room,' he reassured her. 'But you finally got that right – though I've had a helluva time getting used to the wicker swing in the bedroom. And hey, who knew you could write – much less write a vaguely flattering portrait of me? I was moved, I admit it – to the degree that that's possible. Plus, the idea of committing our little peccadillo to celluloid for posterity intrigues me. Although, I must say, our prospects of finding a third act are fairly daunting.'

Cora shuddered. 'Well, if you're daunted, I'm fucked.'

'Daunted and Fucked – sounds like a vaudeville team. Anyway, at least that's a place to begin,' Vincent said brightly, clapping her on her hunched back.

So, privately calling their project *Daunted and Fucked*, Cora began the arduous task of adapting her story. She worked out something vaguely resembling an outline with Vincent – three acts, ten scenes per act, working by the book, Syd Field's book. She continued to work as an interior decorator, but she also continued to write. The act of writing – fits and starts and happy endings – tamed the beast, the big, unquiet bear that drove her. By the time Cora was thirty-two, she had written three screenplays and, with her partner, Bud, rewritten more than twelve others. She had married a man who looked like her father, and when that ended, she dated and slept with eleven men – give or take a man.

At the moment, Cora was basically at a standstill, manwise, somewhere between the next to come and the last to go. The last to go had been Charles, who was from the Caribbean and smelled like spice. His voice was so rich it made her feel impoverished, and grateful for the loan. He cooked dinner for her and his eight-year-old daughter, who put her hands up her father's shirt to warm them. Cora couldn't recall exactly what they discussed, only that each thing he said to her was spoken in a voice usually reserved for reading poetry by a blazing fire with a few close friends, including Richard Burton. After dinner, he walked her to the car, and there he kissed her. He kissed parts of her mouth she wasn't even aware she had. The Santa Anas blew the warm spice air all around them.

He called the next evening just past nine – his daughter's bedtime. Would she come spend the night?

Cora closed her eyes and considered. 'There are words for this,' she said. 'I can't remember them now, but there are. "Jumping the gun" comes to mind. I can't really remember the rest, but I'll work on it on my way over.' Having established that they would do no more than kiss and watch nighttime TV, she got into her nightgown and robe and grabbed her pillow. She hadn't been sleeping well, so just in case, she grabbed a loose sleeping pill from her bedside drawer.

Twenty minutes later, she arrived at his door. There he stood, his open shirt revealing a copper-colored chest. 'I remembered the other word,' she said. 'It's "premature." '

They kissed violently in the chair in front of the TV. A few hours later, they got into bed. Charles fell asleep easily, his body warm and near, one arm slung protectively over her. Cora was wide awake. She stole out from under his animal nearness and groped in her purse for the sleeping pill. She came upon the rogue item in the side pocket and retrieved it eagerly. But what she triumphantly clutched turned out to be a button. She tore apart her purse, but that was it – a button, a white button

11

from her bedside drawer was all she had to put herself to sleep. She stayed awake until three-thirty, watching movies she had seen hundreds of times before on cable while Charles slept noisily beside her, his spicy body burning in the dark.

He awakened her at ten to seven in order to get his daughter off to school. She drove home in the dawn, exhausted, leaving the telltale white button on the dark blue carpet near his bed. The corners of her mouth were cracked and raw as she headed down Mulholland, a layer of smog hanging over the basin below.

He called her the following night, but this time she avoided him. His smoothness overshadowed the spicy warmth. Another phrase finally came to her – 'cart before the horse.' He called her several more times from Toronto, where he was editing a film. He couldn't wait to see her when he returned. In the end, in a fit of cowardice, she changed her phone number and let it go at that.

Cora must not have recognized Ray at first as the person she would soon be seeing all the time. She had been raised to mistrust men generally and lawyers specifically. But lately she had begun to mistrust her impulses, so that she approached those she'd been taught to resist and resisted those she might normally approach.

'Are you seeing anyone?' was a phrase she enjoyed – it implied that there are people you see and people you hear. And those you saw, you dated. The rest you experienced by phone. God forbid you saw and heard someone simultaneously, that way pregnancy lies.

Apparently she'd met Ray before at one or two parties. These meetings neither could recall. But then maybe that was good news. People she remembered meeting

12

frequently turned out to be the ones she'd be better off to forget.

Recently, this was happening a lot, though, her inability to notice or recall when someone had arrived in her life. Maybe she'd continue to grow more and more forgetful with each moment, until the present itself would elude her like a fleeing convict, a passing fancy, the words to a childhood poem. Cora hoped that she could gradually accelerate the process until she would forget things before they happened, so that the future would effectively slip her mind along with the misbegotten past. Sometimes she thought that everything in time was frozen and you simply warmed it into reality when you ran into it, thawing thoughts and feelings as the events blazed all around you, the only difference between the ebbing then and the flowing now being temperature. So remembering and recognizing and ESP and déja vù actually warmed what was around them with premonition, perception, or memory, and yes, sometimes you even found yourself in a multidimensional world. Unless, of course, none of this was true, which was quite often the case with Cora's endless theories.

Another theory was that her voice had somehow swallowed her and trapped her underneath it, burying her with her own words. So that if she were to say, 'Help, please come get me – follow the sound to its source, track me to the end of my voice' – right where the bright sound ended you would find her, under a heap of communicated feelings. The talk was effectively a map to bring you to her. Listening with something other than your ears, you would be able to break the code of all her chat.

So Cora was waiting to see who would spring her from her trap of talking, whom she would find tangled up in her web of words – who would break her sound barrier.

13

Waiting, done at really high speeds, will frequently look like something else. Maybe that's what Ray was doing when Cora first met him, but it's futile to speculate – those moments are gone forever. But lackluster as the initial glance that passed between them may have been, it was closely followed by a careful scrutiny across an enormous variety of foods.

She first remembered seeing him in her kitchen. Consequently she connected him powerfully with nourishment, with food. That, she knew, is how they hypnotize you. Men arrange themselves among a variety of tastes, they gratify one appetite with the hope that it will open a door to the other – nudged inward with a hurled, half-eaten steak.

She felt him notice her when she was talking. She rhapsodized in his scrutiny, flourished under his gaze. The following day when he called, she tuned her eagerness down to pleased, to pleasing. 'How did you get my number?' she asked, settling back into her pillows.

'I just kept calling different combinations of seven digits – I have to say it was fairly time-consuming.'

She laughed. 'But worth it?' she asked lightly.

'Mmmm – that depends on whether you'll have lunch with me tomorrow.'

'More food.'

'What?'

'This'll be the second time I've seen you around food. Never mind – it doesn't matter. Where do we meet?'

They ended up meeting at Thai Me Up, a restaurant in Westwood Cora had suggested, more for the chicken *satay* than the name. The night before, she'd dreamt that she was trying to feed a baby – her baby – peanut butter. She didn't know that it was wrong. She'd been dreaming about babies a lot lately. Babies and spiders and socks.

Cora arrived late and smoking. She was ashamed

14

that she smoked, but the shame only made her want to do it that much more. A baby was at the next table. Cora stubbed out her cigarette, flushing and glancing apologetically at the parents of the lovely, drooling child.

'Sorry I'm late,' she said, taking the seat across from Ray, feeling more like his hapless chess opponent than his date. He wore a well-tailored suit that was unabashedly becoming. Smoke from her discarded cigarette clung to his smooth jacket like fog on a lake.

'That's okay,' he assured her. 'Do you want a drink?' Cora brushed her hair off her face distractedly, peering into the endless green ovals of his eyes. 'A Coke.'

Ray signaled the waiter, ordered her beverage, and asked for menus. The baby at the next table began to cry. Cora leaned forward. 'I always think when they do that they've just found out about mortality,' she whispered. 'That it's just hit them. The horror of it.' She wiped her clammy palms on her skirt, in an effort to smooth herself. Smooth herself like him.

Ray's face furrowed briefly. 'Do you remember finding out about that?' he asked earnestly. 'That you were going to die? Not you, particularly – everyone.'

Cora raised her eyebrows in mock astonishment. 'Am I? God, if I'd known that, I would've worn something completely different.'

Ray laughed, lowering his head as if to conceal the startling white of his teeth. 'Well, you don't have to die,' he said, tucking his teeth back under his full upper lip. 'Not if you get a good lawyer.'

Cora smiled and felt a rush of relief. Lunch was going to be all right. Maybe everything was going to be all right. Maybe their baby would have Ray's eyes and wear suits, smoothly holding the air at bay all around him, obedient and sweet.

Or maybe none of this would happen and she'd get crushed in an elevator, incinerated in a plane crash, and no one would care. Not really.

She stared at Ray's long, ringless fingers; his pale, careful hands; his straight, dark eyelashes. He made a minor vocabulary error and she inwardly, magnanimously forgave him. He told her that he was an entertainment lawyer, and she almost forgave him that, too. She couldn't imagine him sweating. He said he came from the South, admired William Faulkner, had never really been in love. She told him of her ex-husband, how they'd tried to have a child before he left her. Ray nodded gravely. 'He couldn't step up,' he remarked sadly. The term confused her. 'You know, make a commitment, take the next step. Go to the next phase.'

'Ah,' she said, nodding, really only half-seeing, as she inhaled his cologne and wondered how he'd made it to twenty-eight without having loved someone, without 'stepping up' himself.

The baby next to them threw up all over the table. 'A sign of good fortune,' Cora declared.

'Or bad food,' proposed Ray, signaling for the waiter.

Cora had several early memories of her and Ray in restaurants waiting for another course to arrive, another food to pursue, to see if things were right enough with them to continue. Wait at high speeds and see. They ate together in a variety of places. His teeth seemed to her very even and very white. Once he wore suspenders. His hair was gold and thinning.

One Sunday Cora's friend Cliff called to ask her to a screening and dinner at his house. Actually, he claimed he'd asked her weeks ago, but it was possible he was only pretending that he had, to put her on the friendly defensive, so that he could say, 'Come. What are you doing anyway? So?' His voice grew pleased and teasing – 'So, sweetheart, is this a date? Is he cute?' And then commanding, charming – 'Look, just bring him, come early so we can talk.'

Cliff was an extremely successful entrepreneur who was better at getting what he wanted than anyone else Cora knew. It was as though other considerations or obligations didn't make sense to him. He had a plan, a desire, a fixed point of opportunity, and he removed anything that lounged between him and his very best-laid, impossibly well-paid plans. He wanted with a will so powerful that once he put his mind to something, armies couldn't move it, it clung like white on rice.

Cora had known Cliff for most of her professional life. He was a good person to know if you were in a profession of any kind, so successful was he at everything he endeavored to do. Cora didn't so much like him

17

because he was successful, she loved him because he was a relentless communicator, he thought in his mouth. You arrived at his conclusion with him – right on time or even a little before. He loved language and Cora loved it with him. He went at it with her, forehead to forehead, always in an effort to get to the bottom of things. Perceptive, intense, dangerous, he attacked everything he felt or thought with both barrels. Cora loved to hear him blaze. 'Why are we so crazy?' he would ask her, without waiting for a reply, or, 'Honey, is everyone as crazy as us?'

He once advised her to go to bed early 'because everything bad happens to you at night.' Ever since he was twenty-nine, he had gone to bed at ten-thirty and gotten up before seven to talk to New York, read the papers, and eat an egg. He was very protective of Cora – always defending her when any relationship tragedy befell her. 'Look Cora, I am your warrior. I am a six-gun at your side – but you must be careful how you use me.'

'What do you two talk about all the time?' Bud would ask her jealously. But Cora couldn't remember. 'Maybe it's because we so frequently agree. We pile hurried insight upon insight, gossip disguised as psychological analysis, until someone's phone rings or he has to go to sleep.'

Bud nodded. 'He hates me, right?'

Cora rolled her eyes. 'He doesn't hate you. He finds you desperate and a little too butch.'

'Ah,' exclaimed Bud merrily. 'Well, that's okay then.'

All the biggest had begun like Cliff – ruthless and warm and glad. Access was everything, unless you didn't know how to use it properly. Which was Cora's little claim to fame. She had started early, somehow intuitively knowing the people whom a lot of people would later want to know for other reasons. She used to like to

18

say she knew all the right people in all their wrong ways. It still counted for something, Cora's coterie of intense acquaintances. But what Cora had been drawn to in surrounding herself with a pack of powerful pals was their complexity, their indefatigable overalertness and their sprawling, mauling expertise. Theirs was a kind of strip expertise – no matter how many layers they slithered out of, they always had something on.

Cora hoped Ray would fit in with Cliff's crowd, but she wasn't exactly sure what it was she wanted him to fit into. Anyway, she was leaving for Paris the next day, for a month. She and Bud were doing a rewrite on a cable film. It was the last time she would be able to see Ray until she was sure she wanted to see him again.

Cliff's house was on the beach, which was hard to forget as the ocean was lit by floodlights and visible from every room. An Edward Hopper painting of a house lit by honey-colored sunlight hung over the fireplace, which was blazing behind a thick plate of glass. The furniture was white and spare on light wooden floors. Cliff was wearing his usual white T-shirt and jeans with fairly new tennis shoes and affordable socks, impossibly white. An English butler, also named Cliff, served drinks on a silver tray. There were sketches on several walls by an English artist whose name Cora always forgot. She asked Cliff to remind her.

'Hockney,' he replied briskly. 'So, sweetheart, you look terrific. Look at you.' He held her at arm's length.

Cora flushed. 'Stop,' she said, looking around with some alarm for Ray, who seemed to be examining a photo album of Cliff's fortieth birthday on the custom-made stone coffee table near the fire.

Cliff drew her toward him conspiratorially. 'So, sweetheart – he's adorable. Have you done it yet?'

19

Cora hit him on his tanned bicep. 'Get out of here,' she said in a low voice. 'I barely know him.'

He laughed and fluffed her hair. 'So?' he replied. 'Don't wait until you know him too well – that could spoil everything.' Cora nudged him as Ray squinted in their direction. Cliff the butler announced that dinner was served.

She was nervous for Ray among all Cliff's assembled people. Marshall Klein, the head of Brandeis Corporation, one of the most lucrative recording studios in the world, was there, with his longtime wife, Sheila. So was Curtis Freiburg, the chairman of Majestic Studios, and the clothing czar Morris Westin and his new wife, Patty. But Ray seemed to do so well around food that she gradually noticed that she needn't worry at all. It was as though nourishment were a sort of talisman for him, and then there was the business of his hair shining like gold florins.

They shared a large white upholstered chair during the movie, which gave them an enormous amount of proximity to contend with. Cora had worn a tight little black dress – the kind she would never be able to wear again. She kept pulling her skirt down toward her knees to show Ray that she was at least conservative in some departments. Generally departments that didn't involve talk.

Her skin came alive under the flat of his hand on her back. She gazed at the black-and-white image on the screen and made a concerted effort to put her skin back to sleep under his palm. They sat there in the darkness, sharing the chair as if they had done it countless times before, instead of never. Cora hadn't even admitted to herself that this was a date they were on. She hadn't yet fine-tuned their configuration to that frequency.

'A man needs a little madness or else . . . or else he

may never get the strength to cut the rope . . . and be free.' The film they saw that night was *Zorba*, and Cora never forgot that line. It was what instigated all the music and dancing and brought the entertainment effectively to a close, and it was the first song she was aware of hearing with Ray.

Cliff and Ray shook hands warmly as they parted company. 'Thanks, Clifton,' said Cora, kissing him. 'I'm going out and cutting the rope.'

Cliff looked at her. 'Yeah,' he said dryly. 'But then we'd have to do that stupid dance, and I look horrible in cutoffs.'

Cora nodded sympathetically. 'You may have a point.'

Ray and Cora passed into the cloudless Malibu night. She bumped into him as they made their way down the steps and felt a minute twinge of embarrassment that he might sense that he was attractive to her. Some parliament of her pheromones had just named him pope, and she was doing all she could to keep her cardinals from sending up the telling puff of white smoke from her hair. It took an enormous amount of energy to conceal these facts from him. These facts about her sexual feelings. But to conceal is the most effective, popular method of revealing. It always gives away the suppressed pope smoke, the deciding vote.

Her black heels clicked on gray flagstone as they headed to Ray's practical car. His hands were buried deep in his khaki trousers.

'You and Cliff have known each other how many years?'

Cora crinkled her nose. 'Fourteen?' she said uncertainly. 'Sixteen.' She laughed. 'He wanted to be straight with me.'

Ray opened the passenger door and Cora slid in. He got in and started the car. 'What does that mean?'

21

Cora leaned her head back and smiled. 'It meant that I was the new girl in the city and a lot of these powerful men decided they wanted to go out with me. Partly because they all knew each other, and these were very competitive males. One of them likened the situation to this story about a Baron Von Theisen and some Bible. Apparently a very rare Bible was coming up at auction, and the wealthy baron was anxious to add it to his collection for not too enormous a sum. So he phoned all the other collectors he assumed would be interested and talked the Bible down. Said it was a fake, that it was damaged – whatever he needed to do to call into question its true value. I don't remember whether he got it at a discount or even got it at all. But supposedly there was a parallel to the situation between these men and me. Maybe they all called one another and said I was deeply flawed, and young. Anyway, I was very impressed with these guys. I mean, I hadn't actually gotten it together to want to meet a lot of them, much less date them. And Cliff was one of them.'

Ray nodded thoughtfully. 'But he was gay.'

She smiled. 'He used to say that he liked men for sex and women for relationships. But I was very intimidated by these men. I mean, they were very accomplished and bright. I wanted to be around them and I couldn't understand why they wanted to be around me. Oh, I was cute and everything, but I figured they just wanted to sleep with me. And once I either did or didn't, they would gradually drift away. I used to work so hard to be smart and witty for them. Anyway, Jesus, you just asked me how long I knew Cliff, right? I've known him almost half my life. More than half of yours.'

She felt self-conscious about the minor disparity in their ages. She figured that even if they were the same age, she'd end up looking worse first. She would be test-driving imminent decades years before he even glimpsed the taillights. What was the phrase? Younger women make older men look younger, while younger men make older women look . . . silly. Maybe it was 'feel silly.' In all likelihood, this wasn't a saying at all and was just an articulated terror of Cora's.

'I love to talk to him,' she said dreamily as she gazed out the window at somebody jogging down the center of San Vicente. Sam Cooke sang softly on the radio and Ray kept the beat on the steering wheel with the inside of his thumb. Cora gazed at his well-honed profile. He felt her eyes on him and looked at her, streetlights glinting off his glasses. 'What?' he said, squirming happily.

'Nothing,' she said, looking out the windshield. 'Thank you for taking me to that thing, that's all. I didn't realize until we got there that they would all be checking you out to see if you were – well, checking you out. I guess you're not supposed to do that until you really and truly are seeing one another, you know? Now they'll all call me tomorrow and say, "*So,* what's going on with you two? He's *cute.* How long have you guys been together?" ' She hit her forehead with the palm of her hand. '*Oy.*'

'So what will you say?' asked Ray quietly, while Sam Cooke held the vibrato of his last note.

Cora stifled a practically authentic yawn. 'Tomorrow I'm going to Paris, remember? They'll either have to call you or work it out amongst themselves.' Ray smiled a smile involving arched eyebrows. 'Gee, thanks,' he said ironically. A police car sped by and disappeared around the bend.

They pulled into her driveway. Ray stopped the car and stared through the windshield, waiting for further instructions, for the sexual shoe to drop.

'If I lived here, I'd be home now,' she offered feebly.

His hand swept the curve of the steering wheel, as if to give it one last brush before it was bronzed. He cleared his throat.

'I'm not good at this,' he confessed in a low voice.

'Driving?' she guessed. 'Not at all – I actually felt you had a real knack for it.'

He smiled, shaking his head. 'I'm fresh out of knacks,' he insisted softly, and then, 'You know what I mean.' He looked at her, then away.

She leaned toward him, her face drenched in shadows, just the way she liked it. All over the world at this moment, people were doing unspeakable things to one another. 'Every five minutes, seventy-three women are raped in America, six point five men die of AIDS, and two thousand forty babies are born with birth defects,' she intoned solemnly. 'So why don't we contribute to a sunnier statistic?' She leaned in and kissed him. His lips and tongue were cool and slow, as if he were memorizing her mouth, preserving it for later when it was off at the end of a sentence somewhere in France. One hand cupped her shoulder dumbly, like a banister. He drew back and peered at her as though to place her.

'Get out of the car,' he said gently, imploringly. She blinked in astonishment. Then she realized he meant it as a compliment.

Cora watched Ray back down her drive and wave before he turned into the street. She stood with a small smile playing on her mouth and stepped out of her high heels, picked up one in each hand, and turned toward her home. A light was on in her kitchen and she moved toward it, feeling warm and wanted. Feeling silly. She pushed the door open and found Bud standing at the kitchen counter eating a piece of fried chicken, grease covering his mouth and fingers.

'Hey,' he said, licking his thumb and forefinger, 'who's the guy in the car?'

Cora dropped her bag and shoes on the bright linoleum floor and crossed to the open refrigerator. She gazed into its depths. 'The lawyer,' she answered finally, removing a raspberry Jell-O and crossing to get a spoon.

Bud frowned, his forehead shiny in the light. 'What lawyer? Did we talk about this?' Cora was about to answer when Bud suddenly brightened. 'Oh, yeah, the guy from lunch. Okay, okay, I'm up to speed now. So, what happened? Is it happening or – wait, we aren't supposed to like lawyers, are we? Or is that like an eighties thing?'

She laughed and patted him on the arm, leaving the spoon in her half-eaten dessert. 'We're not supposed to like anyone,' she reminded him poignantly. 'That's our tragic plight.'

He cocked his dark head to one side, pouting his ample mouth to comical effect. 'Oh, Caesar,' he said, hugging her side, 'I'm so glad you're home. I heard a good one today – wanna hear?'

She laid her head on his tattooed arm. 'What?' she said softly, breathing his musty scent.

'What are the saddest two words in the English language?'

She smiled into the curve of his arm and waited.

'What party?' he intoned, laughing his breathless, squeaky laugh, his shoulders shaking. 'It's good, no?' he insisted brightly.

'Yup,' she conceded. 'If we didn't work together, I'd steal it.'

Bud, like Cora, was a screenwriter. In fact, they had met at a screenwriting workshop in 1983. They soon fell into a routine of unofficially working together on their separate projects, and finally they hired out as a team. When they weren't together, they spoke on the phone at least twice a day. Every few months, they drove up to Santa Barbara to work at Bud's mother's place. As his visits grew more and more frequent, Cora gave Bud a clicker to her gate and a key to her house. He kept an assortment of towels there, which were his required writing garb. After a while, he would stay overnight or 'slumber,' as he referred to it, as in, 'Maybe I'll come by Friday and slumber. Okay, Caesar?'

After several months of this, they awoke in the middle of one night and moved together for a protracted four a.m. soul kiss. Like two people drawn together through a common tragedy, they wordlessly wrapped themselves around each other and kissed themselves back to sleep. It was as though they dreamt it.

When Cora was young, she had thought it was impossible to feel pain underwater. In a similar way, the interlude with Bud, surrounded by sleep, did not seem to abide by the laws of waking sensuality. They had stolen across the borders of friendship into a lawless underwater world of half-conscious, semicarnal kissing, briefly trespassed there, then ventured back, virtually unscathed. She woke before he did, fed the dogs, and showered. They were in her backyard, writing, by ten-thirty. It was an isolated incident and they never spoke of it.

So far, Bud had had three films made, two released. The first he'd written with his girlfriend Mona Stulen, a woman ten years his senior who took every opportunity to talk about her ex-husband or tell long, exhausting anecdotes about Tolstoy. He moved in with her and they stayed together on and off for the next seven years. The relationship eventually disintegrated, but it set in motion Bud's propensity for crazy older women.

Unfortunately, Bud was not able to have casual relationships. He simply wasn't a casual person. Not only wasn't he a casual person, he was a bipolar person. That is to say, he was a manic-depressive person, which is to say he had been on lithium for well or unwell over ten years. Actually, it had been more or less well. He drew distinctions, made comparisons, lived with contradictions, struggled with opposites.

The only problem was that the lithium made him forgetful. Or maybe he simply was forgetful, and his forgetfulness was infectious, causing his lithium to forget what exactly it was supposed to do. It was meant to inhibit mood, but instead, every so often it made its way over to a little parcel of memory and swallowed it whole.

Once at a party, he'd been standing talking with a group of people and a girl came toward him, a pretty girl. She looked familiar, but then all pretty girls looked familiar to Bud – they looked like someone he was going

27

to know and fuck soon. Also, besides the memory thing, Bud had taken a lot of drugs – so there were various chutes this girl could've slid down. She was standing next to him now, smiling and nodding, and he was smiling back and nodding and finally he said, 'Do I . . . am I . . . supposed to know you?' Her face went flat, and boom – she turned and stormed away from him. So Bud went after her and they talked and it turned out Bud had lived with her for three months.

This was a story that Bud used to tell as funny, but now he was remembering less and less, and the story wasn't hauled out as funny anymore so much as scary.

'You remember Bryn?' Bud was saying as he helped himself to some two-day-old fried rice. 'You know, my first major girlfriend? Well, a couple of weeks ago I was talking to her and she said something about London and I said, 'What about London?' And apparently some incredibly emotional thing had happened between us in London and I had totally forgotten it and she was furious and hung up on me and wouldn't speak to me for days and finally I got her on the phone and told her about the trouble I've been having lately with my memory and I apologized and she softened and I begged her to tell me what happened in London and she did and we made up.'

'So?' said Cora.

'So what?'

'So, what happened in London?'

Bud stared at her. 'I forgot.'

Cora tried to comfort him. 'As we have discussed, you are not a casual person. You have an enormous number of very important, emotional one-night stands. It appears that you are forgetting emotional peak exchanges and one definite whole girl, complete with three-month cohabitation, correct?'

Bud nodded gravely. 'Correct.'

'Well, what I say is that you just have more of those things than most people and can afford to lose one or two. For these women, those are some of the high points of their lives, but for you, they're pretty routine experiences. Well, a lot of people forget routine experiences – hell, that represents a goal for millions.'

'Yeah, but I like a lot of these – what you call routine experiences.'

Cora shrugged. 'Well, you don't get to remember all the experiences you like. I doubt if I remember an eighth of mine. So I'm not terribly concerned for you. My grandfather's got real senility, okay? Last week he said to me, 'Vivian put the popcorn outside.' I said, 'Really? Why?' And he said, 'Safety precaution. But the noisemakers are in the living room.' Now that's someone with memory loss, okay? You're suffering from something more sinister on the one hand and less sinister on the other.'

Bud looked thoughtful for a moment. 'So are you really serious about this guy, or what?' he asked, his mouth full of rice. Cora sighed and started out of the kitchen, carrying her nightly glass of orange juice, her bag slung over her shoulder. Bud followed, take-out container in hand. 'Hey! Was that too heavy a question? Or should I phrase it another way?'

Cora stopped abruptly just shy of her bedroom, causing Bud to almost collide with her back. 'Look,' she began sternly, 'I don't want to discuss this with you if you're going to trivialize it. It's too soon for you to trivialize it. At this point he seems like this – I don't know – gentleman-type person. Like he's all this stuff I – well, maybe I encounter it, but God knows I'm not drawn to it. The joke is, he seems kind and patient and loving and decent and – oh, never mind, never mind.'

29

Bud looked crestfallen in the half-light of the hallway. Cora's television droned soothingly from the bedroom. 'Tell me,' he pleaded, wiping sweet-and-sour sauce from his chin and mouth. 'I promise to be well behaved.'

She sighed again. 'I can't believe he'd ever do the wrong thing. Which combined with his kissing skills is an unbeatable, unheard-of combination. I just wish he had a different job.' She turned and entered her room.

Bud cleared his throat. 'Did he try to finger-fuck you?' he asked innocently. Cora slammed the door in his face and locked it. 'Hey!' he cried mournfully. 'Wha'd I say?'

So Cora went to Paris, to do a four-week rewrite on a little cable movie. She wandered the streets, bag slung over her back, her eyes tearing from the wind, staring into shop windows and at the beautifully dressed Parisians, listening to church bells chime, darting through traffic as she made her way back to her hotel in the dusk. She was staying at the St.-Pierre on the Left Bank, nestled among the shops, the bakeries, *le drugstore*, St.-Germain. She worked in the mornings in the director's office on the set and spent her afternoons plotting how she would spend her salary – on Christmas gifts, fabric, clothes, antique music boxes sporting stuffed birds in stiff brocade dresses. She gazed at explosive floral arrangements wrapped in crisp cellophane, smelled the herbs in the dark shop whose shelves were filled with shampoos and soaps and scents made in the workshop in the back. Her pockets jingled with five-franc pieces and centimes and crisp franc notes. It was a wonderland for her.

'*Puis-je vous aider, madame?*'

Cora smiled. Can you help me? You have no idea how much. She scouted for purchases and doctored her script – a benign punishment to fit all the rewards she hoped to have tailored to her. Her toil was fairly trouble free. She befriended the Swedish director, Charlotte; the Dutch hairdresser, Paul; and Virginia, the costume designer from Alaska.

One afternoon, after a few days of jet lag and letting the city work its magic on her, she bought a beautiful

31

nightgown at the lingerie shop two doors down from her hotel, picked up a croissant and a Coke, and returned to her hotel. She removed the lacy satin finery, the indulgence, the unpardonable sin against the starving, the hopeless, the scarred for life or left for dead, and slipped it over her head. She popped open her soda, unwrapped her croissant, lay down on the bed, and lifted the telephone receiver. Finally she felt ready for Ray, knowing he wouldn't be prepared for her with the time change. He would either still be sleeping or have just recently rumpled into the world.

'Yeah,' his voice managed. Cora curled onto her side, cradling the phone to her ear, lullaby style. 'Hello,' she said, smiling, the pillow cool on her cheek.

'Hey.' He cleared his throat. 'Is that you?' he said sleepily.

'That depends. Which you would you have me be?'

He laughed. 'Cora. I've never said your name just as I was waking – I like it.'

'Are you flirting with me?'

'I guess so. I mean, if you think so, I must be. You're the word person.' He yawned.

'You're not?' she asked, rolling onto her back, giving him time to get where she needed him to be.

'I don't think so,' he answered. 'Not like you, anyway.'

'Does that mean I'll have to draw you out?'

'Mmmmm . . . definitely at this hour.'

'I'll have to come after you.'

'How do you do that?'

'I'll have you tell me stories.'

He laughed. 'That'll be a neat trick.'

'I don't know how neat it'll be,' she informed him. 'It's not as much fun if it's neat. In case you haven't noticed, I'm a messy person.'

'You're a busy person.'

'*Busy* being a synonym for *messy*, no?'

'I guess.' He was laughing again now. 'You can't expect me to have a conversation like this at seven a.m.'

'This isn't a conversation, it's a kiwi.'

She told him about the time she was sitting in her trailer on the set of her first movie, the one she'd written for Vincent DiBiase, working on the ending, when someone tapped at her door. 'Yeah!' she had called. '*Willkommen, bienvenu*, welcome, come on in!' The lead actor tugged her door open and poked his handsome head in. 'Could we have a . . . conversation?' he almost pleaded. Cora had laughed and moved her computer off her lap. 'You say 'conversation' as though it's some rare, exotic thing. Like it's a kiwi.'

'In this town, it is,' the actor had said.

'So,' Cora asked Ray, 'when can I expect you to have a kiwi like this?'

Ray paused. 'When you teach me,' he replied simply, hopefully.

At first they spoke every few days, then every other day, then if they missed a day, it was weird. Dusk was the easiest time to reach him, with the time difference. Her new dark was his new light. She liked knowing she could always find him, even if she couldn't have him for long. Although Cora liked to talk long. Really long.

'Cora, I've got a phone sheet three pages long – I could call you later. What time will you be up until?'

'Until you call,' she said stoically. 'Until I get my kiwi. No ticky, no washy – no kiwi, no sleepy.'

'Jeez, don't you ever get tired?'

'All the time. Tired doesn't have a thing to do with it.'

He was only truly beyond her reach at meals now – ironic, considering that food was the locus of all her initial associations with him. He also got taken hostage in conference calls. Or Brenda, his assistant, would say, 'He just went into a meeting,' as if it were a fit of sorts, or a trance.

'Get him out of the meeting,' Cora would urge. 'Turn on the fire alarm. Call in a bomb scare.'

'Is there something you want me to tell him?' Brenda would inquire gently.

'Mmmmm . . . not in English. Thanks.'

They went on this way, settling into something long on distance, close on comfort, short on lackluster, on Blixen. With phones cradled between shoulder and ear, faces turned sideways into their pillows, muffling the talk, they spread their histories out before one another like Middle Eastern traders tenderly unwrapping treasures – 'For you, special price.'

At first, he seemed reluctant, as though he'd never discussed these things in this particular way.

'Haven't you been in therapy?' she asked him one morning.

'Sort of,' he said. 'I just started a couple of months ago.'

'Well, what do you talk about there?'

'Mmm. . . . Well, you know . . . my childhood and all that. The thing is, he doesn't say much.'

'No kiwi?'

'No kiwi,' he said. 'You're the first person I've ever really kiwied with. This was . . . this is what I basically left South Carolina to find. I thought that somewhere in the world people actually talked to each other – but I never really found it until . . . this.'

'That's because you're so well-mannered,' she said softly. 'Somebody has to come and get you behind all those manners of yours to find out what you really think.'

'But doesn't it get incredibly exhausting, always saying what you think?'

'Oh, no,' she said rapturously. 'It can be one of the most exhilarating things in the world. Manners seem to me like they would be the tiring thing. Always running for office.'

She could feel him cringe all the way from Los Angeles. 'Is that what you think I'm doing?'

'Sure, sometimes. You shake hands and smile and nod and somewhere behind your face something else is going on. You have to be that way in your job, though, don't you? Schmoozing?'

'Ugh, I hate that word.' He shuddered. 'But then, so, why do you – '

'Kiwi with you?' she interrupted. 'Because . . . because most people bother me, and you . . . don't. There are things that happen between people you can't vote on – they begin sometime before you're aware they've started, and then they curl up and threaten to stay. I don't believe that you decide what you want, I think you discover what your imperatives are – what gives you pleasure – and then you figure how to get it, what it costs. And I don't just mean coinwise.' She paused. 'When I told my mother I'd gone on a date with a lawyer, I had to whisper it.'

'Why?' he asked, disconcerted.

''Cause in my house it was a very bad thing to be. My father was cheated by this lawyer and he lost a lot of money and all that. It doesn't matter. My point – if I can ever possibly achieve such a thing – is that every relationship is a compromise of something. And you just have to weigh whether what you're getting is worth what you're giving up. A relationship with me would be extremely unconventional at best – I mean, I'm not the most attentive woman in the world. I have this incredibly time-consuming job and am virtually unskilled in the ways of dotage. The tao of doting. I have what one of my many friends calls a big loud life.'

'Are you trying to warn me away from you?'

'I'm attempting to educate you in the ways of me, so you can best decide whether or not to keep this within the confines of telephones or move out into the world of – '

'I thought you said you couldn't decide things like that.'

She laughed, running her hand over her forehead and through her bangs.

'What?' he said. 'What's funny?'

'Nothing. We're having an A T and Tea party. Look,' she said, 'you can't decide about how you respond to me, but you can evaluate whether or not you want to deal with all the things I bring with me or that you might end up having to do without. Anyway, this is a lot of . . . figuring or whatever you want to call it after one kiss in a driveway and an extended phone schmooze.' 'It was a good kiss,' he said softly.

'Yes,' she said. 'It was.'

'So all I have to do is change jobs and put up with a lot of interference and inattention.'

'In a nutshell, yes.'

'You didn't say anything about nutshells,' he deadpanned. 'That I'll have to think about.'

She looked forward to his calls, came to count on them, and found that she could. He was prompt, reliable, earnest, patient, and interested. These sounded to her like the qualities of a good Scout, but there was a depth behind the scoutdom. A depth and a warmth and a joke. Making him, for her, the scoutmaster with a twist of lime and mayhem. She was such an exotic creature, obstinately quirky, mercurial, intense. She thought of something a friend of Bud's had said when Bud and Bryn split up. 'Yeah, well, you were both such exotic creatures, man. Like flamingos. And what's gonna happen when one of those pink kids gets sick? Who's got the medicine for the sick flamingos?'

It was as though Ray and she were keeping their relationship alive on life-support machines, curing the illness of low levels of physical intimacy, nursing their acquaintanceship through the disease of distance with their initial important impressions of one another. They were responsible about their almost daily dosages of doting. Halfway around the world alone in Paris, the city of romance or shopping or people who looked down on Americans or whatever it was, Cora felt Ray healing her flamingo, quieting it, soothing it outside of sleep. She stimulated his mind and he cared for her emotions – cared for her in such a quiet, conventional way that sometimes she held her breath, so that she could feel it stealing over her.

A week before she was due back, he asked her if she would accompany him to his office Christmas party. She considered carefully.

'Cora? Are you there?'

'I'm here. I'm just thinking. This isn't going to be one of those parties where people get drunk and Xerox their asses, is it?'

'Boy, your family really did a good job getting you to hate lawyers.'

'I was just thinking, though, that it was going to be weird seeing each other in person after being on the phone for so long in such an intimate sort of way. What

37

if we have an allergic reaction or something? I mean, we don't even know what we are, besides two people who have enjoyed an intense nonfrivolous flirtation long distance paid for largely by your company and spanning a short lifetime.'

'You have a real knack for complicating things, you know? All I was asking was if you wanted to go to this stupid little holiday party the night you get home, and you turn it into this Chinese puzzle. It's just that – well, I have to go to the party anyway, at least drop by, so that's all we'd really have to do. Otherwise I guess I wouldn't be able to see you until the next day.'

She closed her eyes and gripped the phone cord. 'Do I get a corsage?'

He laughed, relieved. 'Whatever you want.'

Cora yawned, pleased. 'I want a gardenia,' she announced. 'A gardenia, flamingo medicine, and an enormous bowl of kiwis.'

'Done,' he vowed. And she knew somehow it would be.

The night before her departure, she was up late with Charlotte and Paul and Virginia packing up all of her purchases when the phone rang. 'Uh,' exclaimed Paul in his pointed Dutch accent. 'It is the Carolina lawyer, I think.'

Cora made a face at him and picked up the phone, lighting a cigarette. '*Vous êtes sur la ligne,*' she pronounced in her half-assed *français*.

'I just thought,' he greeted her, as though they had been having one long conversation that was only bent but never broken, and so they could begin without beginnings, pick up where they less and less left off, 'I thought I might leave the office early and pick you up at the airport. I mean, if you didn't have other arrangements. Or even if you did.'

'Sort of for new times' sake.'

'Sort of.'

Cora blew a smoke ring toward her toe. 'You'll have to have a pretty big car,' she said. 'I did all my Christmas shopping. I may even have done somebody else's.'

'I'll have a big car.'

'I hope that's a euphemism.'

'I'm sure you'll let me know.'

'See, you're getting good at this. Which might be a bad sign.'

She gave him her flight number and arrival time and waited while he wrote it down. 'I guess we've tried it apart enough for right now, huh?'

'Yup.'

'What if we hate each other in person?'

'I'll put you on the first plane back to Paris and try to get my old job back at the firm.'

'Good kiwi.'

'Good-night,' he said. 'See you tomorrow.'

*T*he office party was an enormous affair given yearly at the Hillcrest Country Club, a place where Cora had spent many irksome Sundays as a child. She recalled ice sculptures and a dessert table, which she mentioned to Ray as they drove, sitting side by side in the dark and staring out the windshield with awkward intensity. Somehow they had to physically acquaint themselves up to the speed of their pen-pal status. They were like strangers who, having found themselves in sudden darkness, talking out of nervousness, little by little coming to know each other well, tend to talk with their faces averted when the lights come on. Cora played with her corsage nervously, wishing she'd gotten a manicure, a bikini wax, an easy way of talking to others, to men, to this man. He smelled of cologne that was familiar to Cora, though she couldn't remember its name. Old Spice? Mennen? She thought not – or was it hoped not.

Half an hour later, they were sitting to the right of a poor rendering of Clarence Darrow in ice and watching the secretaries sing a joke version of 'The Twelve Days of Christmas' that used the names of many of the lawyers in the firm. Everyone thought the lyrics were hilarious. Everyone, that is, but Cora, who had no idea who anyone at the party was, except Ray, and didn't know why it was funny that on the ninth day of Christmas he would get 'double mint juleps.' Ray seemed pleased, though. Cora watched as he moved through the merrymakers, grinning, laughing, clapping people on the back.

'Hey, Doctor – how're you doing? . . . Professor,

long time no nothing – how's the little lady? ...
Señor Wemmer – you're looking nifty in your little
suit there, huh?'

Ray was wearing a paisley ascot that Cora chose
ultimately to evaluate as a style choice beyond his
control. He sipped his double vodka and smoked half
a cigarette without inhaling. But for all of her feeling
like an outsider, hopelessly albeit temporarily trapped
on the inside, Ray kept her afloat amid the swirling
festivities, steering her steadfastly through the sea of
suits, introducing her proudly to everyone he knew. She
couldn't remember knowing anyone with such a store
of elegant manners, so considerate of her, so pleased
with her presence there beside him. He seemed to her
so steady, so patient, so alert to her needs. Her pulse
quickened with excitement at the nearness of him. He
seemed to have no need to conceal his interest in her,
in encouraging her continuing interest in him, and
the seemingly limitless possibility of what they might
gradually become.

Halfway through dinner, their legs touching under
the table, she knew that the evening would end with
more than a handshake. He seemed so certain of how
he could come to feel about her that she felt herself inch
toward his mile. He emanated values and constancy and
intentions that knew only the best sort of bounds. No
one had made her half so comfortable whom she'd also
yearned to kiss. Perhaps the evening was long for her
because it lay between them and discovering what else
they could do after all that long distance, after this
country-club bash, after all.

They wound up necking on Cora's couch and she lost
an earring in the process. She lay on top of him as his
hands smoothed her skirt and stockings. He squeezed
what her mother referred to as the 'Dutch blub' they got

from her side of the family. She stiffened and rearranged herself so that he was directed away from this unsightly ancestral contribution to a happier bodily inheritance.

The one casualty of the catching up was the earring, which was never recovered. It was as if that was the token they dropped in the slot to get on the relationship ride.

Dear Esme,

A lot of what I dreaded about pregnancy are the things that actually occur. People squeal over you with delight. Strangers feel free to reach out and run their hands over the curve of your abdomen. It's as though because you have, in effect, lost control of your body, you have also lost control of your mind, causing people to emit loud noises when apprised of your maternal state. As though because you have been trespassed upon within, those without can feel free to rub you like some recently well worn rabbit's foot. I have taken a liking to the term hysterical pregnancy, *though in my case the term's redundant. (Get it? Term/s redundant.)*

I haven't had too many strange cravings, though. I think middle-of-the-night hankerings for pickles and ice cream was a notion popularized by James Garner films in the very early seventies. The only thing I've yearned for in the middle of the night is less indigestion and more sleep. I have, however, developed a real passion for cottage cheese, yogurt, milk, string cheese, and other high-cholesterol snack items. And, let's face it, I have a carnivorous inclination that is satisfied by drive-through – the only way I can obtain food without waddling conspicuously through folks far less weight-ridden than myself.

I am doing a lot of driving and swimming – the only activities, as far as I can make out, that make me feel virtually weightless. The great thing about driving is that, in addition to feeling weightless as I skim over the asphalt, I feel powerful and defiant. I make my way through traffic, shrieking obscenities and giving the finger to male drivers (preferably in dangerous large trucks). So if one day you go into some sort of hypnosis and find yourself feeling whipped into a frenzy and ready for a brawl, it's not a past-life regression – it's simply you exercising your in-vitro invective on an assortment of men whom I blame for the more unpleasant aspects of my current state. In a fully estrogenized experience, it's nice to have the occasional testosterized triumph. I also plan for the birthing process to bring along a VCR and an assortment of Vietnam war documentaries, my reasoning being that childbirth is a female ritual in extremis, and war is a male ritual in extremis, and I am forever attempting to achieve a kind of balance where I can. Besides, I think it's important for you to have a taste of authentic androgen before it comes for a taste of you.

Being pregnant feels to me like a whale sounds, all mournful and down below. Flesh has collected on me like dust, like something left too long in a sealed room. Did you know that women have extra fat cells, to protect their unborn children? That is why men get craggy good looks that give them character as they get older, while we get the bleary, melted, overage-broad option. So enjoy your youth – or get a sex change (although I hear the technology is far from perfected).

In the meantime, everything grows rounder and

44

wider and weirder, and I sit in the middle of it all and wonder who in the world you will turn out to be. I phoned an astrologer with your approximate date of arrival, and she said that if you were born on the tenth you would have dimples – on the twelfth, you wouldn't. She said that you would be very civic-minded and a good dresser, someone committed to saving endangered creatures and a talker to boot. I do not believe in astrology anyway. I was just checking.

Your motel,
Mom

*B*eing a few years older, Cora felt silly at first with Ray, as if she were admitting something embarrassing. She had grown up in such a solitary way – she and her parents so spread out in the big square house – that proximity to people for a protracted time was tricky for her. She longed for variety and intensity and spaces in between. But Ray seemed very collected, very presentable, and Cora was, in fact, looking for someone to be with. Someone to squire her around, to steer her through large groups by the elbow, shining and sturdy beside her.

She went on a couple of other dates, one with a fairly accomplished musician and the other with a successful physician. But the spirituality of the first and the squareness of the second bothered her. And the squiring continued, and the longer she waited to run into something she couldn't put up with in Ray, the more she didn't. Until eventually it seemed less and less likely that she would.

Still committed to a gentler pace, they refrained from having sex until their sixth post-Paris date, when the AIDS issue had been covered and a lack of impulsiveness prevailed.

Cora despaired that she generally found pleasantness and good-natured people suspect. Occasionally, though, it acted on her in another way. She felt that people impacted on you in a way that you couldn't predict, and she was drawn to the cool day of Ray's demeanor, a shady haven from her greenhouse effect.

The idea of him did not loom larger, but the reality, the quiet force of him, stole into her sideways one night when she lay next to him and made its hungry home there. He was like the sigh that came on the porch when you just noticed the sun was low and orange and you heard the floorboards creak behind you and felt a mouth on your warm, tilted neck. There was home with him now and she had always been such an uprooted thing. So she gave in to his gentleness, to the highest-class problem in the world: being loved.

His power over her was that he never seemed to attempt to have power over her. He didn't insist, demand, or persuade. His impassive, cool face, like a smile set loosely in stone, made the softest impression in mattresses and pillows, the strongest impression on her. His scent was heavy on her, smoothing her rumpled disposition, a cool breeze in her hot day. Water. In a word, she liked him.

She couldn't find the darkness in him without looking very hard. So she stopped looking, breathed easy, and called all her friends. 'He's great,' she concluded. 'A lawyer, but great.'

She was a worrier, a veteran of warlike relationships. She talked with a limp. He was careful with her, like bone china recently repaired, the glue destined never to dry completely. She told herself that she had given up hope, in an irrational, doomed moment of course, but it was still quite, quite gone. They tiptoed around these things like good Indians, not wanting to wake the irritating sleeping aspects they were so eager to live without. She remembered him now. He was the one who was her boyfriend. They slept side by side, straight as corn stalks, accumulating time together. Amass enough, win a prize.

It was as though she'd woken one day to find herself

in someone else's life, in someone else's relationship, acclimating herself to the strange landscape, the breezier climate. She fidgeted, attempting to accustom herself to this fit, instead of having one.

Initially she had, along with several of her snobbier friends, considered this an interim relationship, an experiment. If she could let Ray love her in his reserved, Southern, unconditional way, who knew what that would allow her to do next? Part of her thought of it as a preparation of sorts – a relationship that had harmony instead of acrimony, support instead of competitiveness, acceptance in place of the pain of being a disappointment. At first these things meant only one thing to Cora: Ray was not good enough for her. He seemed so easily affordable that she thought his quality suspect; discount goods were being snuck past her unpracticed heart and eye. But because she found herself unable to break away from his hypnotic gentleness and apparent strength, she decided that she would stay with him until she couldn't anymore. Or until someone better came along. Someone more tumultuous and familiar and sick.

Every night in the beginning when she came home, she'd fix herself up for Ray's return. She wanted to see if she still wanted him as much that day as she had the day before, and he her. It was as though they had agreed upon it literally instead of figuratively – that is, with each other's figures, figure skating until everybody got their money's worth, and apparently everybody did. They pulled at each other's bedclothes for the better part of a year – she wasn't sure how she knew that's how long it was, but she did. Probably because Ray told her. She believed anything factual he told her because he squinted when he said it as if he had to squeeze a little to get it out.

49

She had been seeing him a few months when one of her dogs got out and didn't come back. She'd never done that, Stella, her German shepherd (her favorite kind of German – born after the wars, short, mute, and stupid). So she and Ray went out driving, mournfully shouting the dog's name. 'Stella,' she yelled. 'Stella!' he echoed, and they drove on, wind in their faces. 'Stella! Stella*aaaa*!' Suddenly they saw a furry white form in the street. Two forms, in fact. Cora's heart twanged with terror. She wasn't prepared to see Stella's body, or the body of any animal for that matter. But it turned out to be two sheepskin seat covers. As if some passing driver just couldn't bear his fuzzy luxury items anymore and had flung them into the middle of the street, feeling a thousand times the better for it.

Cora rubbed her hollow heart with relief, waiting for her body's physiological response to catch up with this ridiculous sheepskin factoid. 'I'm not prepared,' she began. 'I couldn't deal with finding her . . . you know – run over.'

'Unfortunately, I could,' Ray said with grim irony.

'Could what?'

'Handle it. I've buried thirteen dogs back home. Three of them my mom ran over. *Stella*!' he called, punctuating this unusual parcel of personal history.

'You never told me that before,' marveled Cora.

'I didn't?' He frowned. 'Huh, I thought I had.'

She shook her head, sitting back in wonder. 'It's an incredible pickup line.'

'We should go up,' he suggested, turning his car up yet another canyon. 'If Stella went anywhere, it was probably up.'

'Yes.' Cora nodded solemnly. This was just another one of those things Ray knew his way around. He had maps to territories Cora didn't even know existed, much less the exchange rate, the local custom, and whether to tip. Oh, he might grumble about how he was relied on far too much without reciprocation. But finally, he liked knowing he would do the decent, right thing – the thoughtful, pain-in-the-ass thing that would leave everybody open-eyed, amazed. He liked being the guy who did what needed to be done, who made sure that everything was hunky-dory, who checked the perimeters with flashlights. He was just such a good . . . scout. He'd pony up each time and find the camp and warn you of warriors and do you the favor of finding you all-around fine.

Cora hadn't known too many people like this. Her other friends, like her, generally concerned themselves with the task of tending to themselves. She hadn't concerned herself before with finding a person who was concerned about her. She had been drawn to men who were stimulating or talented and a little nonnegotiable – a little out of her reach. Then she'd busy herself with closing that gap and organizing herself around what she'd have to do without, loving them secretly until they caught up. With Ray she felt herself holding him a little at arm's length, until she could warm her liking how she felt with him into something a little more like love.

She could see that Ray was disconcerted by his own emotion for her, was waiting uncomfortably until she let him know it would be okay. He had to deal with her troubling past love ghosts, she with his hopeful, towering ideals. It was so difficult for her to understand how people evened out together. Evened out and went along into an easygoing brand of 'we'.

The thing Cora didn't understand about people like her friend Bud was how they could fall in love with the kind of people with whom you talk all the time about how you love each other so much. What Cora thought you had to discover was someone you could leap to love. Someone with whom you could spend enormous amounts of time without disagreeing much, really enjoying that unarguable time together. That five-thirty at the beach sort of feeling all the time.

She wanted to lie in the sun with Ray, limbs slung over limbs, listening to that music you always turn up in the car radio, maybe even *whop*! hit the wheel. She wanted to warm herself around him and tell stories, including one or two that took a risk, closed the deal, rang the bell. To see the sure thing softly staring from two eyes. To tell it until they were tender enough for spice.

Cora's dogs gravitated to Ray's side of the bed. Even loyal Jim knew the real thing when he smelled it and bounded to Ray when he wandered in, the unsung hero from his battles at the front of his desk.

Cora herself had no relationship to her dogs, couldn't bring herself to care deeply about them. This made her, in her mind, a not very good person. In a lot of ways, she didn't feel like a very good person, and she was not about to be conned into believing otherwise.

And in a sense, as soon as she had Ray, and he her, he was a little lost to her forever. She didn't do things quite as right – he didn't love her the way he had out of the box. She never wore as well as that first protracted fit. He had closed the deal, and despite the fact that it was a dazzling, hungry negotiation, closed was closed. And the next phase was the next phase. But just in case, she touched up her makeup before she got in bed with him at night.

She felt ill-suited to the mystery of being in a relationship. Relationship – that silk purse turned sow's ear, a corridor you wandered too far down and discovered a door had silently closed somewhere far behind you. If the suspense didn't kill you, something else surely would. Ensnared in a relentless beam of scrutiny, the only motion you could achieve was coming up short, Cora had found. She seemed innately proficient in the overlooked skill of letting people down. A world-class disappointer, she had made her way through the world letting men down without even trying. She took it from knack to virtuosity in a heart-beat.

But when you are uniquely gifted, you are in some ways obligated to that gift. What if Debussy had stopped playing the piano because it bored him, coming as easily as it did? Well, Cora was the Debussy of disappointment. She stayed with it as long as they stayed with her.

So she and Ray settled into something that had qualities of a permanent thing, without being the thing itself. They got their bearings from wherever they could. Ray looked for a love he could recognize as something like his own; Cora ruminated about him with her short list of long-term friends. Ray had never felt this way about anyone, and he was elated, hopeful, and at a lonely disadvantage. She had never felt this way with anyone before and felt pressured to trust that this peacefulness was permanent.

'I mean, he has qualities that aren't necessarily stimulating, but I've been stimulated to something just short of a frenzy,' she told Bud.

'Ooh, I love it when you talk dirty to me,' he responded in his huskiest voice.

'Oh, Jesus, it's no good talking to you – you bury yourself with some phony actress person who lies about her age and who at best you could describe as a dumb person with opinions – haughty opinions – and don't see me for months 'cause you're too embarrassed to – oh, forget it. It's just impossible to have a real conversation about this stuff with you.' Bud laughed, long and wheezing, while Cora fumed. 'What's so fucking funny?'

'You,' he said, coming up for air. 'I'm the last person to ask, as you say, yet you rail at me when I don't answer.' Cora considered in silence, playing with a blister on her heel. 'Caesar?' said Bud sweetly.

Cora pursed her lips petulantly. 'What?' she asked finally.

'Do you have to decide something today?'

'Well, pretty soon,' she all but wailed. 'He has five suits here.' She drummed her fingers.

'Well, be with him,' Bud said. 'Hey, I don't understand how anyone stays together, so what do I know? At least he doesn't lie about his age, right?' Cora fought a smile and told him she'd see him at work tomorrow.

She called her friend Norma.

'Well, look, there's really nothing out there, manwise, so – what have you got to lose? He seems like a stable, good guy – but then again, why would a stable, good guy be a lawyer?'

She called her mother.

'Well, darling, lawyers are killers – they have to be, in their jobs – look what they've done to me. But he comes from a very close family, and he seems to adore you. I say, marry his ass – but get everything in writing. I don't want to see you broke and destroyed.'

Cliff said, 'Darling, let me just say one thing about lawyers. They're opportunists. They rely on other people's troubles or talents for their income, and they end up costing more than they're worth. They're expert at making themselves invaluable, at creating a need that wasn't there.'

Cora clutched the phone cord. 'But you were a lawyer in the beginning,' she reminded him in a timid voice.

'For about ten minutes,' he said dryly. 'When I figured that out, I stopped.' There was a pause. 'Look, darling, he seems like a lovely person. If he makes you happy – don't listen to me. In fact, why don't you bring him tomorrow? Ron and Harry are coming. And Denny is bringing pictures of his new plane. Come. At seven-thirty. I love you, sweetheart, okay?'

'Okay,' said Cora softly, replacing the phone.

She called her friend Melissa, who was directing a film downtown in Hancock Park.

'Well, what relationship do you see that you'd want to have, anyway?' said Melissa. 'Hey, what are you doing in August? You want to go to Canyon Ranch?'

After Cora finished calling her committee, she realized Ray was due home within the hour. She began her nightly ritual of reapplying her makeup, just in case she decided she wanted everything to work out. Midmascara, her phone rang. It was one of her more famous friends, Joan. Every so often Cora would look at her and remember how famous she was, her fame dogging her like a needy stepchild through the streets while Cora tagged along expendably. She was grateful to know her, because if she didn't, she'd envy the mystery of Joan's success in virtually every arena: career, husband, children, lovely home. Now that she knew her she wouldn't want Joan to slip and fall en route to collecting yet another award.

'I don't like what he does,' Cora said. 'It embarrasses me. Does that make me a bad person?'

Joan laughed. 'It makes you a snob, baby, that's all.'

Cora bit her lip. 'So, it's probably good that I go out with him – so I can confront my snobbery, right? I mean, I wouldn't want someone to judge me for what I do. Well, maybe I would, but in a good way. Remember the whole Republican Convention was about how awful lawyers are. Their tasseled shoes, their greed – you know.'

'Wasn't Lincoln a lawyer?'

'You mean, besides being a log, a city, and a car?'

'Well, I would never date a log.'

'You're married.'

'But not to a log.'

'So if I confront my whatever – I might end up being a better person.'

'You are a better person – it just so happens that you're also a snob.'

Actually, Ray somehow reminded Cora of Joan's husband, Michael, a handsome, careful man who dispensed seamless advice while he gazed out of kind, patient eyes. Ray would be Michael, she thought, and Cora would be Joan, and they would sail into the Mystery like good swans.

Cora called Noel. 'He's very good-looking,' she told him tentatively.

'Is he a talker?' Noel asked, chewing his Jenny Craig dinner.

'Not really,' she admitted. ' I mean, he talks, but he doesn't love it. It's not an outlet, you know? For him.'

'Well, how does that work?'

Cora considered. 'I either talk to him, or I go and get him.'

Noel choked on his food. 'What does that mean?'

Cora twirled the phone cord around her fingers and smiled. 'You know, ask him questions. I talk to him as if he will talk, and then mostly he does. Also, he's a great kisser.'

'Ah. I figured it must be something like that. Wait, hang on – oh, shoot, they're ready for me in room two, I gotta go.'

'What are you doing?'

'You know I can't tell you my patients' names – it's unethical.'

Cora tapped the phone with her finger. 'Hello, Dr. Discretion – I didn't ask you who, I asked you what. Acne? Collagen in lips? Collagen in face? Skin cancer? What?'

'Sorry.'

Cora sighed with disappointment. 'Well, call me if you need a good lawyer.'

'Good at what?' Noel laughed. 'Look, I'll call you later.'

Cora called her friend William in New York, who was very sick with AIDS. Up to several months ago, he had only two T cells left, whom he had named Mutt and Jeff. Now he had none at all. But he was very optimistic that they would come up with a cure soon, and he would resume his former state of beauty and health.

At the moment, though, he sounded very much as if someone were sitting on his chest. 'I'm fine, Cor – really,' he reassured her. 'I've even put on a few pounds and some of my hair's growing back.' What he failed to mention she knew from their mutual friend Andrew – William was no longer able to walk.

'I want you to come out soon and meet my new boyfriend,' she suggested. 'I can't really go forward until you give me the okay.'

William laughed a laugh that disintegrated into a horrible hacking. 'Hang on a minute,' he managed. Cora clutched the phone, closing her eyes tightly until he was able to return, exhausted, to the phone. 'He doesn't know about us yet, does he?' William wheezed. Cora couldn't recall what they had been discussing – and then it came to her that it had been something to do with Ray.

'No, he doesn't,' she replied with as much irony as she could muster. 'And I think it's probably best until I'm sure whether or not this is an actual thing.'

'You're probably right, as ever. He might not understand it. He'd feel threatened and confused and then where would we be?'

'Just come though, okay?' she urged. 'You know I

58

can't date without you. Think of it as a favor – or flavor – whatever. So long as you come.'

He promised he would, as soon as his doctor gave him clearance.

'I love you, poppet,' he told her, and they concluded the call.

Cora basically didn't believe in her ability to have a relationship. She doubted that she had the appropriate disposition or capacity to boil it down to something even approaching a learnable skill. She would have felt more optimistic if she'd even had the sense that she could fake it. But the parts of her life that felt essential to her – her friendships and her talking and her work – seemed to be the very things that made it impossible for her to enjoy the by-products available from successful combinations of two. For Cora to rely largely on one other person for, well, just about everything seemed like a bet she could never really win. She always hoped that it wouldn't come down to these choices – but for some reason it always did. Most likely it had to do with the men she chose, but what could she do about that? Each time she thought she'd chosen one so different from the ones before. Maybe she had, but somehow, somewhere in the process, something shivered slightly and turned the same. Eventually she saw striking similarities that left her each time a little more stricken than the last.

Yet something in Cora continued to believe it was possible – that you could stay with someone your whole life. She believed it, but she didn't know why. It was a belief based on wishing. Based on the family she hadn't had but longed to wake up and find herself in. There was a study she'd read somewhere, people lived longer when they lived with someone else – turning happily ever after into quite a stretch.

Ray's family, it appeared, was predisposed to things working out. His parents were still married and their parents on both sides before that. He would overcome her ambivalence, she hoped – she'd catch commitment from him like a cold. Everything she and Bud had always mocked began to seem possible for her.

This sort of about-face happened to Cora more often than she liked to admit. The truth was, sometimes she completely forgot what she was like. Which was extraordinary since she was quite like herself – that is to say, she had amassed a considerable accumulation of person, complete with quirks and tastes and peculiarities and sensitivities and recollections of encounters. Yet, she would look up square into a round face running over with expectation, and for the life of her she couldn't remember whom precisely it required her to be at this particular moment. Someone she had been looking for earlier and had somehow forgotten.

She had always been unpredictable compared to other people – but not compared to her very own self. It was a simple case of the ingredients overpowering the dish. Her characteristics had overrun her character – the whole of her had been overtaken by her parts. All the little traits she'd picked up along the way had finally drawn a line under her when she was sleeping, snuck themselves through a calculator of character, and toted themselves up. It was then that they had hatched their insidious plot, all her various aspects agreeing to disagree to function without further notifying one another – then that the predictability of her person ceased upon itself. Even the part that held itself to be unpredictable.

She maintained some outward doubt about Ray for consistency's sake. But she had already begun to count on Ray's love for her. And there was so much novelty here, what with his patience and reliability, that it would distract her generally from her concerns about herself. Maybe this relationship business was learnable after all.

Ray liked to go to screenings, to go out dancing, to parties, breakfast at La Lune Qui Rit. Cora didn't share his enthusiasm for these pastimes, and somehow because she didn't, he felt she loved him a little less. All she could figure was that if she cared for him, as he did for her, it didn't matter what they did. The important thing was sharing the time. 'If that's true, Ray, then we could just stay home.' He ran his hand over the top of his head in frustration. He wanted them to go out together. Maybe she hadn't cared for screenings before, but it would be different with him. He felt that he would do it for her. 'I'm willing to do things with you that I don't want to do, maybe – but – oh, forget it, forget it. Maybe we're just too different.'

So she would go, not feeling important enough in one way, and in another--well, she wouldn't think about that. So they would drive to the studio and park and walk to the screening room on the lot, their shoes echoing in the deserted streets leading to the little theater behind the commissary. They would enter the half-filled room, his hand on the small of her back.

'Hey, boss.' Ray spotted someone he knew and shook his hand warmly. 'Cora, this is Brad Middleton. Business Affairs at – '

Brad interrupted. 'Sure, sure. Cora Sharpe. You did the rewrite on the *Watertown* sequel, right?'

Cora smiled, feeling slightly at a loss. 'Yeah. How's that going?'

'Great, great,' Brad replied, his head bouncing. 'I hear the dailies are great.'

Cora arranged her face into a pleased expression. 'Well, Marcus is a good director,' she noted feebly as someone grabbed her from behind.

'Sweetheart!' exclaimed Cliff's familiar voice. 'What are you doing here?' He turned her toward him and gave her a powerful embrace. 'Darling, *oooh*, it's good to see you.' He released her and acknowledged Ray. 'Hey, Ray, how're you?' They clasped hands.

'Hi, Cliff.'

Cliff turned back to Cora. 'Honey, listen, I was going to call you tomorrow about this thing they're giving me – ugh, don't ask. I'm being honored. Anyway, it's next Thursday and if Ray here could spare you, I'd really love you to come with me. You know how embarrassing those things can be.'

Cora stood, feeling decidedly on the spot. The spot that existed between Cliff and Ray. 'What do you think, Ray?' she asked in her smallest, most well-intended voice.

Ray shrugged and smiled with only his mouth. 'Fine with me,' he said distractedly, looking around the room.

'Great. So we'll talk tomorrow, right?' Cliff held her face with one hand. '*Oooh*, I love you.' He released her. 'Okay – tomorrow. Bye, Ray.' He turned to make his way through the ever-increasing crowd.

Ray didn't look at her. 'We better get a seat,' he said, scanning the room.

Cora squeezed his arm. 'Are you mad?'

He pulled away from her ever so gently and laughed a laugh that bordered on scorn. 'Oh, not at all – I practically have to beg you to come to this screening, but Cliff comes and asks you to this giant thing – this,

this rat-fuck, as you call them – and without a moment's hesitation you say yes. Why would I be mad?'

'Look, Ray, he's being honored – '

Ray interrupted. 'Please. Don't explain. The more you explain, the more upset I get. So let's just drop it.' He started toward the front of the theater where the few remaining seats were.

Sometimes Ray seemed to have pulled back from her to a place just behind his nose. She read it as circumspect, taciturn, restless – but perhaps she was wrong. He didn't communicate as she did. He flourished in feeling – maybe not his own when he was in conflict, then he tended to flounder – but on the whole he was known as a good guy, a comforting soul, a caring individual, and he did everything he could to project that image. Though it seemed effortless and innate, it occurred to Cora that when he came to the end of these things, the end of the manners, the reassuring, the always there for everyone – an uncharted territory must surely begin. A territory filled with disappointment and confusion and the rage of feeling unappreciated and let down.

Running for office is the least aerobic of the socially interactive sports, and Cora sensed that she could never give back to him what he all too often gave to far too many. She felt she had let him down and his disappointment was growing larger all the time.

One morning she asked him what was wrong. Without looking at her he replied, 'Nothing.' He pulled his belt through the loops in his khaki pants. Cora compressed her lips and shifted positions in her bedroom chair.

'Which nothing?' she said carefully, her head tilted to one side in an effort to see his slim, averted face.

'I don't think it's a good idea to talk about this

right now.' He moved to his closet and removed a blue houndstooth jacket.

Cora wiped her mouth with the back of her hand and stared at it intently. 'I don't think it's a good idea to not talk about it, you know?'

The phone rang and she ignored it. It continued to ring. Ray struggled uncharacteristically with his jacket. Finally he pulled it on roughly, ripping the sleeve. 'Are you just going to let it ring?' he almost shouted, returning to his closet for solace, for more cooperation, if only from his clothes.

'Ray, tell me.'

He turned to the wall, throwing his head back in frustration. 'Well, aw, Christ, what's the deal with us, you know? We sort of live here together and I know you've had these terrible relationships and everything, but . . . oh, forget it, okay? It's humiliating to have to say this stuff.'

Cora stood and half approached him, then stopped, crossed her arms, and considered. 'I thought this was . . . good between us. I mean . . .' She stopped and scratched her ear in exasperation.

Ray turned and looked at her, bewildered, affronted, handsome. 'You can't even say it, can you? I can. I love you. I've never felt this way about anyone. I want a life with you. You're the best person I've ever known.'

Cora laughed nervously. 'You ought to get around more. Look, Ray,' she continued, 'I'm a weird enough girlfriend, but I'm just – I've been such a disappointing wife. Please don't think – '

'What can I think?' He sat despondently on the bed. 'Just because you had a bad marriage, now I have to be punished? You were married to a selfish guy, a different guy. Not me . . .' He gazed morosely at his hands. 'Not me,' he repeated without energy.

Cora didn't want to get married. She'd already tried and had been unable to fill those practical fantasy shoes. Weddings intrigued her – she hadn't had one the first time around and had ended up spending eleven hundred dollars on stuff for her kitchen, a trade-off for which she didn't have to write thank-you notes. All those gifts, all that smiling, the lint floating through the air, the moving rendition of 'Close to You' on the organ, the inevitable bad dance band. But vows seemed ridiculous – it was hard enough to keep appointments. She was pleased that Ray wanted to marry her, but the prospect of being tied to someone for life by someone she didn't even know – the operation itself – frightened her.

Still, she didn't want to deprive Ray of the wedding he'd always wanted. Maybe they could compromise.

She crossed to him slowly and sat on the arm of the chair beside him. 'We could be engaged, if you want, and see what happens.' He put his head against her and laughed a small, relenting laugh. 'Let's be fiancés, okay?' she said as he pulled her onto his lap. 'Like in a Henry James novel.'

Ray squeezed her and she turned her face to his to be kissed. He kissed her as a question, then the question answered itself and became a long, luxurious passage in a story they would be telling for an indefinite time. A touching story with less and less punctuation.

Two days later, he presented her with a ring, round, gleaming, and scary.

Dear Esme,

I hope your father at least waited a respectable amount of time after my tragic demise (see your grandmother) before marrying. Of course it's possible that he'll marry someone we know. Like Melissa. I always thought he had an eye for her.

Loud – but not too loud – and too thin in a way
that instead of looking like she is sitting on a chair,
she appears to be draped over it, laughing with
her head thrown back so that the sun falls across
her hair just right. And her voice, always slightly
hoarse as though she'd been up all night yelling at
a Dignity Rally of some sort.

Or he'll marry someone he doesn't know at all.
Someone he'll meet quite by accident – car accident.
She'll rear end him on the way to the publication
party for the cookbook she's just written, following
the publication of two critically acclaimed collections of short stories. A Southern cookbook.
She'll be flustered and very apologetic. He'll be
annoyed until she turns her angelic face up to
his, her hair gleaming, iridescent as the insides
of certain shells. She'll tell him her name in a
soft voice, her face luminous in the streetlight,
basking in the warmth of his soothing disposition.
Mary Louise. He'll tell her not to worry, he never
sees the back of his car anyway. She'll be so
grateful – so grateful and so young. Young but
wise. It will turn out that she grew up twenty
minutes from his hometown. They'll both love
Lyle Lovett, anything smothered with grits, and
going to weird, out-of-the-way museums on rainy
afternoons. He'll put her number in his inside
pocket and look at it before he removes his glasses
and goes to sleep.

From the day they meet, they are rarely apart.
She smells of hyacinth and night-blooming jasmine,
the way he remembers his mother smelling when
he was a child drifting off to sleep in the backseat
of the Chevy. A sleepy, Southern love smell. Her
mouth looks to him like a seagull flying into a

cloud, wings wide above the wind. People always mistake her for Meryl Streep.

At the wedding, they'll play Erik Satie. Her dress of cream satin and lace once belonged to her grandmother. And she'll be a wonderful mother to you, without being disrespectful to my memory.

It would be insane for me to try to turn you against her – especially after she has given you this note, being aware of its contents and all. Fine, sure, I understand, she's an angel – I can't fault her. But no matter how much you like your new stepmother, please don't give her my jewelry. Especially my Essex crystal dog ring or my angel pin. I definitely would be upset about that – I don't care how dead I am.

With undying love,
Mom

B ud had taken an enormous liking to Ray's watches, which included several antiques and a gold Rolex. But it was the platinum – a bracelet style with a light mesh band that had been a gift from Cora – that really haunted his more covetous dreams. Sometimes, before a dinner party, he would ask permission to wear it, which Ray would reluctantly grant. When Ray wasn't there, Bud wandered around the bedroom, rummaging through his closet and dresser drawers, always ending up at Ray's box of cuff links and watches. Ritualistically he'd lift his delicate favorite from the smooth wooden box and slip it onto his wrist, his eyes shining.

Cora had tried subtly to deter Bud from this sort of snooping and poking, but to no avail. Slowly his roaming moved from watches to dress shirts, an Armani jacket, and whatever paperwork caught his eye. Ray was not thrilled with this encroachment, but it wasn't easy to deter Cora's friend and writing partner from his free ways with Ray's private store of personal items, especially as Bud tended to view his appropriation of them as a high compliment he couldn't avoid repeating. Cora had failed to get Bud to see this in any other light.

Bud's other favorite rite at Cora's home – his postwriting rite – was to call for a massage. The sight of him padding through the house clad in the simple adornment of a towel was not Ray's fondest vision upon returning from work. That this habit of Bud's predated Ray and Cora's cohabitation failed to comfort him.

Cora secretly thought that there was something confrontational about Bud's behavior, something that inwardly smiled each time Ray allowed it to continue. But what she failed to appreciate was that, while Ray appeared to take things largely in stride, to keep most things inside, a trembling force was gathering outside the eye of his storm. Each time Bud strode through the house in his trusty semitoga, each time she went to an opening with Cliff, each endless conversation with her endless supply of friends, Ray went stiffer and stiffer with kept silence, with always giving more than he got. Cora had come up with a nickname for this mood. She called it Edwin the Affronted One.

One Friday as Bud lay below, swathed in scented oils, Cora held forth on the phone with luckless Norma, who was inconsolable over the straying of her husband, Burt. 'Just hang in there,' Cora advised. 'Let him have his affair. It'll wear out – she'll become demanding, while you remain indifferent to his tryst, mother of his children, lifelong companion. She has to become demanding – she's thirty-five, he's fifty-four. These are the last years left of whatever remains of her loveliness. Take it from me – I know.'

So concentrated was she on the urgency of her call that Cora didn't hear Ray enter, worn from work. 'Hey, I know what we can do,' she was saying. 'Why don't I give you a party? The main thing he has to lose is the life you have together. You know, friends you've accumulated over the years, people who connect him to his youth. I'll give you a party and he'll come, too, and be reminded that he wouldn't be invited here with her ever.'

Ray's voice behind her startled her. 'Maybe he doesn't want to be connected to that part of his life anymore,' he said gravely. 'Maybe he wants to start over.'

Cora put her hand over the mouthpiece and shifted her weight to look over her shoulder. She hoped the look would convey to Ray her gladness at seeing him, the delicate import of her call, and the reminder that she who was betrothed to him should be treated with unknown, untapped stores of gentleness – all this in a look. But Ray was sitting in a chair facing away from her. He pulled off his calfskin shoes and dropped them with a routine thud to the carpet beneath. Still, she thought, his head looked perky from behind. Perky and solid, with one ear poking out of each side.

'I have to go, Norma,' she said, low, into the phone. 'I'll speak to you tomorrow.' She paused, listening. 'I will.' She returned the phone to its cradle and turned to Ray. 'When did you get in?' she said after a beat, hoping she was wrong about the tension around his mouth.

'I think I walked in when you were planning to save Norma and Burt's marriage with a party,' Ray said evenly, pulling his sweater over his head, leaving his golden hair electric and standing up at the back as though startled.

'Well, what else can I do?' Cora started off the bed, then reconsidered and sat back, feeling misunderstood.

'You could do nothing for once,' Ray said flatly. 'Leave people to solve their own lives.'

It was at this inopportune moment that Bud appeared in the doorway in his scanty costume. 'Hey, man,' he said casually, as if to a fellow voyager. As he reached for Ray, his towel slipped, and he caught it with his free hand – the hand wearing Ray's watch. 'Oops,' Bud exclaimed coyly. 'Almost unveiled Sad Jim. Oh, I hope you don't mind, man,' he continued, oblivious, as they headed for the rocks. 'I borrowed your watch again – I just love it.' He reached for the ceiling, the platinum gleaming sinister in the half-light, turning his wrist one

73

way and another, appreciating its dull shine. 'Oh, I thought of a joke. Ready?' Ray listened in silence, his hair perfectly still. 'Why is there anti-Semitism all over the world?' Bud paused. ''Cause agents travel.' Slapping his stomach with both hands, he looked pleased. Cora smiled a sick smile.

Ray stood. 'I get it,' he managed, retrieving a robe from his closet in one move. 'Funny,' he added, slipping it on.

Bud belched daintily and moved to the doorway. 'I'm going to heat up some chicken,' he announced breezily. 'Can I get anybody anything? Cora? Ray? Coke? Chicken? Chopped salad?'

Cora shook her head slowly.

'Thanks,' said Ray quickly. 'Thanks a lot, but no.'

Bud bounced his head happily to his secret off beat. Making his way out of their room, he called, 'You're making a mistake.'

Ray stood stock-still, until he was sure Bud was out of earshot. Then he said, not looking at Cora, 'Make him go away.'

She explained it to Bud. 'Look, I understand that this is how we functioned before. But now it's different, see? You can't just drop by without calling. You have to treat him like my . . . husband or whatever.'

Bud looked crestfallen. 'I thought that's what I was doing.'

'Then you have to treat him like he's someone else's husband. You know what I mean. We can't act as much like we used to – except on special occasions, okay?'

'Like when?' said Bud moodily. 'Martin Luther King's birthday? Then we can't go to Arizona – they don't recognize it.'

Cora sighed, wiped her brow with the flat of her hand.

'I'm trying to make this work, remember? It's a whole territorial thing.'

Outside of work, Cora saw Bud less and less. He began to see an actress by the name of Camille Fielding, who had starred in his first produced feature, *Grieving Landscape*. Camille admitted to thirty-four, but the actual number was closer to forty-four or -five. From what Cora could gather, the relationship was volatile and depended on crisis and chaos to keep it erotic and new.

Not that she knew most of this from Bud. She missed his confidences, which had included the most intimate details of his affairs – like the time he had helped a fairly well-known artist through her incest traumas (real or imagined) with a series of passionate mutual spankings, at the height of which they had called each other by the names of their respective siblings. Not to mention – but he had – the specifics of his periodic kidney disorders and bouts of constipation. Now when they did speak, he was secretive, guarded, remote. And since Cora was not in much better spirits, the script they punched up in this period, a comedy called *That's All I Have to Say*, was not a lot funnier after the two of them completed their accustomed pass. Cora even mentioned to their agent that it might be better if they rewrote something other than comedy for the moment. A horror film maybe. Or something with a gym-obsessed star.

Meanwhile, Ray became more covetous of her time, more entitled, more jealous of the other people in her life who laid claim to her confidence. There were fewer spells of safety, of sympathy, longer spells of silence.

She told her other friends to stay away for a while. Told Cliff, no more screenings, no more parties without Ray. Kept off the phone when he was in the house. Tried to make him feel how important he'd become to her. To reassure them both that this was where they wanted to be.

The Jamesian engagement ring stuck so far out on her finger that it ripped all her stockings, got tangled in her hair. She tiptoed through the silences, fearful of infractions, feeling her way down the smooth dark walls to the familiar doorway at the end. She hesitated, holding the cold knob in her hand, before stepping into the cold, bright light where Ray would be standing, where all her lovers had stood before, disappointed in her. Where she'd hung her head under their rain of discontent. She, to her mind, expecting so little. They, to her mind, expecting so much.

Cora herself had few problems with Ray – but she was interested in problems. They stood out from the drab world of 'Fine, how are you?' 'Fine,' and she focused on them as though they had a glow all their own.

'But why overcomplicate everything?' Ray asked.

'I don't overcomplicate it – look at how the fucking thing flows.' Maybe she just saw it from the angle that showed its insides – the crying, screaming, glowing side. The side that was all puzzle dying to be done.

'What did you do today?' she would ask. 'Oh, you know,' he would reply. 'Same old same old.' But she didn't know – never would. Responses like these were incomprehensible to Cora. She was hypnotized by the glow and drawn ever downward toward its source. Ray could go either way. To some he was 'Fine.' He had argued with his father only twice in his life as far as she could gather. He had real conversations on occasion with the rest of his family and some of his friends.

But when Cora spoke, he watched her mouth, as though her words had shape and little weight and flew like angels around her unkempt head. He looked at her with some bafflement, more affection. 'I love when you . . . talk.' She spoke to the glow in him, and to her he divested his beam. He poured this part of himself into her and it came to be essential to him. His rarely spoken self bore down on her, big and glowing. These exchanges elated Cora. She dearly loved the ride.

77

'How are you?' Well, put to the Zen master, the answer would be 'Fine' and its essential opposite, 'No fine.' The two existed in relationship to one another, impossible to separate. Cora was no student of Zen, although she periodically wished to be. But she was ever the Countess of Fine/No Fine. She kept a diverse and dark court. Too many courtiers, it was true. But it was to them that she farmed out her need for conversational acrobatics, with them that she worked out her need to be needed. Yes, she was a snob about her strain of malaria, only caught by kings.

Ray's friends were selected for long stints on porches, swatting at flies and shooting the breeze. But for Cora, something was missing. She liked them and could spend time with them, but she couldn't really connect with them. If this were the biggest problem that she and Ray had, then God Save the Queen. But she would ferret out the fellowship of No Fine, and his crowd didn't sit on her side of the stands.

She recalled how Ray snapped at a friend – uncharacteristically, she'd thought at the time. 'When I need your thoughts on this subject,' he'd said coldly, 'I'll let you know sometime in advance.' The dinner had been finished with careful navigation through calmer waters. 'Was I rude?' Ray had asked in the car afterward, heading home.

Cora had looked over through the darkness at his face lit by the lights from the dash. 'If you have to ask,' she said softly, 'then the safest answer is yes. Just like social drinkers don't wonder if they're alcoholic unless they are.'

Ray had stomped down on the accelerator and barely made it through a red light. 'Leave it to you to turn a simple question into a charming footnote in your ongoing lecture series about life.'

Cora had turned her face forward and managed to keep it that way for the rest of the drive home.

Ray had followed her, thumping up the stairs one by one. 'Honey?' he'd said in a light voice.

'Yeah?' Cora had replied in kind.

'Did you know you had a little tear in the back of your dress?'

This was the first time she'd realized that Ray had trouble with saying that he was sorry or with the concept that he was in any way wrong. He was far from wrong, had to be – or the only reason he was anywhere near it was because some schmuck had put him there.

Cora had a ravenous need to talk to people. To feast on the carcass of what they could figure out together. Vultures of reason, of the unsatisfactory why, glow in the eye, they gorged, stripped bones, sucked them scary white. Until they arrived at the nevermind – at least half the time.

This discrepancy as to how they chose and used their friends was not a problem until they decided to possibly get tied and lassoed for life. Then in place of the sweet accord at night came the same old same old, and the little lists they didn't even know they were making scrolled out and unwound down a long hall.

Cora dreamed she was wearing a heavy white satin dress. People were milling around on a lawn, but whether it was for a wedding or a funeral, whether she was the bride or the deceased, recently wed or dead, she wasn't sure. She moved through the gathering, which resembled neither a celebration nor a good-bye. She was searching for Ray, squinting in the sun. David Letterman was there with his wife and four children, and Cora's dead grandmother and her ex-husband, Ben. No one spoke to her or noticed her. Ray would notice, she thought, though she wasn't clear whether he would speak. She was hungry, but for nothing specific, sweet potatoes at the most.

Someone touched her arm. She looked around and found William.

'William,' she tried to say, but he somehow stopped her mouth with his beautiful face. 'I want to come back in water, you know – not in ink,' he said. She thought maybe this had to do with birth and a newspaper article. He seemed to say something about Ray, but she couldn't understand it. 'It's a secret,' William whispered.

She spotted Ray standing on a patch of grass, hands thrust deep in his pockets, hidden from sight. As she approached him, she reached out, but his mother got to him first, stopping Cora in her tracks.

'I'm so miserable,' she heard him say. His mother reached out and touched his brow. It was then that Cora looked down at the ring on her hand and realized she was married.

When she awoke, Ray's arm was around her waist, his face nuzzled into her tight back. 'Ray,' she ventured quietly.

'Mmmm?' he breathed, his warm breath in her damp hair.

'Ray, I think the marriage thing is a bad idea, you know?' She attempted to say this lightly. No Big Deal.

Ray slid his arm slowly from around her, returning it to safety. He rolled onto his back. She turned over to face him, her face eager with entreaty. 'I mean, what does it really mean anyway, you know? We're together, right? So now we'll be legally together. What'll that change – it'll up the fidelity quotient? Marriage is mostly for the woman, anyway – so she'll feel safe or have a more respectable standing in the community. Or so his money will be hers. Well, no offense, but my name has some respectability already – so does yours. And I make good money, so – '

He rose up on one elbow, facing her. 'Stop,' he warned, his voice angry, covering the hurt hunkered down behind it. 'If you don't want to get married, fine. I just don't want to get a lecture along with it.' He lay back down and rolled away from her.

Now it was she who snuggled into him, she who put her arm over his side. She kissed his shoulder and he jerked away, the smallest sort of jerk. 'I don't mean it bad,' she cooed softly. 'I love to be with you. You know that.'

He laughed ironically. 'No, you don't want to marry me in a good way. Right.' He pulled his knees toward his chest.

'Maybe it could be good,' she implored. 'Why don't we see? If it's not, we can always get married. Always as in repeatedly. Heaps of vows and lots of rice.' She could feel his jaw tighten.

'We don't love each other the same,' he said flatly. Upset.

She tried to unlock him somehow. 'No, but I think we love each other enough.'

He sat up and fumbled for his glasses. 'Enough for what?' he asked scornfully, standing.

'Enough to work it out,' she said, a cold terror forming in her plexus. He picked his pants off the floor and pulled them on. 'Enough to not walk out.' He grabbed his shirt from the bedpost and fought to find his sleeve. 'Ray, don't leave.' He scooped up his shoes and socks. She pulled the covers around her shoulders to quiet her pounding heart. 'If you go now, you probably better stay away.'

81

He stuffed his wallet in his pocket and made for the door. 'Fine,' he called as he rounded the corner.

She had always thought that the ideal relationship would be a place where you would feel free to be whatever the fuck it was you were. It seemed odd to fall in love with someone all the while hoping that some fundamental changes would occur, enabling you to remain steadfastly in love – to hold back your acceptance, on the notion that all will be well once she becomes more like what she was going to become once you loved her into learning. Bowed and broken into learning your new law of love. It's that notion, that damnable, crippling notion that things could be – are supposed to be – better. The crippling addiction to the idea of better.

Perfect contentment can rarely be recognized. Maybe in Tibet, maybe in toddlers. It's the happy province of youngsters and the simple. Lost in the wonder of the bells on the jester's hat, the colorful banner, the shiny earring, they examine what passes through their vision one thing at a time, spellbound, unable to perceive the world as a whole complicated mass, unable to fathom the consequences, the bleak implications. They could jump to conclusions, could surmise that the world is a confusing place, if they could remember what they had seen earlier – but they can't.

If only we didn't yearn for beginning things so damn close to the middle. Could be satisfied with a little more than a little. The warm toils in the hushed advancement of the clock. The mutual decisions. The carnival of compromise.

Dear Esme,
What if I turn out to be the type of person who talks like an adult to infants and like an infant to

adults? You can hardly expect me to explain things to you in looping, scooped-up noises, obliterating, in a series of oddly timed felled swoops, the modicum of disheveled dignity I hope to have amassed over a lifetime. So this is a correspondence to whatever jumble of personage you have arrived at by eighteen, shaped, undoubtedly, by things I did or didn't do, said (but not soon enough or loud enough or in the right sort of way) or didn't say.

Still and all, this is for whatever you have arrived at, having passed through our formative family time together or some unpleasant alternative that I do not wish to speculate about at this particular moment. It's hard for me to concentrate really hard while I am pregnant. I don't care what anybody says – you get stupider when you're cooking someone up from a little more than a scratch in your uterus. (This falls under the heading of something called self-deprecatory humor – a thing to avoid whenever real humor is at all possible.)

I rarely think about my childhood. It's a slippery thing I can't keep hold of for long – it slithers out of my grasp. And a lot of the time I remember what was missing instead of what was there. I am a chronicler of absence.

It was as if my family had taken root in our sterile house and grown up around – around, not with – one another, like trees. Just filling in the time, passing the time together until we could leave. (Get it – trees leaving?) We were lodgers whose main common denominator was address. Affection was expressed without being too frequently demonstrated. As my external world didn't seem to provide me with much in the way of nourishment, I became distracted little by little by my internal world. What was it my grandfather said? Find worms – go fishing. I went fishing.

Outside, things came together and fell apart without too much pomp or ceremony. Everything stayed upright. We'd continue to move among one another as before, the occasional crisis standing in our midst like an unmentionable smell. Consequently, I grew into an ardent communicator who has no tools for conflict. Fight to me means flight. Better just to sweep it under the carpet and act like nothing's going on. And maybe eventually nothing will be. Deal with it apparently and all will follow actually – that could have been my family's motto. If we'd ever gotten it together to have a motto, we'd probably have had a motto and nothing else. A motto and a credo and a house.

I tried to tell your father I was too busy to be cruel. What I meant was, I'm so busy grappling with and groping through my insides that I haven't time for deliberate unkindness. I suppose the unkindnesses I am capable of are of the unconscious variety, neglect of others through overconcern for myself. The long way to say selfish. But intent is so important – it's the difference between two to seven and the chair. I would never deliberately neglect the needs of my intimates – or is it my inmates (intimates without their tie).

So you may have found that I was deficient in demonstrativeness, although perhaps they've come up with a vitamin supplement for it. Just remember, I gave what I could and apologize for the rest.

Hope your adolescence was better than mine.

Love,
Cora

Cora had invited her friend William to come stay with her. He had sounded so bad when they last spoke that she told him she had made a lot of money that week on a rewrite and would go to hell if she didn't share it with someone. With him for whom it could really do the most. Neither of them spoke of William's great friend Allan, who'd basically abandoned William when he'd gotten sick. Allan, who'd had the money to help him to die in New York, but out of fear of contamination – emotional or physical – left William no recourse but to come to California to Cora.

So he came, eyes heavy and bright with codeine. A few days before, several cartons of adult diapers had arrived from New York – and that wasn't a good sign of anything, sunny commercials with June Allyson or no. Cora couldn't have said that William was going to die at her house, but she couldn't say that he wasn't, either. Maybe the trip had just spent the last coin his body had for travel. He had looked thin for some time. Thin and eager – eager to live, to be living. He looked like those baby birds, craning for nourishment, for worms. Find worms, go fishing. So he settled in for the short haul down the main hall, next to the living room. His insurance would pay for his nurses for twelve hours a day and Cora would pay for the next dozen.

The night William arrived, Cora sat with him in her room with the fire going, and he told her about his traveling plans and she nodded and smiled and showed him to his room. She unpacked his things while he struggled with his clothes and his walker and his pajamas. Cora handed him her gray silk robe through a crack in the door and shivered. She prepared his nutrition bag, the liquid that drained into the permanent IV hookup in his chest. He referred to his Hickman catheter as Cathy, his one great love. 'Making you Heathcliff,' she warned him ominously. 'And look what happened to him.'

William regarded her stonily. 'He died of AIDS?'

Cora hit his foot, mock hard. 'No Brontë characters died of HIV-related causes. They died in childbirth or of frostbite or drunkenness or just plain rudeness turned to apoplexy. In Heathcliff's case, it was frostbite secondary to Cathy – Catherine Earnshaw coming back to haunt him on a cold night, and he chased her ghost through the snow and in the morning he was dead.' She told him that she didn't want to see him doing the same thing for a big bag of clear nutrients – 'I don't care how good they are for you.'

After William finally fell asleep, Cora slipped back into her room and closed the door. It was going to be okay. They were going to let everything be as okay as they possibly could. An unspoken pact between good companions, doing the thing together at closer or longer intervals and with greater or just pretty damn good proximity.

But there was just one thing. If she was going to take care of William, who was going to see that she was seen to? Who would be her lean-to, her quiet counsel?

She had thought she would feel relieved when she and Ray parted – she had grown so weary of watching him retreat. But already she'd begun to see things from his point of view. Why did all her partners end up feeling so low on her list of priorities? The odd thing was, they were usually wrong about how much she loved them – it always turned out that the depth of her loss came dangerously near her core. She was cut to the quick, wasn't she? And the velocity to her quick was very fast indeed. When she loved people, she loved them like velvet – like velvet and long, for stretches and stretches.

Maybe now that William needed her so much that she was wanting, Ray would take her word for it. Or not her word but her deed – her palpable need. She couldn't think of anyone more adept at meeting needs. She might be the more colorful person, but Ray seemed to her the finer human being. And if he turned out not to be, she would simply be a colorful person who'd turned out to be a bad judge of character.

She slid under the covers and cradled the phone between her bare shoulder and her chin.

'Hullo?' Ray said from his dark, unfurnished house in Beechwood.

'Did I wake you?' she said in a small voice, a voice no more than three inches high.

He laughed, and she heard the sound echo in one of his empty cream-colored rooms.

'Your voice sounds rumpled,' she said, smiling.

'Is that what you called to tell me?'

She was quiet, watching a mosquito bang against the wall, its spindly legs tangling with its shadow.

'Honey?'

Cora drew in her breath and rolled onto her stomach, the phone cord stretched uncomfortably across her midriff. She exhaled, part of her face in the pillow, part held up to the receiver. 'Call me that again,' she whispered sleepily, eyes closed.

'Call you what?'

'Let's just see each other,' she sighed with irritation. 'Let's just be together. This is all just stupid.'

She could picture him wrapping the cord around his hand. Then, low, 'It really is.'

'So . . . ?' Cora said finally. There was an imperceptible beat.

'I'll get my stuff.'

About forty minutes later, Ray made his way into Cora's darkened bedroom and sat in the chair untying his shoes.

'Bay,' he whispered tentatively toward her shape in the bed. It was his shorthand, Southern term for *Babe*, for *Baby*. 'Bay, are you sleeping?'

Cora stirred and sat up in bed, making a movement that was related in some way to rubbing her eyes. 'William's here,' she said. 'William arrived tonight.'

'Is he all right?' Ray asked, slipping in beside her, encircling himself up under her arms and winding his legs around hers.

'Maybe you can stay and help me see,' she said, smoothing the flats of her hands down both his sides to the knobs of his hips. She kissed him near his eyes – she actually did things like that when she felt like it. Those intimate gestures you reserve for your intimates. Reassuring indicators that they did or are doing fine, insecurity inhibitors. You brush their hair back off their shoulders and press their facial flesh in a loving way, letting them know that you think they've done a particularly good job.

Ray kissed her. Their breath mixed. They rubbed against each other harder and harder until they shone, they virtually glowed in the dark.

'Everything'll be okay,' he said as he felt the wetness seep into their kiss, informing their gentle late-night cozy round.

She nodded, though her throat was tight, her hand exploring. 'I know.'

And she did.

Ray told her later that she had fallen asleep and was crying in full slumber for about forty-five minutes or so. When she finally believed him, she wondered if she was crying for a waking thing or a sleeping one. Conversely, perhaps, when she wept while not slumbering, it was for a dreamlike thing. A dream you only remembered enough of to know if it was worthy of the weeping.

There is an artist named Morandi, who paints the spaces between objects, Cora had been told by a director late one night. And then something, she was sure, about the color blue, and those Cornell boxes, the ones with the little snow angels, so blue and pretty and Christmasy. Cora's house was a Cornell box, with so many things just over there in the corner, shining, smiling, remembering your name. Cora closed herself up in a comfortable clutter of color and chip and ray, she kept herself that way, all small with the butterflies. She was happy at her house, the music collected in the walls after years of loud playing, the walls vibrating with the unwound sound. The director had said, 'I think the thing to work for and to get to really hope for is distinguished obscurity.' This had sounded important, and Cora wanted to write it down. But she couldn't find a pen, and besides, she felt certain that the director had said the thing before and, who knew, perhaps he'd say it to her again when she had a pen. Besides, what did the spaces between objects – objects or people – look like?

Cora suddenly wanted to see those paintings more than she wished she had a pen. She wanted to see them in the worst way. She wanted to see what Morandi would paint between William and the race he wouldn't win. She wondered how much blue would be in it. Or if the blue thing was just something she'd dreamed up, and the director hadn't said it at all.

For the next six weeks, William deteriorated in many critical, fundamental ways, but socially he maintained the lifestyle of a suburban show-business sultan. The extraordinary thing Cora discovered from being so close to so much tragedy was that it becomes another thing. This was William's row to hoe, but Cora felt it was her lookout to keep his garden fun. He had manicures and pedicures and massages and readied himself for dinner parties and screenings without the greatest of ease. 'What are we doing tonight?' He was anxious to keep moving, with the aid of his walker or his sugarless candy cane or his wheelchair with the silver spinning wheels. Cora divided her time between the job that was paying for her sultan's final swings and slow drives round the canyon, Joni Mitchell playing, the drizzling air coming through the car windows, the wheelchair crammed into the trunk, making it impossible to see through the rear window.

Initially, Ray moved in enough suits for one week, then two – then three, four, six. Cora took care of William without making it seem as though she was, and Ray took care of Cora, running his finger along the curve of her spine. He had shown up for the big show, but it was her gig. She'd signed on for it a long time ago. Still, he stayed long past when most people – well, who knew about most people, but he hung in there 'cause it was the right thing and William was a good guy, and they ended up doing the last good hard things for William together.

William took the long way home, a slow, circuitous drive, the scenic route, the destination final. Cora and Ray went along for the ride. Cora made up a game called

Sleeping in the Back of the Car. The rules of the game were that William would sleep or half-sleep in the back of the car while Ray and Cora drove and talked. Lying on the warm leather, the motor rumbling beneath him, William was obliged to either listen in or not listen in on Ray and Cora's conversation, their kiwi. Around midnight, when he was truly asleep, lines of liquid worming their way into whatever of him remained awake, Cora and Ray stole home.

When you get that close to death, everything living gets a little more lively, everything looks a little more lifelike, and you love it that much more to keep it near you. So Cora loved Ray more to keep him near her, and she loved William to keep him a bit back from death. His being so near to death upped their proximity. Everyone vibrated and hummed, and she and Ray began pulling at each other's clothes a little harder again at the end of the day. One look from his eiderdown-cast eyes, and she found that she now in fact – and even more in feeling – loved him. He was the one living nearest to her when living and living well made a new sort of sense.

Once during this whole episode Ray gave her a bath. That really got to her. She found that it was really hard to get too far away from someone who'd given you a bath, a washing clean as new music. Looking back, that's probably when she got pregnant. The bubbles, the scented water, the whole washcloth thing. Cora figured there weren't too many forms of contraception that could guard against the bath voodoo and his slipping her white nightgown over her damp head. How do you not have a baby with someone like that?

She wandered through the house at night, turning out the lights one by one, a nightly ritual, making her way to the bedroom in the back, joining him in the darkness there. A comfortable quiet had settled between them.

A silence that was like newly fallen snow. He may even have hummed in it somewhere. It sparkled in certain light, grew deeper over the long weeks, settled just under all the other sounds, took root in their workings and made its home. She felt she knew him. That mattered and so it went on. Hanging by the thread of his voice with one hand, swinging through these tough times.

She could rely on him to keep his word, be on time, talk her through it. Maybe not talk her through it in the way she was accustomed with her committee, her friends. But walk her through it in the way he seemed eminently able to do. She appreciated his effort, respected his too-good-to-be-trueness. His daily I-love-youness. His watchful, adoring eyes.

When Cora couldn't sleep, Ray would pet her to sleep. Now what sort of people do that? Certainly no one Cora ever knew. He curled himself around her and curved her off to sleep, while William's nutrition bag dripped high on its pole into the hole in his chest so he could get drip drip drops of nutrients while he dreamt his arm's length dreams in the outskirts of Cora and Ray's speakeasy, uneasy cozy round, making their curve just that much smoother, guarding the perimeters, leaving footprints in the soft mounds of snow.

Cora was gently awakened at five o'clock one morning. 'He's vomited a pint of blood,' said the night nurse in a low, matter-of-fact voice. 'I'm going to need you to sit with him while I call the paramedics.' Cora groped for the light and sat up, swimming as quickly as she could to the surface of the situation.

'What is it?' said Ray, squinting from his barely imprinted pillow.

'We have to go to the hospital,' she said, finding her clumsy way to the closet. 'I mean, I do. Something's happened.'

Ray flew back his sheet like an angel catching wing and made his way out from under its protective shadow. 'No, no, I'm coming,' he said, sitting on the edge of the bed and groping for his glasses, falling into step with her toward their friend's dwindling fortunes down the darkened hall. 'It'll be okay,' he whispered to her uneasily as they headed toward the brightly lit room and the quaking, shivering William, his bedpan half-filled with bright red blood, his body bent into a wide V, a pink dribbling of bubbles around his mouth, his teeth chattering white and square in his round, gray head.

Everything was clear then – they knew their parts, their designated posts, and the alarming spectrum of what they might have to do. The whites of William's eyes grew whiter with what seemed to be the unnaturally harsh light of the room. But maybe the situation in the room, the events themselves, gave the room its glaring whiteness. Cora thought how amazingly exact everything was. The bed was where the bed was, the TV stared down from the wall. People seemed to move differently in the heightened situation. Everything that happened at that particular moment contained the possibility, the imminent possibility, of death, a formidable equation.

Cora looked at William. She did not look at the blood. His hair, which had fallen out in a previous bout with illness, was growing in in little tufts. His head looked like something a child would do with a razor. Cora winced, trying to recall whether your hair and nails continued to grow after you died. She sat near William and gently patted his leg.

That first night William was in the hospital, he grabbed Ray's cooler hand. 'You love Cora, yeah?'

Ray swallowed, didn't look at her. 'Yeah,' he said quietly.

'I know you do 'cause you're being so lovely to me, yeah? Anyway, here's what I want – and I'm a sick person, so you have to give me what I want. It's the law, right, sweetheart?' He looked at Cora, who only smiled.

William continued. 'Cora's the family sort. We've always been family to each other. Well, I want you to do a favor for me. I want you to make Cora a baby. I don't require an answer now, but it is the request of a man in intensive care. I know what the baby would be, 'cause where I am, I'm closer to her than you are. Now, I don't want you to think I go in for all this heebie-jeebie kind of thing – but it stands to reason that as I've lost a few faculties, I've gained a few more. Your baby wants you to let it come, okay? It's ready now – and as far as you two go, there is no ideal time. Things don't fall into place like you think – but maybe they do in another way.

Ray, you're the only person I've met who could take care of Cora – who Cora would let take care of her. And if you took care of her, then she'd be able to take care of the baby. She can be counted on for the big things, and you seem like the sort who can be counted on for the details. And you know what they say – God is in the details. So if God is there, as far as I can make out, you're right in there with him and Cora is everywhere else. Surely there's room for a baby in the midst of all this wisteria.'

William turned to Cora. 'Can you buzz my nurse, Cor? I'm getting that old feeling again. Where's the TV clicker? Don't want to miss "Nightline."'

As she handed him the remote control, he whispered, 'Who is that girl over there in the corner?'

Cora looked and no one was there. 'There is no girl in the corner,' she reported apologetically.

William looked relieved. 'Oh, good, then I don't have to pretend I know her.'

Two days later, William started to die. At the beginning of the journey, a doctor drew Cora aside. He had the face of an apoplectic frog. All lips and no music. 'Are you, uh, in charge here?' What could that mean? The doctor didn't wait for her to answer. 'How does he seem to you? His attitude, I mean.' Cora didn't understand the question. 'Well,' said the doctor, 'to me he seems to be very, very depressed.'

Cora looked at the face of this very greasy man. 'I think I would be depressed, too, if I were in his situation. I think it would be weird if he weren't depressed.'

She went in and sat with William, who was conscious, fluorescent almost, giving out the last of his light. He drifted off, playing Sleeping in the Back of the Car. Ray and Cora and William's friends Jon and Michael and Louisa stood around the bed and rowed him through

95

it, talking to him when he broke through the surface of consciousness and swam toward them, stripped of his usual layers of accumulated sense.

'Where are my slippers? Where are my slippers?' he said, like a character in a bad English play. But you couldn't bring any personal effects to intensive care. Wouldn't it be great, Cora thought, if you really could go to a place that provided you with intensive care – code for 'whole lotta love.' You'd get a room and pad around the hallways in your pajamas, and everyone would be just great to you. They'd care about you in this really intensive way that was designed to ultimately make you feel better about yourself. How could all these really lovely, impressive people who were being nice to you be wrong? As it turned out, you were, in fact, a terrific human being and should never question it. This was the rest of your life now.

But that wasn't the intensive care that Cora was currently in, waiting out the day and a half William had left of his life. Although this one was homey and nice, as intensive care units went. The nurses were quiet, Asian, disconcertingly neat and prim, and very efficient. Everyone navigated carefully through the hush, dotted intermittently with tiny beeps that indicated something critical or activated something even more electronic and solemn-looking. This was serious. A lot of people didn't get out of this unit. Cora mentioned this to Ray and he gave her a strange look.

'I know you know that, Ray. I was just marveling at it. Can't a person marvel anymore?'

Ray smiled and swung around so his back was against the high-gloss white walls. He pulled Cora to him, his elbows resting on her shoulders. Cora moved to him, stood on her toes, and inhaled his particular, necessary neck. He moved his hands down her arms and across her back, lifting her, kissing her. The kiss traveled to remote, lucky parts of their bodies. A match was struck and *boom*, the whole forest went up like a tinderbox. She was greedy for him in her grieving.

William lay in bed and made funny remarks about the stylishness of his backless hospital gown. 'Cor – do you really think it's me? I don't think it does a bloody thing for me, if you want the God's honest truth.'

Cora sat on his bed. 'How about I get you some contraband Coca-Cola?' William's eyes widened, her hungry baby bird. He was allowed ice chips and what looked like an enormous Q-Tip, drenched in water. 'So if I dip your Q-Tip once in Coke instead of water – what're they gonna do, give you AIDS?'

Ray stayed with William while Cora haggled with the nurse in the doorway about when they could get him his own room. 'Have you alerted his family?' asked the greasy doctor, passing by. Cora shook her head and fell into step with him. They'd tried, but were having trouble reaching them given the time difference, and the odd fact that the phone numbers from William had seemed outdated. 'Well, I think it's critical that they be notified. This boy may not live to see Monday.' The doctor reached into his pocket and removed his wallet. He handed Cora his card with something like aplomb. She turned it over in her hand as though it might carry some special magic explanation, an insight about life, about death, a talisman – but no such luck. 'Call me if there's anything you need,' he said, patting her shoulder. 'He's fighting the good fight.'

Cora nodded again, not knowing what to say to this man – he perplexed her severely. 'Thank you,' she said, pocketing the card.

'That's okay. He seems like a sweet kid, your friend.' He shook his head. 'What a waste.'

Cora nodded, parted company with him at the nurses' station, and headed off in search of a Coke for William. For some reason, she began to imagine herself falling deeply in love with the fat, insensitive doctor through all the grief and displacement and rage. She began to do the ICU love polka in tribute to her imagined healer. 'I'm in love I'm in love I'm in love I'm in love I'm in love with a wonderful guy.'

At the elevators, she stopped singing. At the elevators, she began to feel upset. There was so little time to get hold of his parents in England, to get someone to bring a nicer pillow, a softer blanket, some music.

After twenty-four hours of trying to connect with William's mother and continuously missing one another – which was a lot of time in the all-or-nothing land of this – Cora was told that there was a call for her at the nurses' station. She picked up the beige receiver and placed it to her ear. 'Hello?' She heard the hot breath of the overseas connection.

'Hello, this is Wilhelmina Cadell,' a powerful voice boomed, trouncing the distance between them.

'Hi, Mrs. Cadell, I'm Cora.' Somehow she explained that William might not pull through this time. It struck her that 'might not pull through' was an easygoing way of saying that someone might die.

Mrs. Cadell was stoic, courageous, and devastated, and through all of this, Cora couldn't help noticing that apart from the English accent and the timbre of age to the vocal structure, there were common denominators between her and William's mother that finally enabled her to understand why William had agreed to come to California – come to her – to die. She was the next best thing to a replica of his beloved mum that he could travel to at his advanced stage. Mrs. Cadell had the sound and feel of someone who would get you through it, make it all right – or close enough to all right that you could feel the heat of it, smell the bangers and mash.

Cora was frequently frightened by the certainty crowded and cheering in her own voice. Hers was a hybrid of her mother's rowdy sureness and her own efforts to rally herself over the finish line, through the hoop, straight over the astonished heads of the crowd in the bleachers and out of the park. But force of will didn't always translate into a more festive fact of life.

Cora had a nurse put the call through to William's room. 'Oh, I'm all right,' he told his father as he lost control of an important bodily function. His way of coping with his death was to reassure himself and those around him that it was not going to occur anytime soon, if at all. 'Had a bit of a scare last night, really, but everyone's being fab here, Dad, so not to worry . . . love you.'

Cora and Ray and the nurse cleaned him up and got him ready for bed. The call had exhausted him. Ray waited outside the door until William fell asleep. Cora approached him, put her head on his chest. 'I don't know how he's doing it,' Ray remarked with a kind of wonder. The nurse, whom Cora regarded as the seraph of the HIV unit, told them they should go home and get some sleep – tomorrow would undoubtedly be another eventful day.

Arm in arm, they left the hospital – lucky, lucky – unable to keep their hands off each other, hands creeping into clothing, field hands stealing a break while the foreman's back was turned. Ray steered with his left hand, exploring with his right, her mouth on his neck, his jawline, his chin. They kissed with all the life they had left in them, with the luxury of living, barely getting the car into park. Watching William die pushed them into a panic of passion that neither of them had experienced before. Exhausted, they tore into each other, wordless, impatient, flushed with common purpose, wet with fear and exultation. They found the fleshier parts of their anatomy and squeezed, gorging themselves on the life still left there, left and hopefully not leaving. A scramble of limbs, imploring, frantic twin shapes, their Siamese serpent shrouded in sheets shed an old skin under a new moon. Fugitives from an informed world, beyond abashed, they crash-landed there, making their home together out in the dunes.

'Wow,' one whispered reverently, their coin spent and rolling toward slumber. Cora closed her eyes and curled herself into their cozy round.

They slept.

The phone rang, again at five a.m. It was the seraph. 'Better get over here,' he said. 'He's doing it.'

'What?' asked Cora, leaning up on one shoulder. 'What is he doing?'

There was the smallest of pauses. 'He's gone into reverse labor. He's started to die.'

Apparently there is a sort of reverse labor that goes into effect in the final stage of dying, only the rhythm rides you out, not in. Ray and Cora dressed in silence and drove to the hospital. A Robert Cray song came on. 'I'll be there to hold you – don't be afraid of the dark.' It was the hour when the streets are cleaned, a mist covers taller buildings, your breath comes out smoky, you talk in whispers. They drove straight toward the mystery, Cora clutching Ray's cool undriving hand.

They arrived at the hospital as things were promising to turn a lighter shade of blue. She looked at Ray over the top of the car, but there was absolutely nothing she could say to him about what he was about to do with her. This difficult, important thing. Ray scratched his blond-stubbled chin and looked up at the hospital as if it were a formidable opponent. He sighed and adjusted his collar, and he and Cora strode into the building that would soon swallow her friend.

William's room was a deep blue. There was a warm hum. Transparent bags hung around him, tinted clear to deep red. Cora went to his head and began to talk to him, touch him. If this was some kind of relay, she wanted to make certain that William would be passed like the beloved prize he was.

As the day grew brighter, he grew dimmer, and more of his friends gathered around his bed. They took up their oars and rowed with him as far as they could. 'You've done everything you've had to do. You've done it and you've done it well. Now you have to do just one more thing. And that thing is nothing at all. Feel all the colorful warm liquids passing into you. Let them do their magic, let us work our charm. Okay?'

'Okay,' William said with the gentlest resignation. 'All right.' His eyes closed, skin yellow.

They made the crossing with him as far as they could, and the morphine took him the rest of the way. William's sister, Rose, arrived from England. The nurse believed he had stayed alive to see her. She sat beside him and stroked his wasted hand, weeping.

Cora couldn't bear to watch the lines go flat. She drove home with Ray and they had sex, brought each other back into being, long after William could stay alive. They slept until noon, Ray's hair wet on the back of his neck.

A sort of hush fell over them for the rest of the day. They were gentle with each other, tender even. They looked out of questioning, frightened eyes, gripped hands fiercely in an effort to stay near, to keep each other from being plucked from the earth randomly, suddenly, never to return. William had had the most difficult, unspeakable, painful task, and what remained of him in the end was his extraordinary courage, his humor, and . . . something like willingness and appreciation. Maybe death was less terrifying now that they'd participated, assisted, loved him from this place to the next. Maybe, after they'd clung so closely to him, he'd left them nearer to each other, left them loving. Loving through the various points of no return and back again.

William's brother, Simon, arrived early that evening. It was decided without the aid of decisive communication that Rose and Simon would stay at Cora's house. Having temporarily exhausted their skills in making tangible plans or choices, they all found themselves back in her kitchen, talking in hushed tones about the difficulties William's siblings had had organizing flights. Cora busied herself heating up odd combinations of food that everyone seemed grateful for but no one could quite bring himself to eat. At some point during the evening, William's wife, Adele, whom William had married to get a green card long ago, called from New York.

The twilight staggered and then fell weightless on all of them, as if not wishing to add to the burden of losing such a featherlight brother and friend. Cora showed Rose and Simon the room where William had passed his final weeks. The three stood in the doorway staring at the space that had so recently been his as Ray struggled down the stairway to the guest room with Simon's bags. It had been tacitly decided that Rose would stay in William's old bed.

Simon scanned the room. 'Well, it's nice he had such a nice place to be in when . . . I mean, well, it's great that you were so lovely to him,' he said awkwardly. He cleared his throat and crossed to William's black cane, which leaned next to the closet by the bed. It reminded her of the cane Natalie Wood found by the stairs in *Miracle on 34th Street*, allowing her to believe in Santa Claus after all.

'I loved him,' said Cora as lightly as possible, not focusing on the love, this bright feeling that ached at her insides. Simon could very well have been William's twin, except that his features were slightly more pointed and he had a decidedly heterosexual air. Cora was transfixed by this healthy image of William, moving through the shadowy silence as though he were dancing. Rose watched him also, under the same spell. His hand hovered over the nightstand and the medications there as though feeling for any shreds of his dead brother's spirit that might still be clinging to them. Simon's face caught the light from the bedside lamp, caught it and held it before Cora realized they were watching him cry. For a moment, she grew dizzy, dizzy from all the tears she hadn't shed. She was not an unabashed person, was the consoler, not the consoled one. Now that William was gone, she found these tender feelings coming unleashed. Feelings she had fastened onto him, that he had not taken when he'd gone.

Rose went to her brother and wound her arms around him. Three had been their charm, and now their magic number had been reduced to this tangle of two. It was impossible to think that other losses such as these could and would be endured in a life.

Back in the kitchen Rose made tea, Celestial Seasonings. Ray made himself a drink, alcohol of some sort with ice and lemon. Simon had taken a shower and changed into dark, clean clothes. Cora was trying to think of things to tell them about William's passing. Nice, neat things that wouldn't make anyone cry. 'He liked me to drive him slowly around Mulholland listening to R.E.M. on CD. He planned to return to England to be with his family. Not to die. To see you, his parents, to live.'

Rose stirred her tea thoughtfully, steam rising into her

face. 'I never thought he'd die, really,' she said softly. 'He's had so many close calls before.'

Close calls, mused Cora, like labor. Calls that came closer and closer until there was no time left at all. Calls that were heralded without an abundance of ringing. Something left forever after the last, lonely beep. 'So what are we . . . ,' began Simon haltingly. 'What do we do now? I mean, he's still at the hospital, isn't he?' It was hard for Cora to imagine William anyplace right now but trapped in the crosshairs of Simon's and Rose's gazes.

Ray leaned against the oven, nursing his drink, still unshaven, restored to an uneasy calm. 'The body has to be transferred to a mortuary,' he said hollowly. 'One that accepts . . . HIV deaths. And then we have to decide where – or if – you want to have him buried.'

'He wanted to be cremated,' Rose informed them, staring into her cup as if the teabag told this plan. 'He left some instructions with his friend Peter in New York. He didn't want to go home in a box, wearing a baggy suit and funny shoes.'

Cora smiled. 'Those are the words he used?'

Rose swallowed her tea and looked up with a serious face. 'He didn't want to rely on anyone to dress him. He always said it was too momentous a fashion decision, to commit to one suit for the rest of his life. Anyway, he told Peter he wanted to be cremated and his remains put in some sort of container that made a statement. And then one of us was to bring him back home to Mum.'

'So, who's to pick the container?' asked Cora.

'Well, I assume we three.' Rose turned to Ray. 'Unless of course you could join?'

Ray looked to Cora for help. 'He can't miss any more work,' Cora said quickly. 'So why don't we three go in the morning?'

Ray bid them good-night and headed off to bed.

Cora made Simon and Rose hot cocoa with marshmallows and showed them how to turn off the lights, leaving them to smoke and call their parents to let them know that all was more or less well, considering.

In the bedroom, Cora found Ray ritualistically lighting scented candles on either side of the bed. 'You're not one to stand on ceremony,' she said, coming up behind him and slipping her arms around his chest.

Ray squeezed her hand and pulled her down onto the bed on top of him. 'How do you stand on ceremony?' he asked kissing her. The smell of jasmine permeated the room. She kissed him without passion as he smoothed the hair from her face. 'First you must get special stand on ceremony shoes,' she answered him, but she saw he wasn't listening. She remembered he'd lost five friends by the time he was eighteen – an unusual number unless you'd been caught in a battle or a bombing. He rarely discussed this period of his life, and she wondered how he'd weathered these losses. Had they left him with a fear of attachment? Did he feel safe with her because he could concentrate on her ambivalence rather than admit to his own? Somehow it felt as if they'd gotten as attached as they were capable of – anything beyond was fraught with reticence and the wrong sorts of shoes. Their shapes flickering on the walls, they fought for whatever closeness remained to them, enveloped in the jasmine and the expensive flannel sheets.

After Ray fell asleep, Cora watched him, his face peaceful, vulnerable, spent as someone's last hard-earned buck. She noticed, watching him, how soft his features were when disengaged from their usual inscrutable configuration. What energy it must take him to appear so closely engaged from such a faraway place. She couldn't help but wonder if he had actually made it there at all. Or whether a part of him had watched and waited, measuring out how much he was putting out with each exhalation of generosity, and how close every intake of breath brought him to the person he longed to be with – or longed to be.

He frowned in his sleep and rolled over, disengaging himself from the sharp, silent claws of her scrutiny. How would she ever return this gesture of his – of having been so long in the right place at the wrong time? She felt herself poised once again on the high dive of disappointment. How soon would they return to whomever it was they had been before? The couple who had been unable to marry and unable not to marry, but able somehow to partner together so that a dear friend could slowly die?

The next morning, Cora kissed Ray good-bye as though he were going to war, then breakfasted with Simon and Rose. Rose made them all cheese omelettes, and toast topped with butter and jam. They planned to drive to the place where William's body had been sent to be cremated to pick the urn and make whatever other arrangements needed to be made. It was way out in the Valley, farther out than Cora had ever gone before.

They went through William's clothes, looking for something suitable for him to wear while he was reduced to ash and bone. Simon put on one of William's jackets, still suffused with his smell.

'What about this?' Cora suggested, raising a blue and white work shirt. 'He always loved this one because it was so soft.' They looked at one another, each of them fondling articles of William's clothing. All at once, as if a gust of wind had descended from the heavens, they collapsed in laughter, still clutching the clothes.

'It's so ridiculous, isn't it?' said Rose, wiping tears from her eyes. 'I mean, it's not as though he's going to feel it, his soft shirt – and who besides us is going to see?'

Cora gasped for breath, holding the shirt in one hand and William's red bandanna in another. 'You never know who he'll run into. It is L.A., after all – appearance plays an all-important part, whether you're no longer living or just unknown.'

Simon was the first to attempt a return to the seriousness befitting their situation. 'C'mon now, ladies, we've got to compose ourselves.'

'Before he starts decomposing,' added Cora, causing a raucous renewal of their morbid mirth.

'He'd want us to laugh, wouldn't he?' Rose ventured in an attempt to rationalize their possibly disrespectful merriment. 'He'd want us to laugh and he'd want us to dress him in the style to which he'd become accustomed.' They settled on the blue shirt, his best jeans, a bandanna, and socks. Comfort had been such an elusive state in the last year of his illness that they were determined to get him there in this final phase of his physical life.

Cora had been in such a frenzy of concern for William that she could not break the momentum, for to do that was to confront some unspeakable peril. To do that was to accept that William was really dead. He couldn't have died so long as there were still ways to attend to him. So long as he had clothing and family – as his sweet, doomed scent still clung to his bedroom and clothes. His situation had so required her. She had been critical to him, he had given her the honor of easing his sizable pain. It was the only situation she'd ever been in that had told her over and over exactly what it was that she needed to do next. She – and Ray – had risen to someone else's last, towering occasion. She'd been able to do something she hadn't dreamed she could do. She hadn't dreamed she could, but the dream she hadn't dreamed had been the waking-up sort.

The day was uncharacteristically overcast. Simon clutched a scrap of yellow paper with the directions to the mortuary. He sat at Cora's side as she maneuvered them farther and farther toward the low mountains half-hidden by dark clouds. Rose sat in the back, smoking with the window open, the damp, warm wind blowing onto her face.

'Ray seems a good chap,' said Simon amiably. 'So kind to do all of this for us. I mean, it's not as though he knows us at all.' They passed car dealerships and appliance stores, doughnut shops, and low buildings that boasted 'Authentic Mexican Cuisine.'

'Not that we really know you either,' Simon continued forlornly. 'But you've been friends with Willie so long and we've heard so much about you.' They ventured farther on into the Valley, past storage buildings and mattress stores and very little green.

'I don't know what I would've done without Ray,' said Cora wistfully. 'Not many people . . .' She trailed off, looking for the cross street, unable to adequately complete her thought.

Their destination turned out to be a low building off the main drag that you entered through the back. 'Aftercare Mortuary' was written in gold lettering on the glass door. Funny how the word *care* kept cropping up in this process of death and dying. Home care for the nursing, intensive care for the dying, and aftercare for the cleaning up. There must be a point in the not too distant future when you got past all the various points of caring, but Cora couldn't foresee when that time would come.

A bell rang as they entered a hallway with low ceilings. The building seemed to be airless, but perhaps there just wasn't enough oxygen anywhere for their current task. Cora missed Ray, missed the clean nearness of him, the flat of his hand steady on her lower back. The situation had pulled her down through illness and dying, finally dropping her from death into this cramped and creepy place. A neglected plant stood by the door as they looked around for some sign of life. Cora found herself looking at Simon's profile. It was hard not to touch him, so much of William was there. And in her highly charged state, all her senses pushed to their limit, she was distressed to discover an erotic component to her otherwise bereaved involvement with him.

She flushed, looked away from Simon as a door down the hall opened and a little man with dyed black hair and mustache made his way slowly down the hall. He wore powder-blue pants that were too short for him and black boots with a buckle at each side. He approached Rose first, extending his hand. 'I'm Albert Blackstone, manager of Aftercare Mortuary,' he said carefully, looking out from under his considerable eyebrows. 'How do you do.'

He led them through a small doorway into a low-ceilinged room. The room was lined with shelves that displayed a variety of ornate vaselike receptacles. In the center of the room was a table covered with six or seven scrapbooks and a small container half-filled with business cards and brochures. 'This is our selection of urns for the ashes of the recently deceased.' He gestured around the room to the various containers, ranging from plain to ornate. Many of them looked like music boxes to Cora, and she wondered what theme for the recently deceased each of them would play.

She made her way over to what appeared to be a marble rendering of the globe. 'What kind of person would someone put in this?' she asked no one in particular.

'We like to have an assortment with something for everyone,' said Mr. Blackstone, proudly gesturing around the room. Cora wanted to ask him how he'd arrived in his particular line of work. Was it a calling or something you fell into, like a destructive love affair or a freshly dug grave? 'We try to keep a variety of receptacles for the loved one in stock. So that each person can find one they'll feel comfortable placing in a prominent position within the family home.' Mr. Blackstone handed them a price list, and the three of them browsed through their macabre, expensive choices as if it were something they were accustomed to doing, something they would undoubtedly do again.

Simon ran his hand over a low rectangular box sporting a small gondola. 'Will always did like Venice,' he remarked sadly. 'But I don't know if he liked it enough to lie under it from this point on.'

Rose turned from an urn that looked something like a rocket. 'This is really absurd, you know,' she observed brightly. 'I mean, it really is, isn't it? Or am I still so jet-lagged that nothing seems real?'

Cora lifted something heavy and bronze-looking from a corner table. 'I think William would love this. It looks like something from *Indiana Jones and the Temple of Doom*.' The three clustered around the powerful object she held before her, appraising it solemnly.

'Yeah,' said Simon. 'It's perfect. It has irony and majesty.'

'Just about everything but a jaunty little hat,' said Cora.

After selecting the urn, they proceeded to the coffins. They pored over the scrapbooks in the hot room, drinking coffee and perspiring. 'What's the point of an expensive coffin?' said Simon, staring at a white

111

coffin lined with satin. 'They're just going to burn it.' Cora frowned. The coffin was three thousand dollars.

'There has to be a compromise between the royal treatment and the plague,' said Rose. The term struck Cora as an unfortunate choice. But in this climate, everything had so many meanings. An undercurrent with a powerfully grim pull attended all their dealings. They were silent for a moment as they perused the boxes for the dead. Simon was still wearing William's jacket, and as he grew warmer, the scent of William was dense and disconcerting in the room. They finally selected a simple mahogany model lined with something akin to wool and cotton. It seemed almost elegant. Or not. But what else could they do?

While they waited for Mr. Blackstone to draw up the invoice, Cora found herself thumbing through a book of coffins for infants and children of various sizes. She wanted to slam the book shut, but it held her attention from front to back. A life unlived, without even a partial vocabulary. She hoped that doomed infants lacked the wherewithal to grasp the horror of their situation. But the parents – what of the parents choosing a box for their baby beloved? Should it be the one with the tiny angel, the one with the wreath, or the one with the baby bird? She shuddered and wandered over to the small gray window. Rose was looking at the flyer for a burial at sea.

They decided on the Traditional Funeral with Cremation, which included embalming or 'alternate care' of the deceased. Cora found it funny that you were required by law to get a permit for disposition of the body. Meaning you paid the state seven dollars to be allowed to have someone reduced to ash. There would be taped music and prayer cards at a place called Chapel of the Pines. Cora wrote a check for ten thousand dollars and they readied to leave. 'Jesus, it costs a lot of money to get off this planet,' she said. 'I wonder how it compares to the tariff on birth.'

Neither Cora nor Rose was anxious to attend the cremation, so it was decided that Simon would go and dress William the following morning and follow the body to the cremation site to witness him going into the incinerator – not only William but his clothing and his casket and its woollike lining, mused Cora as she started her car. Indivisible for all eternity, this three-part puddle of person, clothes, and casket – robbed of its spirit and resting in Indiana's Temple of Doom. Did the body resist the fire? How long did it take to pulverize the bones? Things you couldn't possibly find yourself wondering about they'd be well versed in all too soon.

Cora woke in the morning to the feeling of Ray snuggling up to her. She rolled toward him and they wound their way into each other awake. But more of the urgency had tiptoed out of their lovemaking; at least Cora heard the whispered footfalls as they came to another rest. She found herself thinking of Simon driving out to Van Nuys now, out to the building with the smoking chimneys and the Chapel of the Pines. Was she thinking of Simon or of William? One seemed to have passed into the next. She felt Ray breathing next to her, felt him watching the side of her inwardly gazing eyes. For the first time in a while, she found herself with nothing to say to him. Now that they had dispensed with the urgency of William's dying, the situation that had knit them so closely together, there was more sunlight between them, more time to take for working, for telephone calls, or even sleep.

They had looked at each other across William's death-bed with such gratitude and trust and relief. That's what death gives to the living – the love for a fellow soldier in battle, won by a higher order of losing. Of watching life slip away into something less than death because of the company they were able to keep. Survivors of someone else's storm, they'd been whipped into whirlwinds of love and fear and stillness. Ray had been her hero, she William's – he the biggest hero of all. They'd clung together in the foxhole, bullets singing over their heads, kissing the urgent kiss of companions in battle. Ray had been her confederate confidant, together they'd roamed

115

through the valley of death, shouting 'Yea.' A man like this would not be so easily dispensable. But somehow, with all the activity slowing now, she found herself in sight of another sort of end. And Cora was an ambivalent person, as she had warned him. Ambivalent, and now, the morning after the fierce battle to keep hold of losing ground, of good friends, of common cause – spent and alone.

'Ugh,' said Cora.

'What?' asked Ray, kissing her face and frowning mouth.

'It's just a thought-dispersal technique I use to crowd out unpleasant thoughts.' She turned into the crook of his arm.

'The cremation is this morning, right?' he said quietly.

Cora held her breath imperceptibly, then said, 'Right.'

Ray left for work, natty in his smooth gray slacks and white shirt. Cora, by contrast, was wearing something slipped on in a dark wind tunnel, rumpled and ravaged from her ambivalence fête. It hung on her forlornly, the hem anxious for the floor.

She had an appointment with Bud to prepare for a rewrite they'd be doing in New York in a couple of weeks. It was on a romantic thriller, their first, called *Dead and Married*. The problem was the setup, a relationship that was eroding from the outside. It needed to be reworked so that it was eroding from within. 'It's an inside job,' Bud had mocked, using jargon he had picked up from his lengthy, unsuccessful stint in AA. Cora felt she had a raucous and eerie affinity for the material, especially a speech the mother made to the daughter: 'Marriage is a pact, in its original inception, without outs. Our generation understood that. Your generation does not. If you give yourself an out, make no mistake, you will take it.' (The 'make no mistake' was later cut.)

It wasn't that Cora was actually versed in this motherly advice. True, her mother had rarely been unmarried – first to Cora's father, then to the unbelievably nonverbal Bob, a real estate developer who spent most of his time in Florida. Viv didn't so much like men as require them in the abstract:

'Men are basically selfish stinkers, they're very competitive and they just hate you if you have a job – particularly if you have as good a job as they do or better. Now, I've always been a worker, so it takes a very secure man to live with that. And there are no truly secure men in my opinion – except maybe Ross Perot, who has those horrible little teeth. So you just have to put up with it, that's all. It's an imperfect situation, and in the final analysis, most women are just too good for most men. They don't deserve us. The main thing they're good for is making babies, only nowadays you can go to a sperm bank. But I got you out of one of them, so that makes up for the money he lost me and the pain he caused me. My point is, always keep your finances separate and don't count on them for much. Look at Paulette Goddard. She was independent and rich all her life, and she died in Paris with a smile on her face.'

Bud swung his door open to receive her, with an exaggerated, forlorn expression on his expressive face. 'It's the angel of mercy,' he said sadly as Cora swept by him and into his strange, spare loft.

'What happened?' she said.

Bud frowned, then laughed an odd laugh, a laugh without anything akin to merriment, even his ghoulish brand. 'Camille and I are getting divorced,' he announced lightly. 'Is it "getting divorced,"' he continued, looking perplexed, 'or "getting a divorce"? Is it a verb or a noun? Divorcing is an action, right? And a divorce is kind of a thing, isn't it?'

Cora stared at him blankly.

Bud put his head back and gazed at the ceiling. 'I married her, okay?' he said flatly. 'I married Camille six weeks ago and now it's over. Look,' he said, standing and beginning to pace, 'I was trying to be a human being – but whenever I do that, I always end up being confronted with what an alien I am.' He paused, interlaced his fingers under his chin, and jerked his hands up, cracking his knuckles noisily. Cora cringed.

'That's not clear, is it?' Bud continued. 'I want to be precise.' He resumed his pacing. 'I woke up with this woman every day not knowing where I was – what country I was in. She used to say to me – now this is daily, mind you – "What's the matter?" And I would consider – I'm a Jew, remember, "What's the matter?" is a very provocative question – and I would think and then say, "Nothing. Why?" And she would say, "Oh, it's no big deal. You just seem so – hey, never mind. Forget it." Forget it? I would be totally thrown – well, thrown, anyway. So then these hideous silences would ensue, and finally after like two weeks, we go to see this marriage counselor.' Bud began to laugh and shake his hanging head. 'You should've seen this therapist's face when we said we'd been married a month. Anyway, the guy tells us that we should never fight in the house, that whenever we feel a fight coming on – as if we're talking about a cold or something – we should jump in my truck and go to, like, a coffee shop and have the fight there.' He slapped his forehead and ran his hand over his face.

'Why were you not allowed to fight at home?' asked Cora eagerly from the edge of the bed. She was happy to have her friend back.

'Aw, please, don't ask. Something to do with having the house get too toxic. Or maybe so we didn't associate the house with fighting. Unfortunately, I've got bad associations with about nine coffee shops – including the Hash House, which was one of my favorites.' He sat next to Cora on the bed, drained and winded. Then he turned to her and said with exaggerated perkiness, 'So how've you been?'

Cora reached into her bag and removed a pack of cigarettes and a lighter. She lit up and inhaled, then exhaled the smoke through her nose. 'Let me ask you something frankly, no jokes allowed.' Bud sat expectantly before her, awaiting his charge. 'What do you think of Ray?'

Bud looked at her for a moment, blinking. 'Uh . . . well, well, give me a second. You've caught me off-guard. A real question. What do I think of him how?'

Cora rolled her eyes up, thinking. 'Me and him. What do you think of me and him as a . . . unit?'

'A unit?' Bud pursed his lips. 'Well, he seems really good to you, right? I mean, he's a sweet guy, very solicitous. Remember that party you had for Norma? He was great. He made drinks and, you know, seemed really engaging and such.'

Cora scanned her memory for a vision of this solicitous, engaging Ray. 'Did he . . . ,' she began slowly, 'did he make too many drinks?'

Bud looked confused. 'You mean, get people drunk?'

'No,' said Cora. 'No. You know what I mean. Did he . . . make too many drinks for too many people?'

Bud scratched his face. 'Well . . . I mean . . . he's a lawyer, right? A solicitor – they tend to be solicitous.' He looked up, a gleam in his eye.

Cora stubbed out her cigarette. 'Thanks,' she said tersely, pushing her hair back off her eyes.

Bud fell to his knees before her. 'Oh, Caesar, don't be mad. I'm beholden to you. For that matter, I am Bill Holden to you.' He touched her knee tentatively.

119

'Did I answer wrong?' he asked imploringly, gazing up at her.

Her eyes met his, her brow furrowed. 'No.'

Cora left Bud's just after five o'clock. The sky was overcast and a breeze was blowing cool air from the sea. The writing partners had found themselves too distracted to get much work done. Cora had a chilly, anxious feeling. They decided to resume the following morning, giving themselves some time for the ravages of emotional stress. 'Good-night, you gladiator,' Bud called to her from the door. But Cora was already gone.

She arrived back at her house close to six, stalled by an accident. She pulled up to her gate to find Simon trying to climb over it. She got out of the car and approached him as he turned to her with a pale, alarmed face. 'Oh, thank God!' he moaned as he gathered her into his arms.

'What's going on?' she asked, returning the embrace, squeezing his lean frame tightly in the fading light.

He held on to her, swaying and smelling vaguely of marijuana. 'Oh, it was awful, just terrible,' he moaned, pulling back slightly to gaze remorsefully into her face. 'I watched the box – the coffin – go down this moving sort of surface into the terrible thing. And as it was almost through the doors, I saw his sock coming out the corner of the box. This white sock. Or maybe I imagined it. But it was moving through those little doors. I spent the rest of the time outside on a bench.'

'I'm so sorry,' said Cora.

He exhaled softly, losing his balance slightly. Cora steadied him. 'So I found this joint in Will's jacket and I smoked it in the parking lot in back of that awful place. And then . . . well, it felt like I drove for hours with his ashes and this awful headache – I couldn't figure out where I was. After a while, I just started talking to William, just telling him everything. How I missed him, how I loved him – how sorry I was about the sock and the dope.'

He embraced Cora again, and she patted his back. 'It's okay. Everything'll be better soon, I swear.'

He nodded his head next to hers as the wind whispered through the trees overhead. She felt like an ass making this sweeping kind of assurance, the kind of assurance Ray made to her, the sort she rarely believed. But it was nice to hear and Cora had said it because she hadn't known what else to say.

'The other thing,' Simon said softly. His breath was on her neck, his British accent pronounced, his voice low and crushed. 'This terrible thing they told me. I just can't get it out of my head. This man there told me that after they burn you and reduce you to ash and pulverize your bones – after that, he said, you're three times the size of sand. That's all that's left, you know? Or anyway, so he said. It's not the sort of thing someone takes the piss out of you on, you know? And it just . . . bothered me on top of everything, to think of Will as little as that.'

They stood in the driveway in silence, holding each other, regulating their breathing and beating hearts, as lights came around the corner and Ray pulled up next to Cora's car. Simon jumped back from her and put a nervous hand over his head. 'Hey,' said Ray easily, rolling down his window, 'what's the deal?'

'Simon couldn't get in,' Cora explained briskly, moving to her car. 'He had a bad day with the urn.' Oh, God, don't let this be an incident, she thought, not on top of the rest. She followed Ray up the driveway and parked. In the rearview mirror, she watched Simon making his way gingerly toward them, William's urn tucked protectively under his arm. Three times the size of sand, she thought, that's a good title. She made a mental note to tell Bud and made a point of trying not to think about anything else.

That night in bed she waited for Ray to mention finding her in Simon's arms on the street, but he only slipped in beside her, twining his chilly feet with hers. Winding their way into their cozy round, which wasn't quite so fierce now, had grown susceptible to other shapes, looser forms. 'I love you,' he said, pulling her on top of him. She didn't reply, just squeezed him back, her eyes shut tight.

The love they had left for one another seemed to be at a greater distance now. In the beginning their love had been a big thing that threw shadows on all that was missing. He still told her he loved her. 'I love you, g'night.' 'Bye-bye, I love you.' But now she wondered if it was to remind himself or to coax an ember of their infatuation into flame. Sometimes it echoed hollowly, like the catechism of a lapsed Catholic.

There must be other kinds of relationships, she thought. Of course, you couldn't help hitting pockets of disenchantment, stretches of desert, but from the outside, most looked like fairly amiable agreements. Agreements to walk side by side, to point things out to one another. To interact, to run errands, to lean in to hear what the other was saying. To be good about most things and let the little ones go by. To say how you feel without the you-make-me's. To propose solutions to the hurt feeling you've amassed over a lifetime. To lie twined together, waiting.

Cora listened as Ray's breathing slowed to a kind of snore. Her finger moved from his jawline to his shoulder. A confusion of heartbeats pounded between them. His teeth ground slowly, etching swirls in the round silence of his mouth.

She pushed herself slowly from him, easing her weight

off, careful not to wake him. His eyes flashed open. Startled, he grabbed her. 'No!' he cried. 'I've got you.' He looked at her through the dark, blinking, orienting himself to awakening. She looked back at him, waiting; he released her, relieved, one hand pushing his hair back in wonder, his eyes to the ceiling, remembering where he'd come from, exhausted, breathless from the trip.

'Jeez. Sorry. I dreamt you were falling out of bed.' He patted her, rolled over, and resumed sleep.

Her hands groped for the clicker; she turned on the television, her very complicated wallpaper. On a cable access show, a woman read poetry on the loss of her breast to cancer. What if she were alone right now, like William, trapped on all four sides by something intangible, something untouchable, inescapable? She reached out to touch Ray, to get from him her measure of peace, but he did not stir. She wondered whether someone like herself would be there to send her off when it was her turn to leave this life. And then she thought, but someone like me will be there. I'll be there.

'I love you,' Cora whispered to William, staring into the dark. Ray's arm heavy over her, she slept.

The winds blew hard the next morning, clearing the basin of its usual smoggy congestion. Everything gleamed, causing Cora to blink back from this blanket of brightness. They were going to a noon mass at the Church of the Good Shepherd, where William would be remembered and receive his last rites from the God of his childhood.

She brushed her teeth next to Ray, who stood shaving in the nude. 'Do we wear black?' she asked, wiping toothpaste from her mouth. 'I mean, it's not really his funeral, right? It's more like a remembrance at a mass.'

Ray pulled his razor along his throat. 'It doesn't

123

really feel like you need me for this conversation, do you?'

Cora couldn't tell whether he sported a grimace or a smile. 'Maybe a kind of dark blue,' she continued, applying moisturizer to her face and neck. 'Not really sunny and not really sad.' She nodded to herself with satisfaction as she started from the bathroom. 'I could see your penis, you know, Ray – it's bad luck before church.'

Church – the vaulted ceilings, the colorful windows, the prayers for mercy and peace – always made Cora want to sob. If she could cry enough, maybe she could become one of them, a humble member of a parish. Even being a lapsed Catholic would be better than being a spirited person sorely lacking in spiritual life. Christ hung on his cross above the altar, looking less like a savior and more like a survivor of Auschwitz – like William in the end, with a beard and long hair. The wasted body, the head dropped to one side, the air of exhaustion – of exhausted, exalted peace.

Sitting between Ray and Simon, Cora listened to the words of the priest. 'May we live as disciples, supporting and nourishing each other,' he intoned. Cora closed her stinging eyes. He spoke of the 'glorious mystery' and asked Jesus to 'renew us – lift up our hearts.' He urged them to advance peace and salvation for all the world. 'Father, hear the prayers of your family whom you have gathered here.'

Cora ran her hand over the light, smooth wood of the pew before her. Maybe if she were full of grace she wouldn't have to sob when surrounded on all sides by forgiven sinners and stained glass. T. S. Eliot had been religious – just because she was a hack writer, surely Christ wouldn't turn her away.

Ray reached for her hand. His felt warm and rubbery

– not spiced with spirit and glory and the kingdom of God. The helping hand of a handsome boy from the South. The illness and decay that had surrounded their union, that had pushed them closer than ever before, had finally brought them to this church and under the compassionate eye of a merciful God.

Kneeling next to Ray, bathed in the soft light coming through the panels of the colored windows, the candles glowing, the flowers fresh and sanguine, Cora felt the intense events that had bound them so tightly together coming to a close. They had been the best part of a bad set of circumstances. Ray had loved her as William was leaving her, making his departure easier to bear. She had offered up a shoulder to die on; he, one to cry on. Now the crying and dying were almost at an end, and she realized that beyond lay only disappointment. She would never be able to equal for Ray the fierceness or commitment she'd shown to William in death. Ray wasn't dying of anything in particular, but over time, he would come to feel neglected and undernourished by her. Having taken care of the caretaker, he would require something of the same in return. He had courted her mightily, a loving pretender to her throne. Coming together out of need instead of want – in deed instead of common speak – had been a fierce and glorious thing. But it was the hardest act in the world to follow. How could they make the leap from death to marriage and a good life, from dark blue to virgin white? He seemed to worship her, a dangerous devotion. Things could only go downhill from there. And though she knew that beginnings were often a fine way to start, this beginning already contained the seeds of a predictable ending, an ending they'd arrive at after a stretch of comfortable reassurances, reassurances that neither would really believe.

The priest said a blessing for William, 'a fellow disciple from overseas,' and Cora felt her composure begin to betray her. Her sweet companion of nightly cozy rounds was falling through her hands. Without William, there was no cause to intensely connect them; without William they'd be together alone.

Her eyes filled and she shivered. Ray drew her to him and kissed the crown of her head. She leaned against his shoulder, patting one hand on the buttons of his soft, white shirt. The priest assured them that those who had left everything and followed Him would now be 'repaid a hundredfold and given eternal life.' Cora doubted, missed William, and wept.

Cora and Ray had been invited to Ron Silton's birthday party at his extraordinary beach house just outside of Malibu. Ron was an extremely successful studio executive who lived with beautiful Harry, the young producer, who everyone agreed looked almost exactly like Daniel Day-Lewis. Like Ray, Harry was also from South Carolina, and Ray had recently taken him on as a client.

Ron was a very young looking man in his early fifties, who took a lot of time and effort to maintain his youthful appearance and trim physique. He kept up a strict regime of vegetarianism and yoga and acupuncture on top of his meditation and massage and Noel's collagen injections to eliminate whatever wrinkles the creams and the diet and the stress-reducing meditation couldn't quite obliterate. Every year for Christmas, Ron had given Cora crystals for her bath and gardenias floating in a crystal bowl. To the best of her recollection, Cora had never seen him in anything but a cheerful, jocular mood.

Cora knew that Ray truly enjoyed these parties – the events of the world of privilege in which they lived and worked, while others failed to make ends meet and suffered and starved and drank hot billy beer. This was a world of events where ponies were rented for children to ride on the warm stretches of clean beach, and ten thousand dollars was spent for five minutes of fireworks shot off a barge reminiscent of something docked outside Kowloon.

They knew there was a world in which people did

127

not go out after dark and accustomed themselves to the sound of gunshots and screeching tires and an abundance of indignities. They could sense this other world just at the edge of theirs, its atmosphere swimming with fumes. This was the high cost of the fireworks and the ponies and the cashmere houndstooth jackets and the twenty-two-karat-gold bracelets hand-crafted from Victorian buttons and worn with immaculately ripped jeans. So it was all-important to be extra successful in all that you endeavored, so that you could go to the parties and partake of the ponies and the fireworks and the raspberry parfait. The parties of the famous and rich and their fun and feigning friends, clustered tribal and tittering, while just beyond the hills and through the swimming air, the Crips and the Bloods and the gangs with far less range and magnitude but more inventive names struggled over imagined and real insults, struggled between the netherworld of prison and the street.

Ray had been drawn to Hollywood, to the place that held these wonderful parties. Parties that Cora shunned and he discreetly adored, while claiming that they bored him. As a gesture, once in a while she agreed to go mingle and be seen with him. Appearance nearly always won out over experience in Hollywood, a place committed to the depiction of life as seen in moving pictures and rarely to the living of it, or so Cora thought. It was *what* you were doing that counted, not *how* – never just that, unfortunately. Because how Cora was doing at this time wasn't particularly well at all.

She had gone to her closet and gazed at her array of clothing, finally selecting a red velvet dress that Ray had bought her following their first Christmas together. After fighting to get the dress on, she exited the closet and practically collided with Ray.

'Oh, sorry,' he said, distracted. He took a step back and appraised her. 'Isn't that the one I got you?' he asked, reaching around her and retrieving a white shirt from a hanger.

'Yeah,' she replied, avoiding looking directly into his eyes. He reached past her again for his green Hermès tie, the one with the small seated Buddhas. 'Looks good,' he said to his reflection as he wound the smooth silk perfectly, bringing it over and through the loop and tugging it up under his neck.

'I'm amazed that all guys can do that.' Cora attempted to marvel, crossing to the other side of the mirror and checking the corners of each eye. She ran some cold water and rubbed her face with almond-avocado cleansing scrub, avoiding her mouth and underneath each eye.

'Not all guys can do it,' he said, tucking his shirt into his trousers. 'I doubt if Aborigines can do it, for example. Or Zulus. Or Eskimos.'

Cora wiped the scrub off her face with a warm, wet towel. 'Peruvians have more than eighty words for potato,' she said, reaching for her moisturizer. 'But I don't think they have one for marvel at all.' Ray ran a comb deliberately and smoothly through his wet hair. She watched him watch himself in the mirror. When he didn't respond, she said, 'Don't you think that's weird?'

He replaced the comb on the tiles with a plastic *click*, then looked at it as if it had somehow betrayed him. The lines were tight around his mouth. 'It's not weird,' he said sternly to the comb. 'Not if you think about it. I mean, what is it you always say? Find out what's essential to you. Find out what matters to you and then do it.' He strode past her to the bedroom, smiling at her with something close to satisfaction, a smile she hadn't seen for a while and hadn't really missed.

'I hardly think that I *always* say that. I'd like to think I have a little wider range of subject matter.' She stood staring at the sink. Something had gone terribly wrong without her noticing, and now she was afraid. Afraid because she didn't know if she wanted to fix it.

'You don't have to go to this thing,' Ray said pleasantly, startling her. She wiped the line under her eyes until it was straight again and pulled back from the mirror to face him. He rubbed his neck. 'I mean, I know you hate them.'

Cora smiled and exhaled through her nose by way of a laugh. 'Yeah, I do, but . . .' She shrugged sheepishly. 'You never know, right?' She looked at him. 'But maybe we could take separate cars in case I want to leave before you, you know? Would that be okay?' Ray looked at her, his face unreadable, his attire perfect.

She followed the swirling curves of Sunset, a series of asphalt S's leading to the sea. She watched the back of Ray's nodding head as he chatted on his car phone, his shock of pale hair silhouetted by the taillights of the car directly in front of his. He picked up speed and suddenly she had difficulty keeping up with him. Cora had the vague sense that he was trying to lose her. He swerved dangerously through traffic, and Cora tailed him valiantly, her radio turned up high, her hair whipped by the warm wind. Several times she almost ran red lights to stay behind him. She felt as if she were in a car chase scene from the kind of movie she generally managed to avoid either watching or rewriting.

In the Palisades, she almost got into an accident with a Volvo sporting an early Christmas wreath on its hood. After much honking and shrieked obscenities,

Cora decided she preferred to survive the drive and let Ray continue at his own frantic pace. As she pulled up to the stoplight at Pacific Coast High-way, her car phone rang. She liked people to think that she was busy fixing her hair in the rearview mirror and was unable to answer on the first or second ring – this, at any rate, was her private joke. She picked it up on the sixth ring. 'I couldn't keep up with you without peril for my life.'

'You never could keep up with me,' said Bud's unexpected cheery voice. 'So what else is nude?'

Cora headed on toward Malibu. 'I thought you were Ray.'

'That's such a coincidence,' he said, turning his radio down a notch. 'I thought I was Ray earlier, too – and then I looked down on my wrist and that beautiful watch wasn't there. *Oy*, was my face red. Where're you headed, creature?'

'Rat-fuck at the beach,' she reported, watching a wave curl sleepily down below to her left. A three-quarter moon shone on the sparkling water and across a barren stretch of sand.

'Silton's rat-fuck?' he shouted hopefully.

'Yup. The very same. How come you're going?'

'Oh, thanks. Thanks a lot. You mean how come some lowly hack writer like myself is invited to some putrid above the line hullabaloo?'

'Well, I wouldn't have said it quite as kindly, but now that you mention it – yes.' There was a pause at the other end of the line, which after a few wheezes Cora was able to identify as laughter. 'Buddy?' she said, smiling.

'You kill me, baby. Agh . . . agh . . .' he moaned in a happy falsetto. 'You really do.' Cora imagined him reaching under his glasses and wiping his eyes.

'You're a really easy audience tonight,' she teased. 'I'll kill you more later.' She hung up and drove on, looking for Ray, but she never saw him. Belatedly, it occurred to her that that must have been his intent. He'd seemed a little distant to her earlier. Come to think of it, he'd seemed a little distant in general since the flurry around William's dying.

Perhaps it was only natural. They'd been so strangely close during the whole episode, or whatever you wanted to call it – huddled so tightly together around William's last light and heat. Now that it was over, someone was bound to have to open a window or two to let in a breeze. Or did she mean, it was only human. What humans did when they were afraid. As long as William drew them closer to him and to each other, to his imminent death and a little toward their life, there wasn't time to ask too many questions. There wasn't time to be anything other than what the situation called for or demanded them to be. They'd been courageous enough to be scared together, to be at a loss. Not a loss for words, but a loss of life – with a craving for, a terror of living.

But now, with all that past, they were returning to who they'd been together before – returning with more information and less energy to know what to do with it. They were together again, as before, still not married; he was still with her and her clutch of powerful friends in whose company he felt unimportant, unappreciated as ever, still not loved by her in a way that enabled her to put her feelings aside in favor of what he wanted her to make him feel like. After all he'd done for her, she still didn't love him enough to change enough to please him. And to her mind, he still didn't love her enough to let her go on being who she was, loving him the best way she knew how.

Expensive cars lined Ron's street in either direction as far as the eye could see. This looked like the biggest party Cora had ever seen in her long, party-riddled life.

She eased up to the parking attendant, a girl in a tuxedo who handed her a ticket and a single white rose. Cora took a deep breath and made her way down the flagstone path toward the music and the brightly lit mansion at the end of the drive.

She entered through the open doorway, her head hanging down. She made her way down the hall and spotted Ray in the distance, on the far side of the enormous living room. He was laughing with his head thrown back, a drink in his hand. Cora shivered. He reminded her of the guests she used to see at her parents' parties. Life had worked out, their gestures seemed to say, the rest was just parties. Parties where people were laughing at jokes. How she had longed to grow up and appear so certain, so easy. How do we sustain such ideas? she wondered. If you pretend long enough, does it actually become true? If you get enough people to believe it, is it any truer? Cora made a note to look up 'idea.' She wondered if her idea of herself was based on reality or wish.

When she looked up, Ray was nowhere in sight. She worked the party like a scullery maid, drawn this way and that. At one point, she spotted him at a table, miles away. He was bent over, listening furiously to a troubled-looking gent who Cora had to assume was gay. Most of the men at Ron's parties were, below a certain age. Some of the older men in the cashmere jackets were endlessly straight, married – two people stuck in the soil side by side. Or they were accompanied by another in an extended line of pretty, lost-looking girls, long of limb, lips parted, as though they inhaled the party discreetly or felt it settle on their skin like fairy dust, like ash from a faraway fire.

By the time Cora worked her way to the other side of the room, Ray was gone again. She felt that the party was a giant animal that masticated her over and over again, and she was hopelessly lost in its entrails. She located the buffet and got in line beside an astonishing-looking female wearing a halter top and a black beret. Her pale skin was astonishing, her lips red. Near the pasta primavera, someone whispered to the creature and she turned to Cora, smiling brilliantly.

'You're Cora Sharpe, right? Well, I'd just kick myself if I didn't talk to you.' Her accent was Southern and pleasant, a breeze. 'Every time I've gone up on some movie that I love, it turns out you've rewritten it. I'm just dying to do a character who was created by you.' Cora nodded and smiled, lost in the symmetry of this girl's features. Cora took a roll, thanked her haplessly, and darted away. It was no good to be confronted with what she could never hope to look like, and the fact that she made these young beauties sound smarter and funnier than they were was a fate she didn't wish to consider at just that moment.

She ran in no particular direction. She felt unable to enter into the constant chatter of films – weekend grosses, how they tested, how they tracked. This was show business, this was what was served up as the order of the day. What had Cliff once said to her? 'It's called show business, not show friend.'

At the bar she ran into Bud, who was telling a group of people about the rewrite they were doing, the current miracle they were wreaking. The director, Mitchell Clap, he was explaining, was quite literally all business. They had puffed and prodded in their usual ways, but all they could find out about him was that he was not married and had no children, only a dog that had died several years ago. 'I know why the dog died,' Cora interjected, hugging Bud from behind. 'It died from lack of treats.' She and Bud thought of themselves as puppies, all wagging and slobbering for approval. Nichols had cheered them, Spielberg had twirled them around the room and bought Bud a lucky pen, yet all they could get out of Mitchell was 'I like it.' But then, they always complained. That was the motor they got it done on. How bad a bad they had. It was a game they never tired of playing.

Bud noisily unwrapped a stick of Juicy Fruit. 'We'll do things separately, finally,' he was saying to Cora. 'We'll have a really, really bitter, hideous break like Gilbert and Sullivan or . . . or the Beatles . . .' He belched violently, chewing his gum. 'Only no one will really care, so we'll be forced to tell total strangers which lines were ours, and we'll saw our Emmy in half, and try to write tell-all biographies on each other, only the whole give-a-shit component will be eerily absent. Do you think I should shave?'

It was quite a leap, but Cora valiantly sprang for it. 'Yes,' she pounced. 'But only if it's everything. Only if you wax yourself clean. Like a girl, like a fucking child.'

'Poor Caesar,' he pronounced merrily. 'Why are we like this?'

Cora regarded him thoughtfully. 'Will we break up, though, Buddy?'

Bud put one hand on each shoulder. 'You will write your girlie breakout thingie and I'll write my perverse, pretentious tract and be ruined. But in answer to your question, no. Not as we know it in your basic Carole Bayer Sager-Burt Bacharach way. We will always survive in some mutated form.'

Bud wandered off to refill his plate with barbecue chicken and strawberry parfait. He promised to return to her, but when she saw him talking to the girl from the South with the riotously symmetrical features and the black beret, she wandered back up to the veranda for a better view of the gathering.

She caught sight of Ray in his handsome suit, in a clearing near the perfectly manicured shrub overlooking the bay. He stood alone, holding a drink, looking absolutely at ease, rocking ever so slightly backward and forward in his tan suede shoes.

One day in the seventh grade, Ray had told her, he'd stood on the lawn of his school in a panic, telling the principal he had a stomachache. He wouldn't move until his mother came to pick him up. In the car, he had begged her to tell him when he could leave home. When was the soonest, what could he count on? She had told him eighteen – she assured him of that. He fixed his mind on that time and pulled it toward him until it arrived. The year he turned eighteen, he'd gone to four weddings and four funerals, all friends from school. Then he left, as if he'd recovered from a debilitating illness.

Ten years later, he'd met Cora. When they talked, it was as though she came and got the last of him waiting there on the lawn. She'd fluffed the rice from his hair, shaken the petals from the funeral wreaths out of his pockets, found the real, urgent part of him and spoke to it until it talked back.

He'd pursued her like some great, almost attainable idea, wooing her with everything in him that was winning, creeping ever closer to uncovering her willingness. She'd experienced him not as an idea but as a state of being, a stretch of sameness, a small smile hovering just above a suit. A sweetness, a sadness, a hobbling brand of hope that lurked around her exhaustive talk. A character she would have difficulty writing.

Two men and a woman joined him and he came to life, conversing with animation. Watching him, Cora had the odd sense that she was seeing him out of context. Maybe she simply preferred to think of the Ray he was when he was with her as the authentic Ray. Not pure unadulterated Ray, but the Ray that was adulterated with her. Her Ray, of Ray and Cora. Of course, she realized there were aspects of him that he manifested in different arenas, but she preferred to think of him as their mutual creature. The place where they overlapped was a charmed circle, their cozy round in which all things could be worked out – if that was what they wanted to do. And suddenly she wanted to very badly. She was lonely for the person he wanted her to be. But did he? She watched him talking to these intently listening people, and realized he looked a way she hadn't seen him look in a while. He looked as though he was enjoying himself.

Suddenly, he looked up and saw her on the porch watching him. He raised his hand to her briefly and as she watched, she saw the enjoyment drain out of his face. Slowly, he took leave of the people he'd been talking to and made his way toward her through the well-tailored throng. Music was playing, but it seemed to Cora that he failed to keep the insistent beat. She watched as he nodded to folks who recognized him from lunches and dinners, the phone.

At last the distance between them closed, and their lips met. It was hurried for a kiss that would turn out to be their last. 'Hey,' he said neutrally, no trace of Southern in his voice. 'I didn't really think you'd come.'

Cora nodded in time to the music, her music. 'I seem to have, though, don't I? Didn't we, girl?' she said faintly. They gazed at each other for a brief, unguarded moment, then he looked at the ice tinkling in his empty glass. 'Bud's over by the bar,' she said. 'You'll probably want to talk to him. I haven't seen Cliff yet – and of course Joan never comes.'

'Actually, I was thinking of going pretty soon. What do you plan to do?'

Cora scratched her head and wondered if his remark was intended to make her feel as anxious as it did. She scanned the outer reaches of the gathering in search of a friendlier fate, a warmer voice. 'I thought I might stay on for a bit.'

Ray squinted at her blankly, leading with his smooth chin. 'Sounds like a plan,' he returned. 'Sounds like something you might actually do.'

They stood together looking out at the ocean. Cora felt that something enormous was about to happen and they were simply waiting for their cue. Her heart began to pound as she realized that the first line wasn't hers this time. Events had organized themselves outside of her control. Out of nowhere, Ray touched her arm. Suddenly, things were happening out of nowhere.

'Cora, can I talk to you for a minute?' He'd never said that to her before, had he? Or maybe it was the tone. Maybe he'd never used that tone. She looked into his face as far as he would let her. His skin seemed taut over his skull, his hair strained with shine. Something was wrong with his eyebrows – they seemed to have very little to do with the rest of his face. And then there was this air of resigned determination.

'Yeah,' she said nodding. 'Talk to me.' Of course, she knew now that something had gone wrong. But nothing serious. How could something serious have gone wrong without her noticing? Well, she'd been very busy, of course.

He steered her to the side of the house and she moved with him, obedient, powerless, wishing that whatever was bad in this wouldn't be too bad and would be over quickly. Whatever was happening seemed to be going so terribly slowly, and yet it moved in a direction that she would have found fast at any speed. Their heads down, they made their way toward a small patio with a fountain in the form of a girl spilling water from a jar. Her bronze head was down also. Ray stopped by a bench and took his hand from her elbow. He sat. Cora looked around as if acclimating herself to her new environment. She noticed fish in the pond. Fish and a lily pad with a lit candle on it. Maybe the bronze girl's head was down because she was looking at it.

Ray cleared his throat and she looked at him. His eyes were wide, the whites whiter than she could ever remember them. Suddenly, he crossed his legs neatly and folded his hands, an elbow on each knee, and looked up at her. She'd never seen him so handsome.

'I can't be in this relationship,' he announced almost listlessly. It was the last sentence she'd expected from his mouth, yet when he said it she knew that in some form it had been true for quite some time. She stared down at him, not knowing what to say. In the distance she could hear the party, and farther off still, the surf. 'I don't want to work on it, I don't want to talk about it, I just want to go.' She held very still to hear all of this, to hear it with her whole being. She examined her shoe. The tiles on the ground were red ceramic with tufts of grass in between. She began to nod. There was something familiar about how strange this was. Mustn't get too attached to people – they either leave or die.

'Is there someone else?' she asked evenly. She had not moved at all, found herself captive to this being set free.

'No,' he said, looking straight ahead.

'I wish you wouldn't do this,' she said, a sick feeling beginning inside. 'I just wish you wouldn't do this.' She wanted to say more than this. Don't do this. I know I have too many friends. I know I'm selfish, that I pay too little attention, that I keep you up late, that I make fun of your job, hold you in mild contempt for not being an ardent conversationalist, for having friends who shoot the breeze instead of . . . instead of . . . I know I'm a snob, but please . . . wait . . . But she said only, 'Did you ever really love me at all?'

He looked up at her again, hunched over now, his face openly frightened, but he was nearly there now – almost free, almost free. 'The funny thing is that I still love you as much as I ever did – it has nothing to do with that.' She began to pace, her hands behind her back. He was falling away from her, back and back and back, further and further out of context.

'Look, if it's about getting married, let's go and get married. I can be – '

He interrupted her again. 'I don't want to get married anymore. I'm a different person than I thought I was when we first met. We've been . . . we're just very different people and . . . I don't know, we've been growing apart for quite a while. We're just so . . . estranged. I don't know how else to describe it.'

Cora felt drained. She listened to the fountain as though it were the last of her energy going out of her life. 'Estranged,' she repeated, trying the word on for size. 'Estranged.' She nodded.

He looked at his hands and sighed. 'I mean, I guess I have to have AIDS or be going through some unbelievable depression to get you to pay some sympathetic attention to me. That or be some powerful celebrity. Oh, never mind. I promised myself I wasn't going to do this. I'm just tired of waiting in line is all. I mean, just once after I spend the day listening to people's problems at the office, I'd like to come home and have you ask me how I am for a change, you know? If you're not interested in me, why were you with me? If you don't appreciate me, why hang around? It's all fucked. It's all fucked. Some forms of estrangement just can't be fixed. There are things you can't do, and unfortunately this is one of them. Now I know how your ex-husband felt.'

Cora had stopped listening somewhere in the middle of what he said, concentrating more on the rhythm and the tone until his voice stopped and she could pluck herself from this place of hurt. Eventually she realized that Ray had stopped talking and was staring at her.

'Well, what can I do?' she said, in a voice that bordered on bravery. 'I can't talk you out of it, right?' He put a hand on each knee. They were finished. The conversation, the kiwi, was officially and forever closed. Huh. Something else to get used to.

'Right,' he said. She looked at the platinum watch on his wrist, wanting it away from him, for Bud.

'If we do this,' she said carefully, feeling her way, 'we can't talk for quite a while, you know? I mean, we just can't.' Ray nodded. Looking at him, she knew she'd never understood him, never known him really, and now she never would. 'Well,' she said, a sick smile on her face now as she looked out over the bay. 'I can't believe this is happening, you know?' She shook her head. 'I'll send your stuff to the office.'

'Bye,' he said. She listened for some emotion, but all she heard was her heels as they clicked over the flagstone away from Ray and the sad little bronze girl.

At eleven o'clock, Cora announced that she had officially become a gay man. The party had taken a decidedly other turn. Beautiful men clustered everywhere. They draped themselves over chairs or sat on sills, slowly sipping at something half-filled and chilled and looking off affectedly. The older, successful gay men wandered among the stock, eyebrows engaged. The preyers and the preyed upon. The players and the played upon.

Cora met a model agent named Trey, who herded these magnificent creatures to wander among the millionaires and moguls. She had wondered how it was done. She encountered the troubled man Ray had been talking to earlier, loitering in the hall by the bathroom with two Morris Westin models of different hues. He turned out to be a director who had just made his first film. To prove it, he had a picture in his hip pocket of himself behind a camera, and another with an actor, his star. He said that he was on the antidepressant Zoloft. 'Sounds like a Yiddish superhero,' Cora observed. She watched him for a minute, acting like himself in front of others, very Hermione Gingold, very *Suddenly, Last Summer*. He made himself large enough to be noticed – strange, more wonderful still. 'You're weird enough as it is,' she told him in parting. 'Stop now.'

She asked a collected author who sailed on cruises with these Larry, Curley, and Moguls – the sorts of people who could afford to collect widely read authors – whether she wasn't afraid of becoming a pet. 'I'm too prickly to be a pet,' replied the widely read author. To which Cora retorted, 'They like their pets prickly.'

She found Ron, the curliest mogul of them all, sitting in the kitchen giving career advice to Pia Zadora. Later, he told Cora he had fallen asleep in the process. He took Cora upstairs and offered her half of a German quaalude. 'Leave it to the Germans to maintain a time-honored tradition,' she said, declining. She told him about dreaming that she had an electric mother – 'and I have to unplug her.' Ron nodded heavily, the daiquiris and quaaludes and whatever else weighing him up and down. 'Why did everyone give me drugs for my birthday?' he asked no one in particular. Cora was simply a warmth at his side. She had all her wattage and warmth because of her electric mother, but she'd been born with a broken dimmer. She remembered that an actress friend of hers who'd appeared on David Letterman had said there used to be a sign just before you went on that read, 'Hit the chair and run,' as if your mind could run in front of you on a flat, clean surface, grinning.

'Let me ask you something,' said Ron, squinting at her. 'You're the sort that knows things.' Cora waited, sensing Marianne Williamson on the lawn below. She was a sort of makeshift shaman for the well known and wealthy. Or not. Or they shamanized her. Either way everyone made sure some shamaning was going on. 'What do you do when you're old?' continued Ron. 'I mean at the end?' He scrutinized her through one bloodshot eye.

'Well, I mean, you're already at an age that you thought was really old at an earlier point, right?'

He pondered this seriously. Finally he said, 'Yeah . . . I guess. Sure.'

'So I'd say you were doing all right for over fifty. The fireworks, the cashmere, the boys to look at, and your very own very good companion. I'd say you were doing very well. The only thing maybe is you could find a very old person, in their late seventies or early eighties, who's doing it even better and befriend them, get them to teach your companion to coax you to row.'

Ron looked startled. 'Row?'

Cora nodded and shifted on her tiny teetering heels. 'That awful rowing towards God. Anne Sexton. You know.'

Ron pursed his lips and considered. 'I wonder if Harry could do that.'

Cora patted him. 'Harry can.'

'You did it, right? With your friend?'

Cora nodded. 'I did it. I'll teach Harry. Or I'll come to yours and you'll come to mine. It'll be fine. I'm good at it. Harry will be good at it. You'll be fine.' She kissed him good-night.

Later, she pulled over by the side of the road, her mascara running. Not crying, not crying – really. Not crying for the German quaaludes and the Crips and the Bloods and the fireworks and William, good Ray – and all the beautiful, beautiful men out there on the lawn.

Cora flew to New York to meet Bud for their rewrite. Better single and alive than Dead and Married. She sat next to an overweight man who worked his computer fanatically for the entire flight. Cora read magazines, ate dry chicken, and watched an unfortunate film.

In the limo, she called Bud at the hotel. 'Oh, Caesar, come quick,' he said.

'What's wrong?' 'Oh, nothing. I've just found out that Camille has a new boyfriend,' he replied bitterly. 'It's really nothing to me at all. Can you believe it? That was how little our relationship meant to her. She just walked out on me, combed out her hair, and met somebody else.'

Cora turned her face to the receiver and lay down on the vinyl seat. 'I'm sure it's not like that,' she said in an attempt to be reassuring. 'She can't be in a serious relationship.'

Bud groaned. 'Oh, God, I hope she is – 'cause it's such a horrible-sounding thing. Like a seedy motel in an Eastern-bloc country. A serious relationship. God, please let her be in one of those.' He sighed tragically. 'What do you want me to order you from room service?'

'Rice pudding, onion soup, and a case of Coke,' said Cora.

She returned the phone to its dark cradle and watched Manhattan gradually begin to blaze in the distance. Uptown, downtown, seething with culture, taxis, and homeless. Cora rubbed her bare arms and thought of Ray. She wondered if he had gotten all of his stuff out of her house yet, or would little knickknacks keep turning up in unlikely places for years? The dogs would be devastated – especially Stella.

What had he expected? That she would fall at his feet sobbing, beg him to reconsider? Make some sort of heroic try? No. But better now, before her wayward attachment cut her an unnegotiable wound. She turned her face to the back of the seat. She had loved his good manners, his soft touch, his impassive, handsome face – but in some critical, fundamental way she hadn't known him, hadn't known him at all. She thought about what he'd said. 'I can't be in this relationship.' She shook her head. 'I don't think so,' she said out loud. They were talking about a relationship, not putting a house on your back. He'd been the first one of countless generations of his family to get out of that little town and make money and have more success than any Beaudrilleaux down through time. It was what he had wanted to do. He would do anything for his family. He was their hero, their designated hero.

But Cora and Ray had been unable to call each other kin. As familiar as they were, they weren't family. She wouldn't follow him down the flower-strewn aisle, and he wouldn't comfort her unto death.

Suddenly, her ex looked like a fine individual. They'd disagreed but had understood the subjects between them, and the inevitable stakes. He never came out of any shade of blue and brutalized her. She had thought Ray would love her longer than he had. When was the first kiss? When was the last? She'd miscalculated this time – not to mention every time before. It was her pride, her fucking pride that lead her down back streets, whispering, 'If he really loved you . . . if he really loved you . . .' What? As though love were a license that let you drive and drive and drive. Good

146

lyric for a country-and-western song, she thought. Must remember to tell Bud.

She'd been so absorbed in the details that she'd missed the big picture. That's what troubled her so tremendously, had her going over and over her time with Ray in her stunned, distracted mind. There was a Morandi that she wanted very badly to see – the composite he might do of who Ray had seemed to be and who he in fact was.

She had a sudden longing to talk to the director who'd told her about Morandi when she hadn't had a pen. Surely he'd know if there was a way to situate herself in these circumstances. She wondered what the Morandi of herself would look like – herself between now and the next time she was okay again. This time there would be no blue in it. It would be the color of sand – the white, sparking sort that burned the bottoms of your bare fleet feet. And not sand three times its normal size – no, not that either. She longed for the time when she'd stroll through the recent painful past as if through a museum, gazing at pictures and pleasures now quite dry, with no blue for cruel things to come out of and blow her to kingdom come, to snatch from her the last vestiges of perspective, ruin her hair.

She hoped Bud wasn't as despondent as he'd sounded. Maybe they should just get a room on a higher floor and plan to leap to their doom together. Only they'd probably disagree on the wording of their joint suicide note, and by the time they finally worked it out, the black mist would have lifted, and they would breakfast joyfully on French toast and bagels and cream cheese.

She arrived at the hotel suite followed by a man in a silly blue outfit and hat. Bud greeted her in the hallway in a hotel towel and a pair of black socks, his hairy, tattooed arms wide open. 'Oh, Caesar . . . thank God you've come.' She made her way to his open arms and he wrapped them around her. She noticed that he was weeping copiously, soundlessly, tears streaming down his dark, bearded face. They rocked back and forth silently, while the bellman waited at a safe distance. 'You are a godsend,' Bud mumbled.

'Just don't make me pay the postage,' she said, gently freeing herself from his tenacious grasp.

He followed her morosely into their shared living quarters. 'You're telling me this will go away, right, Caesar?'

'It will go away,' Cora assured him. 'I promise you. It feels like the realest thing you've ever known, but it isn't. This has all the earmarks of a physiological depression.' She glanced at him. 'And some of the skid marks, too.'

Bud slowed and regarded her with brief, mute alarm. 'You don't hate me now, too?' he asked in a voice subdued by dread, a mere echo of his customary rumble.

Cora put her hand over his mouth. 'This is us, Monster,' she reassured him. 'Remember? If enormous depressions were all it took to alienate us from one another, we would've parted company years ago.'

Cora situated herself in her room and changed into her paisley pajamas and Oriental robe. She met Bud in the living room, which lay between their private quarters like a comfortable moat. The room service table sat under the frosted window, through which Cora could hear the muted noise of traffic sixteen floors below. Bud stood at the table holding a plate of vegetables, alternately weeping and shoveling spinach into his mouth. Cora situated herself next to him and lifted a plate from her now tepid soup.

'Ray and I split up,' she mentioned lightly, looking for the large spoon amongst the other silverware on the table.

Bud's eyes widened in astonishment and his mouth opened as though to say something, but Cora cut him off by raising the flat of her palm toward his face. 'Please don't make me talk about this with you now – it's no good both of us being upset.' She turned away from him and he followed her with his sorrowful eyes. Just as she was about to arrive at the window, she turned toward him, smiling. 'See?' she said, almost laughing. 'I'm melodramatic even when I don't talk.'

Bud gazed at her imploringly. 'Tell me just a little – you have to. I told you about mine.'

Cora sat on the window shaking her head in exasperation. 'Yeah, right – but only after like sixteen years.' She frowned and crossed her arms, staring into the space before her and waiting for it to tell her the bottom-line answer to her recent conclusion with Ray. None came. She pursed her lips in concentration and returned her eyes to Bud. 'There is no way to condense these relationship things into a sentence or two, am I right? If there is, you've got to tell me.' She tapped her little foot.

'But I thought everything was – ' He stopped and corrected himself. 'Oh, no. I guess I didn't. Well . . .' He sighed and took a breadstick from the room service table and bit into it with a loud snap. 'So, how do you feel, if I may be so bold?'

Cora closed her eyes and considered. Finally she said, 'Two ways. Like a failure and overconfident. An overconfident failure.' She frowned at her feet. 'No, that's not true. That's just something to say to get it over with.'

Bud stopped chewing and bit his lip. 'Oh, Caesar. I don't mean to add to your problems – '

'Hey,' Cora cut him off. 'This is your depression, not mine, okay? I'm just keeping track of you from the

149

outskirts of your tortured soul, at least until we can get you back on your lithium. Until you feel so much better that you no longer know what to do with your arms.'

Bud smiled. Or rather his mouth smiled, and the rest of his face failed to cooperate. The smile hung on his face for a minute, then retreated into its little cave behind his prominent nose. 'Don't you wish they had patches for other stuff besides just stopping smoking?' he said. 'You know, a mood patch, or a patch that infused you with a knowledge of Latin.'

Cora sat forward excitedly. 'Yeah, right. A relationship patch that would reproduce the infatuation phase. A dream patch. A chess patch – '

'A chess patch? You're not interested in chess,' Bud reminded her.

'No, but if I had the patch, I would be. Hey, I'm not really interested in relationships right now. No relationship I've had anyway, but if I had the patch, they wouldn't trouble me so much.'

'So you're sort of okay, right?' asked Bud tentatively.

Cora kept her eyes closed. She considered a variety of answers. Define *okay*, she thought to herself, pursing her lips and running her hand through her mussy red hair.

'The weird thing is,' she said, 'that my feelings for him must've run a lot deeper than either he or I thought, because this has really hit me like a hurricane. It turns out that he was way off – I did appreciate him, a lot. It's just that I'm difficult, as I told him in the beginning – in such detail that he asked whether I was trying to chase him away, if you recall.'

Bud sighed. 'Yeah, but they can't hear anything early on. Besides, the coming attractions never quite do justice to the feature. Maybe differences grow stale way before similarities do. Mystery gives way to frustration at the inability to understand and to find a common bond. I wonder if that's where the term *stalemate* comes from,' he mused, looking thoughtful for a moment.

'I used to have these horrible fights with Camille,' he continued. 'And at some point she started using the words *thus* and *therefore*. I started calling her Thusly Thusly. The last fight we had she actually used the word *nay*, like a scene being played out in an Elizabethan stable.'

'But you must've laughed.'

'Of course I did, which only made her more furious. Sometimes I think there must be some mechanism in us that enables us to forget the ridiculous things people say in relationship arguments.'

'Like how they say women forget the pain of childbirth – because if they didn't, no one would have more than one child.'

'Yeah. If you remembered how ridiculous the arguments were, you'd only have one relationship.'

Cora nodded moodily. 'That's the difference between us. You see the ordinariness of relationships. You know what the person will mutate into, how you'll love them and learn all of their idiosyncrasies and one day you won't love them anymore, or in the same way, and then you'll leave and find someone else and start the process all over again. Or, God forbid, you'll stay and find yourself giving each other shit at fifty. And all this ends up repelling you. You're horrified that you might turn out to be like everyone else, that you might turn out to be ordinary. But I'm afraid of being different. I'm terrified that I might not make the cut of suburban domesticity.'

'The cult of suburban domesticity,' Bud interrupted. He shuddered. 'Ugh, don't get me started. I have come to the conclusion that I don't believe in relationships, pets, or children. People have them because they don't want to be alone, you know? They build this elaborate, intricate superstructure designed to ward off their loneliness, which is a fantasy, 'cause you're alone at the end anyway, right? Either in pain or hallucinating or whatever.' He pounded his fork on his plate for emphasis, then got up from the table and began to pace. 'People don't pick people, they pick solace. That's the real opiate of the masses, the insane agenda of the middle class. It makes me want to scream, "Wake up, everybody! Get real! There are tumbleweeds on Main Street!" ' He stood in the center of the room panting, sweat standing on his ample brow back to the middle of his head where his hair began.

Cora watched him, wondering if she made all the men she knew lose their hair – maybe she acted on them like lime.

'Solace is a drug,' Bud said softly. 'It'll just numb you to the rest of what's possible.' His towel loosened and fell to the floor, giving Cora a full view of Sad Jim. She started to say something, but Bud stopped her. 'Nothing you could possibly say would improve this situation.' He picked up his towel with extraordinary dignity and wrapped it once more around his middle, covering his genitals and ample butt. 'Let's pretend none of this happened,' he pleaded, and strode from the room.

'I will not allow you a clean, earnest exit!' Cora called loudly. 'It's just not Jewish!'

Bud stopped in his tracks without turning, his shoulders shaking. 'You're the Caesar,' he said tenderly. 'You're my little Caesar.'

She and Bud had an appointment with the director the next morning. Afterward, Cora headed for Fifty-seventh Street, hoping to buy something dark and slimming.

Something with a scooped neck and three-quarter-length sleeves – something extremely Natalie Wood, very Cardinal Wolsey. Something to mourn William's passing and the disintegration of her recent relationship. It occurred to her that they should have a mourning shop, like they have bridal shops. Attire suitable for wearing at a cremation or behind a hearse, or for a feisty day in court.

Crowds of people made their way up and down the street. A woman laden down with gift boxes moved to one side to avoid a baby stroller and ran right into Cora, throwing her off-balance and onto her rear. 'Oh, I'm so sorry – I'm so terribly sorry,' the woman insisted, restacking her booty. But Cora barely heard her. She was listening instead to the pain the collision had caused, especially in her generally uncomplaining breasts. She didn't budge from the sidewalk as the astonishing realization took hold that the breathtaking pain in her chest and the belated arrival of her period might add up to something more far-reaching than clumsiness. It was as if a bubble of knowledge had fought its way up from her abdomen, finally bursting in her brain and bringing Cora to her knees.

Actually there was no sure way for her to determine whether her period was late, as Cora had never been absolutely clear on when it was due. And what with all the upset over William's death and the demise of her and Ray, she hadn't been surprised at a delay that seemed lengthier than usual. As for her aching, stinging breasts – well, as Noel liked to say, 'If stress can give you a heart attack, it can certainly give you a pimple.' So why not a throbbing chest as well?

But of course, for all the things stress could do, it couldn't make you pregnant. That was one of the few things of which Cora was sure. She recalled with some

153

reluctance that, in all the unbridled sex she'd had with Ray as William lay dying, she'd abandoned precautions a time or two as well. As if it were inconceivable that she could conceive around all that loss of life, instead of what now seemed astonishingly clear to her – that their proximity to William's death had brought out their stores of life. As if, in dying, he made room for a passing angel – as if her being with Ray had created a revolving door, enabling one noble creature to travel out in a certain style and another bouncing being to travel in. It was the ultimate in auld lang syne.

'Lady, are you all right?' inquired the liveried Henri Bendel doorman.

She slowly pulled herself upright, brushing the back of her plaid skirt and straightening her stockings. 'I'm all right,' she said. 'I just think I'm going to have a baby.'

Discovering that she was in the family way, Cora felt ambivalence rise in her like a genie without wishes to bestow. Her reaction was far from Hallmark. She sensed a quickening, but it took the form of anxiety: she was overwhelmed by the notion of tying herself to someone for the next twenty years. She had had these terrified musings before. She feared she would be an inattentive mother, erratic, unavailable, wouldn't have the patience to play with an infant. If she couldn't play by herself, how much time could she reasonably expect to devote to someone else, lost in a world without language, a place for which she possessed only the most rudimentary of maps? She was genuinely afraid that any child of hers would arrive with an inexplicable predilection to just basically not like her.

But a perverse inquisitiveness persisted in her. She yearned to do whatever it was that humans did – and this was one of their noisier inclinations. The inclination

to see their stamp swamping a smaller human's disposition. What did they say – there's no perfect time. Or
maybe it was she who said it. The bottom line was,
she believed it.

'Are you sure?' said Bud when she told him. 'I mean,
how do you know?'

'Well,' she began hesitantly, 'I've taken five of those
at-home pregnancy tests and they were all positive. Plus
the whole thing of not getting your period – and not
getting anyone else's period, either, for that matter. And
the painful breasts thing. I mean, no rabbits have died or
anything, but I think those are fairly strong indicators.'

She pulled mournfully at the clothes around her
stomach and breasts. This was the onset of what she
came to call her Pregnancy Humiliation. Something in
her, quite apart from the baby, felt caught and foolish.
She was a train track, and unless it was derailed, the little
choo-choo on the distant horizon would grow larger and
larger until it blasted right through her, leaving the place
between her legs in ruins, her mind a blank. Someone
who had oh-so-recently waddled could never be taken
seriously again, she was sure.

'Well . . . are you happy about it?' asked Bud hesitantly.

'You mean like in the Pacific Bell commercials?' she
asked darkly. 'Or the Pamprin commercials?'

'Mumser,' said Bud. 'Wiener's gonna be a mumser.'
She waved him away. 'Preg Nancy Drew,' he teased.
'The drawings on the uterine wall.'

'Fetus scrawl,' responded Cora miserably.

'Caesar, are you okay?'

'I'm okay,' she answered, intent on the pattern in the
carpet. 'I'm just working on – you know, how I'm going
to tell people, how I'm going to keep from gaining too
much weight, stuff like that.'

Bud reached over and patted her on the back. 'You'll be fine, Caesar. If this is what you want, you'll be fine.'

Cora began to shake her head, still staring straight ahead. 'You don't know,' she said hoarsely, a tear sliding down her face. 'No one knows stuff like that.'

While she was in New York, Cora was working by phone on another rewrite for Michael Harding, a very famous actor/producer to whom she occasionally faxed jokes. Michael had asked to work with her alone – he found Bud 'too morbid.' At the moment, however, Cora was extremely depressed and distracted. One night, she found herself weeping to Michael on the phone. 'I'm sorry I'm so touchy. Maybe it's some temporary hormonal hello, right? That happens. Some vomit, some sob.'

'Just keep navigating,' Michael advised her patiently. 'Navigate and articulate.'

Cora thanked him, gulped, and hung up the phone. As she faxed him her latest joke menu, she considered his advice and shook her head, frowning. 'I always navigate and articulate,' she moaned to Bud. 'For me that's not an optimum goal. Maps I can make to all that ails me. I just can't seem to articulate myself an exit to the ongoing overall. I just keep going back over and over the familiar roads, finding a new shrub here and there, isolating the occasional exotic fern.' She stopped and looked up in dismay. 'Do I sound like I'm whining to you?'

Bud cocked his head in an effort to pick up any whine her voice might've left behind. 'Yes,' he said, nodding slowly. 'But it's probably from all the navigating and articulating. It's the motor.'

Cora hung her head.

'What's the matter with the mapmaker?' Bud asked tenderly. 'Is she sleeping?'

She cocked her head to one side, considering. '*The Mapmaker Is Sleeping*. That's a good title.'

'What about *The Mapmaker Sleeps*?'

Cora shook her head. 'No, I'm pretty sure about this stuff. It's *The Mapmaker Is Sleeping*.'

Bud's shoulders shook as he laughed his soundless laugh. 'What's so funny?' she asked, a tentative smile hung on her face like a half-spread fan.

'You kill me,' he informed her breathlessly. 'You're my Caesar – so sure of her title.'

They resumed their task, and it was at least half an hour before Cora remembered that she was with child. Bud gave her a look that made full use of his eyebrows and lower lip. She stared straight into the space before her as though charting its depths, searching for shipwrecks, sunken treasure. 'Maybe I'll do just one more test to make absolutely sure,' she said. 'There's no reason to get all . . . festooned for nothing.'

'Festooned?' echoed Bud.

She waved him away en route to her room on the other side of the suite. 'A combination of festive and marooned,' she informed him absently. 'It's an allusion, from *The Mapmaker Is Sleeping*, chapter twelve.' She disappeared through her door.

'If you're pregnant,' Bud called after her, 'does that mean you've passed the test or failed it?' But there was no reply, only the sound of Cora's bathroom door closing sternly behind her.

She watched the white plastic stick as the word *Yes* brightened before her. Then she stared at herself in the mirror and found four eyes staring back – two from her belly and two from her head. She sat on the cold, hard edge of the tub. Slipping slowly to the even colder floor, she pulled a pad that lay there toward her and dragged her purse across the tiles, rooting around in its depths for a pen that might be lurking there. Discovering one in the side pocket, she drew circles in the margins until a looping blue line appeared trembling before her. She wrote: 'When ruminating about the weather within, it is important to note – see note: the weather is just that much too fine – like silvery strands of unmanageable sand, it slips my mind off both feet and . . .'

She stopped writing and considered her condition – the condition that would draw a curtain delicately over the life she'd led so far. The life she would soon follow around, picking up toys, changing diapers, making ridiculous, high-pitched noises accompanied by idiot donkey faces.

She imagined having access to her very own child whose tiny head she could repeatedly smell, whose little feet she could – what? Bite. Tickle. Squeeze. She attempted to decide, with everything in her that could make any sort of important decision, that the baby was a girl. The parts of Cora that were unable to decide things and could only fear some sort of coming punishment to fit the unspecific crimes she was always and forever committing feared that she would have a boy child, a man baby. A baby she would only come increasingly to misunderstand – who would grow to resent her living apart from his father. A boy anxious to play catch and war and touch football, whose genitals she wouldn't feel comfortable getting perfectly clean. A warring child who hid from her, refused to bathe or eat, and preferred his father's gifts at Christmas, widening the gulf that grimaced between them.

No. She wouldn't think about it. It was a girl who'd taken root in Cora's belly and grew and floated, not entirely free. A girl child, who would recharge her own dimming femininity. An electric baby who would continue to glow and shine even after Cora unplugged her in seven months.

She would be beautiful – pale and startled like Ray, warm with wonder. Cora's devils would dance in the sides of her eyes, depending on the order and size of the tides. A fierce tug would pull the baby down to her depths, where she would lunch at her usual table.

Cora had never thought about herself as a mother – she had feared it, but she had never actually thought about herself as such. So she began to take stock of her relevant qualities. Her friend Joan claimed that the main thing you had to do with babies was point things out to them. Cora felt fairly confident that she could accomplish that. She would certainly be able to give her child the ability, even the passion, to communicate. She had energy, and will. What else? It struck her as pathetic in a way, this niggling around to locate and enumerate her more positive aspects. What was she, after she was lazy and impatient and fearful and people-pleasing and vain? Well, she had a good sense of humor – and she was self-involved for a generous person, as opposed to the other way around.

Perhaps she ought to call Ray and say – no, her hefty store of pride lay in the road of that route. Maybe she could call one of his friends, those amiable, porch-sitting pals shooting the breeze until it lay dead in the dirt. And say what?

She figured that once Ray knew she was pregnant, he'd try to do the right thing. She feared raising Esme alone, of course, felt hopelessly inadequate to the responsibility of raising someone from infancy to long after she was upright and outgrowing all her clothes. If only Ray had been what he had seemed to be, what he obviously wanted to be. A boy scout who would stick by her, who was willing to do whatever it took to stay in the game, who loved her as she was and was likely to be.

But he'd already found a reason to leave, and she couldn't bring herself to call him – to call him back to his den of disappointment. She wouldn't abort, either – she couldn't. Think of the little coffins with the carved angels and the baby birds! In the end, there was so little to decide here, virtually no bulls to take by the horns. It appeared to her that she could do only what she was already doing.

She unstuck her sweaty legs from the bathroom tile and padded back out to Bud.

He saluted her. 'Hail, Caesar, full of grace,' he intoned solemnly. 'I mean Grace if it's a girl. If it's a boy, I think Monster – what do you think?'

She sat down heavily. 'Don't joke. It's bad luck.'

Bud looked confused. 'In what religion?'

'No religion. When has luck been a religious thing?'

'Only when I wasn't in it. Which is most of the time, come to think of it.'

'If you think of it,' she said absently.

'I have one question.' She looked at him. 'As a writer – when it's time, I mean . . . I'd like you to think about letting me breast-feed. You don't have to answer now – I just wanted to put it out there.'

Cora eyed him, the faintest of smiles fighting its way toward her mouth. 'As a writer, when it's time, I'll let you know.' The exchange hung in the air briefly before they returned to the work at hand.

Cora arranged herself in anticipation of calling her committee. She hadn't meant to know so many people. It was just that she worked herself out in interaction, she righted herself with words. It was a way of getting the continuity and consistent contact she'd always longed for as a child. Like Ray, she'd left home in search of this connection. She just didn't have to go so far to find it.

She pulled out her least-wrinkled nightgown, a white one with long sleeves and lace at the collar. Then she brushed her teeth, sprayed perfume on her wrists and neck, and put erase cream under each eye. The logic being that if she looked good, the news would go over better. She looked at herself in the mirror and considered applying powder to reduce the shine under her eyes, then decided to turn the lights down low – just light enough to see any phone numbers she couldn't remember.

She called Joan first. Joan had children, lots of children, and would therefore have the substantive maternal response. Also she wasn't from Los Angeles. For that matter, who was? But Joan had instinctive, well-articulated values that Cora aspired to assimilate over time.

Joan's seven-year-old daughter, Natalie, answered the phone. 'Hey,' said Cora feebly, clearing her throat. 'It's Cora. Is your mom there?'

'Yeah, hang on a second.' Natalie dropped the phone with a bang, and Cora listened as she called to her mother somewhere else in the house. 'Mom!' and then farther away, 'Maamaaa!'

Cora realized that this was a scenario she'd be playing out in several years. Someone would call and her own child would answer, roaming through the house shrieking her name, her new appellation, in a baby-soft scream.

'Hey, baby,' Joan greeted her in her breathless, hushed voice.

Yes, baby, Cora explained.

'Ray's?' Joan inquired gently.

'And mine.'

'Well, now I know who I can give Natalie's crib liners to. They're yellow, so they work with either sex.'

'The thing about it being Ray's is that we split up before I left town.'

There was a beat while Joan considered this. 'For good?' she asked finally.

'Well, I don't know how good it is in terms of the baby and everything – but I guess it's better for him and me.'

'Well, babies are very resilient. And it's not as though it will be accustomed to you two being together so that it has another type of arrangement to lose. Have you told him yet?'

Cora cleared her throat. 'I was hoping that you'd do that for me.'

'Oh, I don't know about that.'

'Well, maybe I'll send him a note,' Cora proposed.

Joan laughed. 'A note? You're going to write him a note telling him that he's going to be a father? What about a fax, or a brief message on his machine?'

'How do you want me to do it? In a heartfelt sixty-page thesis?'

They discussed skywriting and Morse code and E-mail

and carrier pigeons. When Cora suggested loud drums in the jungle, Joan reminded her that the subject at hand was her and Ray's unborn child. Cora made an effort to be more serious. They discussed the best sort of bassinets, the shop on South Beverly that carried state-of-the-art cribs. Joan wanted to give Cora a baby shower, but Cora couldn't think about that yet, so she said maybe and promised Joan that she'd work on a yes.

'When the baby's born, I'll stop joking and become really serious. But I reserve the right to kid around – get it, *kid*? – for the duration of the pregnancy. After that I'll become very earnest and real.' Joan suggested that Cora draft several letter options to Ray and fax them to her, and Cora hung up feeling better about the whole thing.

She called Noel next. She knew he wouldn't ask any hard questions, and that he'd be incredibly practical. His Polish houseman answered. He put her on hold, with the sound track of Disney's *Jungle Book*. Noel picked up the phone breathing hard. Cora could hear the low whir of the treadmill. 'Where have you been?' he demanded. '*How* have you been?'

'Well, actually, I'm not sure. I guess I'm sort of in a pregnant mood.'

'What does that mean, exactly?'

'Well, I'm knocked up, as they used to say. I have a bun in my oven.'

'Wow. Well, I know a wonderful woman ob-gyn at Cedars who you'll love, and she's very close to my office. Let me take care of setting that up.' He was panting harder now, so Cora could tell he'd increased his speed.

'You sound like you're having a heart attack.'

'And you sound like you're having a baby. We're even.'

163

Cora pointed out that long after he turned off his treadmill she would still sound like she was gestating. He congratulated her and hung up.

Cora drummed her fingers. She considered calling her ex-husband so that he wouldn't hear it from anyone else. But she wasn't quite up to that just yet. She perused her phone book and found a number for her journalist friend, Sarah. Not one of her absolute inner circle, but good counsel and good practice.

'Oh, Cora, how great. You have to have a baby. I'm too weird and phobic, so in a way you'll be doing this for both of us – for all phobics everywhere.'

Cora felt more confident. Her news was going over better than she'd expected. Buoyant and nauseous, she dialed Cliff.

'It's me,' she said in the shorthand of their extended interaction.

'Gorgeous – I thought you were in New York.'

'I am. And I'm also pregnant.'

'Pregnant? I thought you and Ray split up.'

'We did.'

'So . . . what does that mean? Are you getting back together?'

'No. I'm having the baby on my own. I mean, of course he's the father and he can see it and everything – '

Cliff interrupted. 'Sweetheart, are you sure this is what you want right now, after everything you've been through?'

'Yes. I want to have a baby. But there's a big difference between wanting to have one and the actual, bona fide baby. I need to be told that this is a good idea in a way that I actually hear.'

'Gorgeous, you know how I feel about you. I love you. If this is important to you, I guess it's something you better do.'

'Will you be the godfather?'

'I'd like to see someone stop me.'

Cora laughed. 'I'd like to see someone stop you, too.'

After she finished talking to Cliff, she called an ex-boyfriend with whom she'd maintained a flirtatious relationship over the years. They had actually discussed getting married right before she met Ray. The wedding party, the guest list, their honeymoon – sailing to Europe on the *Queen Mary* with some friends. It was a great fantasy that neither was really invested in, but on some level – the level where they'd given up hope for anything other than camaraderie and fun – it was absolutely real.

Martin answered, his voice husky, strange. 'Are you sick?' she asked ruefully.

He chuckled, her only friend who did. None of them chortled, cackled, or guffawed. 'Only up to a point.'

'Which point is that?'

'The point that eats.'

When Cora told him, he said, 'Well, now I am sick. When did all this happen? I hope that this won't affect our little plan.'

'No, I just need to take a breather. A Lamaze breather.'

'What boat are we taking again?'

'The *QE Two*,' said Cora, happy to keep this option alive. 'The Festive Line.'

The more people she told, the more real it all seemed to her. It was no longer this secret life just south of her stomach, but a fact that she'd placed in her friends' possession, something she'd said and couldn't take back. She was working it out, wording it out into her expansive world, until, armed with the acceptance of her family of friends, she had made it all right with herself. If she could understand it and communicate it properly, then all would be well. Or thereabouts. She could only do her best, and if that wasn't enough, she'd do it better the next time. Or so she told herself.

After a late night working with Bud, Cora was awakened at nine A.M. by the phone.

'Hello?' she said. There was no answer, only irregular, uncontrolled breathing. Cora raised herself up on both elbows and blinked, listening. She heard a stifled sob. 'Mama,' she ventured. 'What is it?' Whatever it was, for the moment it lay beyond words, but Cora was confident that her speechless caller was Viv, and Viv being Viv, words couldn't be too far away.

Cora tried to establish some essentials. 'Nobody's dead, right?'

Viv managed a tiny, plaintive 'No.' Then suddenly she wailed, 'Sally's put Bill in a nursing home!'

Bill was Viv's father. After the death of Viv's mother, Minnie, he'd married the part-time nurse who'd cared for his wife during her illness. Viv had always regarded Sally as something of a gold digger – although, as Cora pointed out, there wasn't a lot of gold for Sally to dig.

Viv found it difficult to accept her father's new wife, but when Bill's growing forgetfulness was diagnosed as Alzheimer's, she had been guardedly grateful for Sally's profession, assuming that it guaranteed her father would not be 'farmed out to one of those awful places.' But apparently she'd been wrong. Sally had said she found it necessary to admit him to a nursing home because she didn't feel her skills were sufficient to cope with Bill's incontinence and mood swings. 'Skills, hah!' sniffed Viv. 'She was just waiting for an opportunity to get rid of him, so that she could have the house all to herself, that ... that ... *chippy*!'

Cora stretched the phone to the minibar and took out a Coke, then remembered her condition and reached for a 7-Up.

'While my father is wasting away among strangers who talk to him as though he were an infant,' Viv continued miserably. 'Or worse still, an idiot. I know my father. I feel his pain.'

Actually, Bill had a peculiar history with pain. For most of his life, he'd had no physical experience of it. His father would beat him or he'd get beaten up at school, even knocked out, and he'd feel nothing at all. Once, when he was doing some carpentry work, he'd nearly severed two fingers – there was a trail of blood that they'd followed all the way to the bathroom – but he'd felt nothing. Then, when he was sixty, he'd slipped while working on a friend's boat and fallen on his head. He'd heard something click in his neck, and ever since then, everything hurt, as though a lifetime of pain was flooding back on him. The slightest injury put him in agony – he had nothing to compare it to. He'd hold up his leathery little paw and say, 'And now the least little splinter kills me.'

Cora considered the legacy of her family's pain. Bill had amassed the pain of a lifetime, then unleashed it, set it free. Viv had experienced it as much as she could, and what was left over was Cora's to enjoy. The fight in front of Mick's Fly & Tackle where he'd lost two teeth and was unconscious for half a day. The time he fell off the back of the bleachers in Sherman and broke both legs and did something horrible to his back. But what about his emotional pain? Had that also been numbed and then thawed? Was it even now making its way down through the generations to nestle with Esme in her umbilical sac as she prepared for her role in the everlasting show?

Cora mustered what her mother might've called gumption, if she hadn't been so distracted by her ancient father's plight. 'Mama,' she began. 'I have to tell you something. Actually it's more like a couple of things, when you get right down to it.'

Viv exhaled noisily all the way from L.A. 'What is it, dear?' she asked, shifting into maternal gear.

Cora sat on the edge of the bed and crossed her legs. 'Well, the first thing, I guess, is that Ray and I broke up.' She waited for her mother's typically eccentric reply.

'Well, dear, I can't say that this is unexpected. He was a lovely boy, but basically not for you. It's like I always say, men are bottom-line stinkers, especially the sweet ones – 'cause they come out of nowhere and vomit all over your life.'

Cora smiled and hung her head in admiration. Who needed a conventional mother when you had one who'd say stuff like that? 'And the other thing is that I think I'm pregnant.'

There was a barely perceptible beat as Viv had a quick think. 'They're stinkers, but they often make beautiful babies. It's a blessing, a baby. Aren't you thrilled?'

Cora scratched her face thoughtfully. 'Well, I'm not exactly a thrilled type of person even in ideal circumstances – whatever they might be. But given that configuration, I'm as happy as someone like me gets.'

'Good,' rallied Viv. 'That's my brave, strong daughter. Let's just hope the baby has your brains and his – hmm. What do we want it to have of his?'

This was a good question, and Cora had already applied her mind to it. 'His ability to sleep during the day.'

'Yes, that would be nice,' bubbled Viv. 'Almost no

169

one from our side of the family can – ' She broke off suddenly. 'You know, darling, it's just come to me.'

Cora twisted her hair around the first two fingers of her right hand. 'What's come, Mama?' she asked absently. Frequently things came to Viv that Cora wished would go back to the nutty cave from whence they sprang.

'This whole moment in time – daddy in the hospital – you carrying his great-grandchild. Why it's so clear, I'm surprised you can't see it, as bright as you are.'

Cora twirled her hair a little faster. 'Maybe I can't see it because I'm in New York. Or maybe it's the jet lag combined with the baby slowly stealing my brain and ruining my body forever – '

Viv interrupted her daughter's ramblings. 'You know how Daddy has been saying for quite some time that he wants to go home – even before Sally pulled this stunt. In fact, I'd been planning to take him back to Texas, to Whitewright, where he was born. And now I see that that's exactly what we must do. Daddy must be returned to his place of birth, and we must deliver him. When he is returned to where he's from and where he wished to be, then your baby will come to where she will someday be returned – but in the meantime, everything will be all right, because it all will have been in its proper place. That is to say, "So as it is in the beginning, so it also shall be on the other end." Now do you see, darling? It's a Biblical quest we're about to embark on, in order to restore peace and fun.' She hesitated, then amended. 'Well, maybe not restore peace so much as get some for the first time in our lives. For us. For the baby. Do you see now?'

Cora had stopped twirling her hair and had closed her eyes so she could listen to her mother's voice saying its crazy family prayer without distractions, in the darkness down behind her eyes. And the thing was, thought Cora – Cora or the baby, from now on she would have difficulty determining which – from way down there in the warm darkness, the crazy prayer of her family sounded oddly reasonable. But then, perhaps her current condition had altered the criteria for reasonable.

She considered. She wanted a simpler life, the kind you had the time to learn to play the harmonica in. Maybe that was the kind of life they had in Whitewright. A place to return a confused grandfather to and to brew a tiny child. Maybe they knew something about family there that Cora could hope to learn. Particularly before her child came, came into the world without cohabiting parents, as it appeared she would do. Cora had to find some way of thinking, some crumbs of wisdom that would lead her out of this childless forest and into parenthood. She didn't believe that there was something that one could call a normal childhood. Her word for normal was *acceptance*. That's what families always looked like to Cora in those happy family pictures. As though each person had accepted his or her place in this good family life. It had to be like that in Whitewright. Her grandfather had left by mistake – once they returned him, everything would be fine. Fine would flow down through their family from the old and the mad down to the growing fetus.

She heard Viv light a cigarette. 'I say we kidnap him,' said Cora somberly.

'That was my idea exactly.'

And they began to hatch their plan.

Dear Esme,

There is a Jungian joke that someone told me – as far as I know, one of the few jokes attributed to Jung in all of history. (Jung was one of the

171

founders of psychoanalysis – a subject you might find discussed on PBS or A&E.) The joke goes: 'What do grandparents and grandchildren have in common?' Give up? 'They share a common enemy.' Not a hilarious joke, I grant you, but Jung was not known as a great card.

Anyway, this is by way of explaining whatever affinity you may have for your Grandma Vivian (my mother, the one who predicted I might not survive childbirth – as, in a way, she did not survive mine). Your father was not a huge fan of my mother. He found her eccentric and hard to talk to – or rather, hard to listen to. Suffice to say, they never hit it off. Let him say what he wants about her, though – she still owns the ruby red slippers from The Wizard of Oz.

I wish I knew what my mother felt or thought about when she was pregnant with me. (If, in fact, this red-headed woman actually is my mom, as she so frequently asserts.) You will understand why I am curious regarding your Grandma Viv's way of thinking when you meet her. She seems to have discovered some system of reality testing other than the one everybody else uses. When she doesn't like the reality around her, she changes it – not later, but in the moment, in the bright right now. When things don't go her way, she keeps on going until the direction doubles back to the way it ought to be. The truth is, I don't have any idea how she thinks at all, but I know she does it like she does everything – in very high style.

My father called her the Iron Butterfly. My nickname was Miss Ears – not as glamorous or lyrical as my mother's, naturally. I spied on all she said and did, anxious not to miss out on any clues to the furtive ongoing activities some call family life. Not having my mother's gift of reality alchemy, I figured the more I knew about the way things are, the less likely they'd bite me viciously in the butt later on. I was wrong about this – about this whole enterprise of pursuing understanding as a means of mastering your predicament. But as Bud likes to say, 'Nice try.'

All of which, I guess, is a way of saying that no understanding of myself I can convey to you is going to prevent me, in the end, from viciously and inadvertently biting you on your pert butt. . . .

Come on out so I can talk to you.

Love,
Miss Ears

*T*he two writing partners didn't talk much on the flight back to Los Angeles. Bud always got despondent after they'd finished a project, and Cora had learned to just leave him alone when he was like this, to let him walk his high-low wire until they hit the platform of their next assignment. He hung there now, staring straight ahead as if for fear of seeing how far the drop was. He'd even agreed to accompany Cora to Whitewright – in truth, Cora had been fearful of leaving him alone. The fact that Camille had a minor role in the in-flight movie, *The Blinds Were Drawn That Morning*, hadn't helped his mood. Cora slept for the last half hour of the flight, while Bud hid under his blue flight blanket, weeping.

At the airport, they retrieved Bud's truck and drove directly to Viv's. Cora wasn't up to facing her Rayless house just yet, and Bud had stocked up on fresh towels before they'd left the hotel. They rode along in silence until Bud eased his truck alongside the curb beside Viv's house in the Valley, a two-story mock English Tudor cottage from the forties, nestled in a yard of overgrown shrubs and sagging oaks.

Cora swung her legs out of the cab and eased herself down to the curb, slinging her bag over her shoulder. She gazed at the house where she had been raised, then headed resolutely up the steps.

When she rang the bell, Cora heard music within. 'Big band,' she said. She looked up at Bud to see if he heard it, too, but his expression was inscrutable. She doubted it, though, doubted that when people were severely depressed they heard distant music. She lifted the knocker and smacked it to the door three times. There was a stirring from beyond, the slap of small approaching feet. 'That smoked her out of her chair,' she commented.

'Caesar's mother is coming,' Bud said in a worn voice, his eyes fixed on the bottom of the door, his arms dangling lifelessly at his sides.

Suddenly, the door was yanked open, admitting the spectacle of Viv adorned all in green, the hallway lights dazzling behind her. 'Hello, my sweet angel,' she said, wrapping her arms around Cora. She continued playing with Cora's hair, pulling it back off her face and kissing her cheek.

'Let me look at you – do I see a little fullness in your face?' Viv held her daughter's chin firmly in one hand and gazed at her with bright eyes. 'Nope. Nothing in your face yet. Me? By six weeks I looked like a lump of cauliflower. Hi, Bud,' she said, releasing her daughter's face. 'Cora tells me you're suicidal – come inside and I'll get you some juice.'

'Oh, great,' Bud said, starting up the steps. 'Something to live for.'

Viv regarded him sternly. 'You laugh, but a clean colon does wonders for the will to live.' She seated them on the living room sofa and went to fetch Bud's juice.

The room was crowded with furniture that looked as though it belonged to a larger, more elegant house. Overstuffed chairs surrounded a wrought-iron and glass coffee table. There were bronze art nouveau floor lamps in the form of nude Nubian men. The mantelpiece was crammed with every sort of figurine from Vivian's many collections. She had a collection of china soldiers, a collection of monkeys, a collection of kachina dolls, and a collection of silver picture frames with photos

176

from every phase of her life. There were photos of
Viv with her current husband, Bob, Viv with Cora,
with her late mother, Minnie, and her father, Bill, and
last but definitely not least, Viv with all the people
she had worked with. Celebrities and directors and
producers, even stills from the movies whose costumes
she had designed. In a prominent place on the wall a
certificate of nomination from the Academy hung, from
1962, when Vivian had been nominated for her work on
Faraway Hills. She had lost to Edith Head, for a period
piece – 'another period piece,' as Viv often put it. 'One of
those movies where people write with feathers and back
out of rooms bowing at the waist.'

Vivian Ness had arrived in Los Angeles from Mahaya,
Texas, when she was just seven, with her parents and
her older sister, Pearl. They'd come by train, the same
way Viv was determined to return her father to Texas
sixty-odd years later. From the compartment windows
she had watched the monochromatic tones of the desert
give way to the greenest scenery she'd ever known.

When she was nineteen, she got several jobs in movies
as a sort of glorified extra, but didn't like the waiting,
either for the job or for the scene to be shot. But what
she did like was the atmosphere around the film set and
at the studios themselves. So she turned to the one skill
she had, which was sewing – something her mother had
taught her as a girl. And as difficult as it had seemed to
get through the acting door, it was that much simpler to
get through the one marked wardrobe. She spent four
years as a wardrobe woman, taking night classes in
theatrical design. She didn't get a break in designing
until she was in her late twenties, but was constantly
employed dressing stars. She had been a personal favorite of Myrna Loy and Lauren Bacall and was asked
to do each of their films in quick succession. Finally,

she designed the costumes for a low-budget film shot somewhere in the South. It was there that she'd met and married Cora's father. There must have been an immense physical attraction, in Cora's estimation, as neither of them had ever mentioned a remembered phrase of the other's, let alone a conversation of any kind.

Viv was an expert tour guide to Hollywood from the late forties to the early seventies, the span she had worked there. Thanks to her, Cora could watch practically any movie from the early thirties on and know the names of not only those above the line, the actors and directors, but also those who toiled below it, many of whom she'd met when she was allowed to visit Viv on the set. Cora had also inherited Viv's deep appreciation for and fascination with the underside of The Industry, the intricate pulsing network that drove it. Viv knew who everyone was, where they lived, whom they married, how many children they had, whether they had bad tantrums or good angles. Cora heard these stories so often that she began to think of these people as her extended family.

'Here we are!' Viv announced brightly, brandishing a glass of orange juice. 'Now, who's hungry? I have food, food, food, food – food coming out of my ass. Enchiladas, chicken, crepes, potato salad, peas.' She turned to Cora. 'How about some Jell-O for you, darling? Or cheese? I adored cheese when I was pregnant. I used to grate an entire wedge of cheddar and nibble away until it was gone.'

'We ate on the flight, Mama,' said Cora. 'And besides, we'd better get going if we're going to get Grandpa and make the train.'

'All right, then. I'll just leave the TV to keep you company while I get my things.' Viv clicked on the television in the corner. On the screen, Katharine Hepburn and

Jimmy Stewart were dancing outdoors. 'Oh, look, Cora, it's *The Philadelphia Story*!' she exclaimed happily. 'See that dress she's wearing? I own it.' She turned up the volume. 'In absolute mint condition. To die for. I own that one and also the wedding dress and hat from the end.' She turned to Bud. 'Cora's told you about my museum, hasn't she?'

Bud looked confused. 'Museum?'

'The costume museum I plan to open,' Viv explained. 'But not just for costumes I designed. See, about . . . uh, let's see . . . what is it, now – twenty years ago? Fifteen, twenty – something like that. Anyway, all of the studios – Paramount, Metro, RKO, Fox – were auctioning off all of this memorabilia. That is to say sets, costumes, stills, furniture – everything. And I thought that this was a tragedy. They didn't think to protect all this history – they were just throwing it away. So I bought up as much of it as I could afford. And since then it's been my dream to open a museum for it all. Which reminds me.' She turned to Cora. 'I have news.'

'What?' said Cora warily. She recognized an all-too-familiar brightness in her mother's tone.

Vivian delicately exhaled some smoke, looking mischievous. 'I found a site for the museum finally. It's in a hotel just off the Strip in Vegas. For an unbelievable price. I mean, now is such a fantastic time to buy. It's practically a steal.'

Cora stood and walked to the window, opening it a crack. 'How much?' she asked nonchalantly, returning to her chair.

Vivian leaned forward conspiratorially. 'Two million,' she whispered, then sat back, a satisfied expression playing across her face.

Cora paled. 'Two million?' she echoed. 'For a museum?'

'No, dear,' said Viv patiently. 'For the hotel. The museum will be in the hotel.'

Cora sat very still. 'Okay,' she said finally. 'A museum and a hotel. But Mama – what do you know about running a hotel?'

'Darling, I'm not going to discuss this with you if you're going to be negative, like your father. I finally have a chance to realize my dream. And all I want is for you to be a little excited for me, okay?'

Like Cora's father, Viv tended to be either child-like or childish in her dealings with her daughter, depending. When her parents looked at her and were pleased, they saw themselves. When they looked and were disappointed, they either saw her or the other parent's influence.

Viv turned to Bud. 'My husband knows all about real estate. He's put together a lot of very successful ventures in Florida, which is where he's from. Where he remains, most of the time.'

'Where will you get the money?' whispered Cora.

Vivian stubbed out her cigarette. 'I'll use my retirement money and take a loan on my house and Grandpa's house.' She crossed to an end table and opened a drawer. 'Here, I have photos.' She seated herself between Bud and Cora on the couch and flipped to a snapshot of the hotel.

Cora was taken aback by its size. She had pictured a small, quaint family-style building somewhere off the Strip, with low ceilings, a few friendly stories high. Instead, she found herself staring in amazement at a dinosaur of a structure more than twelve stories high. 'Jesus,' she murmured, her eyes wide.

'Yeah,' echoed Bud. He looked from the picture to Viv as if to discover a resemblance between them.

'Isn't it terrific?' said Viv.

'It's gigantic,' exclaimed Cora, lamely pushing her words from underneath so that they sounded lively, optimistic.

Bud cleared his throat noisily. 'How many rooms are there actually?'

'Two hundred, including suites.'

The next picture was of a huge cavernous space that had apparently been the lobby. But the walls had been stripped and the carpet pulled up and rolled to one side. There seemed to be dust and debris everywhere. The wreckage of what had once possibly been a bar lurked toward the back, lost in shadows.

'This is going to be the casino,' Viv said. Bud wet his lips and appeared to be attempting to visualize croupiers, change girls, blackjack tables, jackpots being hit, coins warm from their stay in the one-armed bandit. 'I think I'll call the bar Bogart's and put a collage of old movie stars up,' continued Viv, gesturing grandly with her free arm. 'And here' – she shuffled the photos – 'is the coffee shop. I don't know – should I call it the Hollywood Cafe or the Hollywood Canteen?' She looked at her daughter expectantly.

'Hollywood Canteen,' Cora replied by rote.

Bud looked from one woman to the other, then slapped both his knees with both hands. 'Sounds good to me,' he said in an attempt at good cheer.

'Wait until you see some of the sketches,' said Viv. 'You see, my idea is not to make it a museum so much as a kind of ride.'

Cora swallowed. 'A what?' she asked weakly.

'You know, a kind of hall of horrors, very Hitch-cockian in feeling – a sort of scary costume ride. People will get into a cart like at Disneyland and they're sort of carried through the costumes. For example, when they go through the displays from *The Birds*, a flock of crows will swoop down on them. Or when they go through the *Psycho* set, a knife will come out of the wall while they're looking at Norman Bates's mother's housedress. It'll have loads of atmosphere. Of course, ultimately, I'd love to do some of the sci fi stuff – you know, for the kids – but that is all very far in the future, so to speak.'

'So it would be kind of a scary costume ride, is that it?' Bud ventured.

'You could put it that way, yes,' said Viv, pleased.

Cora felt light-headed. 'But with costumes?' she asked weakly. 'Birds and daggers and costumes?'

Viv gave Cora an exasperated look. 'I know this isn't your kind of thing, dear. But trust me. Your mother has a couple of good ideas in her. You'll see.' She put the photos away. 'Now, if you'll excuse me, I'll just be a minute.'

Cora wanted to climb into her mother's lap and sob. Not this mother. Not this hotel-purchasing, scary-costume ride, kidnapping mother, but the calm, sweet, soothing mother who would smooth your hair gently, gently, and tell you everything would be fine and you could believe her. Not just want to very much, but really for certain believe that everything would be okay.

She admired her mother's guts and vision, her ability to picture things on such a grand scale, much as she feared for the outcome of these grand schemes of hers – this being the grandest scheme to date. Viv was an unbelievable fighter, fiercely loyal, touching when touched or wounded herself, darling when temporarily daunted. To label her eccentric would be a disservice to the word. She was defiantly loony, fearlessly so.

Cora had adapted herself to her mother's brand of kooky, cockeyed optimism by always fearing the worst, looking over her shoulder. Her voice had acquired its sharp tone early – it was designed to wrest people from dreams, to train their eyes on how it was and not how it was going to be when they got through with it. In counterpoint to her mother's buoyant optimism, she was cautious, ambivalent, pessimistic. She wandered through her mother's lifelong dream with dread. She couldn't for the life of her imagine what Viv was describing. She couldn't see what this could become. Even from the photos, it had looked to her like an insurmountable task, a money pit.

'What is it, Caesar?' said Bud. 'Are you feeling non compos Vegas?' Cora smiled wanly and took his hand. 'I think so,' she said despondently.

She picked up a framed picture from Viv's wedding to Bob. All Cora could remember of the event was her mother's dress, which Viv herself had designed. It was the most beautiful dress Cora had ever seen, and she thought her mother had never looked so extraordinarily pretty. Later, she had begged to try on the sparkling white dress embroidered with tiny pastel flowers. Vivian finally agreed, and after much pinning and tucking so that the dress would even remotely fit, Cora stood in front of the mirror with Viv smiling behind her, smoothing her daughter's hair back from her stern, hot face.

'Look how fast you're growing up,' Viv had said. 'Another few years and I won't know you.'

Cora had begun to cry, big, hot tears, and to struggle out of the dress. 'Dear, what is it?' said Viv, taking her wriggling daughter in her arms. 'What's the matter? Is it because I said I wouldn't know you? Because that's just a figure of speech – of course I'll know you, baby – all I meant was – '

Cora hadn't been able to tell her mother that she was crying because the dress had not worked its magic on her. The magic dress had not worked, and for the first time she'd realized that she was going to have to rely on something else to get by.

Cora pulled a clean dress out of her suitcase and began to unbutton the one she was wearing. 'Turn your head,' she said to Bud. 'I don't want you getting enormously aroused. Not on top of all your recent invigoration and depression. You might get Alzheimer's like my grandfather. You're certainly headed in that direction.'

Bud turned to look at a framed poster of *Death in Venice*. 'You know what they say is the upside of Alzheimer's?'

'What?' said Cora, pulling the dress over her head.

He turned and looked at her appraisingly. 'You meet new people all the time.'

Cora ducked her head self-consciously. 'Happy, darling?' she said in her finest upper-class British accent.

Bud smiled. 'Veddy.' And then he began to weep again, in earnest.

Viv appeared in the doorway, holding a large floral-patterned suitcase.

'Bud, dear,' she said. 'Everything will work out over time. As my late mother used to say, this too shall pass. Besides, I talked to a psychic this week who told me that Cora's baby is a very special baby, and that when she comes, she will bring a great deal of joy. She will be a great healer and teacher and everything will be just fine. She also said that she will be the spitting image of me. But exactly.' She picked up her suitcase and made her way to the door.

Cora looked up at Bud's pale, unshaven face. She reached out to rub his lucky head.

'To Oz?' she challenged him softly.

'To Oz,' he echoed. He moved out the door and down

the steps, his boots clucking heavily over the sidewalk as Cora padded obediently behind.

Bud pulled up to the side street next to the convalescent home in Santa Monica where Grandpa Bill had been incarcerated. Viv fought back tears as a crisp-looking nurse wheeled by an elderly man in a wheelchair. 'Come on now, Mama,' said Cora. 'You can't get all upset. We have to look like normal people visiting a little elderly guy.'

'Which'll be tough enough without the weeping,' Bud commented. Viv opened her white leather bag and pulled a gold compact from its depths. She opened it and gingerly powdered her pert nose, and the shiny areas under each eye. 'Okay, I'm fine. It was just a moment. Let's hit it.'

She opened the car door and stepped out onto the pavement. Cora followed close behind. It had been decided that Bud would remain in the truck, as his presence might upset the old people. Cora looked back once as they rounded the corner and saw him patting the side of his vehicle and bopping his head to some faraway beat. Palms lined either side of the drive in a stretch that seemed to continue to the shimmering ocean beyond. It was a beautiful breezy afternoon. 'A perfect day for an abduction,' Cora noted as they approached the door of the home. 'Shhhh,' cautioned Viv as they clunked their way up the steps. A group of white-haired residents lounged on the porch. Viv pushed the door open and a cool blast of air-conditioning washed over them. 'It seems like an okay place,' Cora remarked. Viv gave her a stern look.

187

'Hello,' said Viv to the receptionist, turning on her highest voltage of charm. 'I'm here to see my father, Bill Stone.' Cora tried to look as stable as possible, stable and trustworthy. The receptionist pursed her red lips and tapped a pencil on the registry book before her. 'Let's see. Hmmmm. Oh, yes, here he is, Bill Stone. A new resident, of course. Just down the hall and to your left. Room thirty-six. Mary will show you.'

Viv's smile widened. 'I was wondering – since it's such a beautiful day – would it be possible to go for a short walk in the park with my father? Just over there.' She pointed vaguely in the direction of a green rectangle across the street. The nurse squinted. 'Well, we don't usually allow unescorted outings, but' – she looked them over – 'I suppose a little outing wouldn't do anybody any harm.'

Cora and Viv followed the nurse down the huge linoleum hall. Through the doors they could see the silhouettes of old people sitting and lying down, living out the remainder of their days in square and sometimes sunny rooms. A strong smell of cleaning fluid and Mentholatum permeated the halls. 'Books on tape notwithstanding, this doesn't look like the greatest place to finish your life,' Cora offered.

'Here we are!' said the nurse cheerfully, holding open a door. Bill sat in the corner of the room, with a box of Good & Plenty in his hand and a crocheted blanket over his lap. 'Daddy!' Viv cried, closing the distance between them with her arms outstretched.

The nurse approached. 'Bill, do you know who this is?'

Bill looked at Viv. 'Second prize!' he cried. Viv cradled her father's bald, shiny head in her arms.

Cora tapped the nurse on the arm. 'Do you often ask people with Alzheimer's trick questions?'

Viv looked at her daughter sharply. 'Cora!' she warned. She turned to the nurse cheerfully. 'You wouldn't happen to have any juice, would you? The salt air really parches me.'

The nurse regarded Cora haughtily. 'I'll see,' she replied, and swept out of the room, hips swinging.

As soon as the nurse was out of earshot, Viv pulled her fragile father to his spindly legs. 'C'mon, Daddy, we're going for a walk.'

Bill fixed his gaze on her. 'Nettie?' he said happily.

'No, Daddy, Mother's dead. Now let's move, we're going to the park.' Viv herded her shrunken father toward the open door.

'I wanna go home,' he said sadly, his eyes blinking and bleary.

'I know, Daddy, I know. We're going.'

Cora grabbed a sweater and a hat of Bill's and stuffed them in her colorful quilted bag. Whatever else he needed they could buy en route. They navigated him down the hallway and past the desk. Viv waved with exaggerated merriment at the receptionist as they passed.

'Not too long now. Lunch is in twenty minutes.'

Viv nodded and grinned and Cora attempted to mimic her frantic good cheer. They passed through the front doors and into the sunshine, slowly making their way to the sidewalk. Just as they got to the curb, Bud rounded the corner in his ominous black truck. Viv practically pushed Bill into the backseat while Cora ran around to get in on the other side. Once Bill was ensconced, Viv swung into the front seat and Bud hit the accelerator. Glancing back through the rear window, they saw the nurse running to the curb with a Styrofoam cup in her hand, bright orange liquid slopping over the sides.

'Righteous!' cried Bud, hitting the wheel with the palm of his large hand. They screeched around the first corner they came to and headed east, to the train station downtown.

I'm gonna go right out on a limb and say that the people in train stations are fat, elderly, and wear large hats that make their heads look like the ultimate in unrisen soufflés,' said Bud, surveying the throng grouped around the ticket counters while Viv purchased their tickets to Dallas. Grandpa Bill sat smoking in a red bucket chair near a woman with a humpback who wore short rubber boots and one glove. The place was not exactly wanting for atmosphere.

Viv returned, brandishing a handful of red envelopes. 'We could only get one deluxe sleeping car,' she informed them airily. 'The other is a handicapped sleeper, but the woman behind the counter said it's quite nice. I assume it's a large area in that even a wheelchair is involved.'

Bud looked skeptical. 'But what if it's for the mentally handicapped? Then the compartment might be considerably smaller.'

Viv patted his cheek. 'Bud, dear, please – don't be such a poky old joe. Things could be worse. If this were the eighteen hundreds, you'd be escaping a pogrom or something. And then you'd be lucky to be alive – much less get handicapped accommodations.'

'I think in those days being Jewish actually was considered a handicap. And they had special rooms on trains for them, too, only – '

'Bud,' said Cora sharply. 'Do me a favor and think about how nice the eggs are going to taste in the dining car tomorrow morning. Think about porters and white linen tablecloths, okay? With pogroms in your past,

191

mood swings in your present – I'd pursue a future of eggs and rumbling through scenery if I were you. Things are complicated enough as it is.'

Bud regarded Cora suspiciously. 'Eggs,' he repeated thoughtfully, concentrating on his task.

'Very well put, Cora dear.' Viv turned to her father. 'We're getting on a train now, Daddy,' she said in a slightly louder voice. 'Won't that be fun?'

Grandpa Bill looked vacantly at a point located somewhere over his daughter's head. 'I wanna go home,' he reiterated.

'That's just what we're doing, Daddy. Now take my arm.'

The Sunset Limited stood waiting on track three. Cora and Viv and Bill and Bud pulled up in the little Sky Caps trolley with their luggage wedged around their arms and feet. Arriving at their car, they discovered that their porters' names were, appropriately enough, Elijah and Sinbad. A prophet and a sailor – one to navigate the seas that the other foresaw.

Everyone was so courteous and sweet and helpful that it made Cora want to sob. She felt like she felt in church – hopeful and set apart. An elderly couple wearing pale yellow windbreakers stood breathless and bent at the top of the stairs. 'Pardon me, would you happen to know if this is car twenty-two?' the woman asked Cora, clutching the railing by the bathrooms at the end of the car. End or beginning – it all depended on your approach.

'I'm sorry,' said Cora. 'I have absolutely no idea.' She smiled at them weakly and moved past them toward her overnight home.

She imagined the couple having traveled on the train all of their lives. Down through time, getting aboard at the start of their marriage, deciding to ride it through to the end, getting off at stations just to buy magazines in order to keep up with changing styles. Perhaps they'd even discovered that the slow rumbling over tracks keeps you young, keeps your heart pumping and your organs humming in a rhythm that's just right.

She found Bud in his compartment examining the tiny shower/toilet stall in horror. 'There must be a saying about not pissing where you cleanse, like not shitting where you eat. Would *cleanse* be the word?'

Cora sat down heavily in the lower, bigger bunk. 'I would advise you not to eat in there,' she said, examining their close quarters. 'I think that might even be one of the ten commandments of train travel or something.'

Bud shook his head and laughed. 'Only my Caesar could turn this into some sort of religious quest. Although the whole experience does have pilgrimage overtones. Still, I can't help wondering – if he basically doesn't know where he is, how's he gonna know that he is where he was when he gets there?'

Cora sighed. 'He's just gonna have to take our word for it.'

Bud began to laugh. 'Why – ' He stopped, overcome with merriment.

'What?' Cora asked, wanting in on the joke, banging hard on the joke door.

'Why couldn't we just have told him that he was home? I mean, if he's just going to end up taking our word for it, why didn't we just lie instead of schlepping all the way to Whitehat?'

'Whitewright,' corrected Cora sternly.

'Whatever. Just please tell me and then I promise not to ask again – even if I don't ever understand.'

Cora looked at him steadily. 'He never asked for much ever, my grandfather. Just to leave him be to fix things and play sports. He liked coffee and those

193

plain doughnuts you dunk in them. I think we owe it to him to do this one thing, particularly for such an undemanding guy. I mean, he's lived his whole long life making sure his family was set up right and as happy as they could be. It's hard enough identifying exactly what your imperatives are, much less communicating them to other people. This represents a communicated desire of his at a point in his life when not much else is possible. So I feel, as a fellow human and relative and someone he built a very nice playhouse for when I was a little girl, that it is my duty to follow whatever simple instructions remain for him to give. It's probably very little compared to the list of things I'm going to have to do for the baby, though by that point their ability to communicate their wants and needs might turn out to be of a pretty similar sort.'

Bud pursed his lips and crossed his arms thoughtfully. 'Can I just say one thing? And then I promise to be an extremely convivial traveling companion.' Cora waited, prone in the fluorescent light of the cabin, the sounds of boarding passengers muffled in the corridor beyond. 'My friend Greg's father had Alzheimer's, and he kept saying that he wanted to go home, too. Only he was home. My point being that I think it's a symptom of this condition. A feeling of restlessness, of uprootedness – so that it presents itself as a wish to go home, when in fact – '

Cora interrupted him. 'Here's the thing. I once looked up *family* in the *Oxford English Dictionary* – you know, the one that deals with the history of words and not just their meaning. Anyway, the original meaning of *family* was the servants of a household. It referred to one's retinue or school – as in school of gladiators, I recall. A happy family was a collection of birds – but the real deal seemed to be a group of persons connected by affinity, as in by blood, inclination, or attraction. So what I figured is that I am a servant of my family of inclination and attraction, and my job is to serve them in whatever way they want to be served.'

Bud listened, contemplating the floor. Cora watched him come by slow mule to some conclusion. Finally his head snapped up, and he looked at his friend. 'So let's go to Whitewright, right?'

'Right,' Cora said softly.

Viv and Bill joined them in the compartment. 'Daddy, you remember Bud,' said Viv, sitting him on the low berth. 'You're going to be sharing your little compartment together.'

'Hey, Grandpa!' exclaimed Bud cheerily. 'I hope you don't mind a little snoring.'

Bill seemed not to have registered Bud's presence. 'Two brothers, Teddy and Eddie,' he said dreamily. 'They died one summer when Daddy was away. Had a flu. There wasn't enough food. Brothers just under me.'

Bud raised his eyebrows. 'Wow,' he remarked, sincerely for him. 'Heavy. What'd your father do?'

Bill seemed to look inside himself, scanning whatever landscape remained. 'Mild day, seventy-five degrees. He was the fastest runner I'd ever seen.'

Bud tapped his foot, squinted in concentration. 'Well, it sounds like a great . . . time, ya know?' he said, groping for a fitting comment, waiting for some interaction to make sense.

'One-man band – traveled everywhere. Won every drinking contest in town. Never even staggered.'

Bud tried and failed to establish eye contact. 'This is your dad, right?'

Bill turned to look at him at last, considering him slowly. 'You're not Jim,' he said dispassionately.

Bud laughed and patted Bill on the back. 'That depends on how you mean it. I could always be Jim for you.'

Viv stood up and patted Bud's stubbly cheek. 'Daddy's a little hard of hearing.'

'Should I repeat things over and over in a loud voice or just leave him alone?' Bud whispered.

'I would just leave him be, unless he seems to want to talk. Also, he may need some assistance going to the potty. If he does, just ring for the porter.'

'But . . . ,' Bud began.

'You'll be fine, dear,' Viv said. 'You worry too much, Buddy.'

Visitors were asked to leave the train in preparation for departure. 'Ugh,' said Viv, pushing some stray hairs off her face. 'I haven't taken a train since I was a teenager.' The train jolted into motion and their pilgrimage was irrevocably under way. 'And that's several lifetimes ago.'

The train tracks rumbled beneath them as they made their sleepy, no-haste way out of L.A. The whistle sounded, lonely and long. Cora closed her eyes and attempted to situate herself in such a way as to be the source of the sound, a sound usually associated with transportation from another time, at a slower pace. The city slipped past their window, junkyards, truck stops, trailer parks, gulches. The whistle moaned its retreat from one sort of wild into another.

Viv tucked Bill into his berth and sat beside him, cradling his head to her bosom, her eyes on the darkening sky. Grandpa Bill looked stressed and confused. Where did the rest of him go as the rats nibbled into his nebula? What island of self remained in the Alzheimer's wake? Maybe as the tide of his great lake of a life receded, its waters rose around Cora's baby. Whatever he had been would inform her coming DNA parcel. The baby's eyes would be hazel, it would have inexplicable urges to fish. Traits making their way down through generations, through families, eons and eons amassed over lifetimes of savory stuff. There down below in her belly brewed the baby, in the dark little nursing home from which she would someday be freed.

Bill Stone was born on October 13 in the distant year of 1899. The third of nine children, he was pulled into his mother's bedroom by a midwife. He spent his first seven years miles from anywhere in the rural town of Whitewright, with three churches and one grocery store. Bill's daddy was a schoolteacher, but he drank too much and lost his job. They moved to nearby Mahaya, and Bill's parents separated for two years, his father going to live with a substitute teacher he met there.

Bill had met his first wife, Minnie, Viv's mother, at a baseball game he'd played just outside of El Paso one fine spring day, a day when a Rudiosa Indian dance was held in the town. Minnie was fourteen, the youngest of nine children, but already 'built like a brick house,' in Bill's economic description. Bill's team won, and when they went out to celebrate, Minnie followed him in his athletic wake at a discreet distance with two of her girlfriends. At twenty-one, Bill was a lean man with leathery skin and pale, keen eyes. Minnie watched him through the bar window as the Rudiosas paraded by behind her. He felt her gaze upon him as he tilted back a bottle of warm beer.

Minnie followed him from town to town, each time she knew he was playing. His game improved noticeably when she appeared. Finally, she knitted him a sweater and they went for walks and to a dance, and on August 11, 1922, just three days after her sixteenth birthday, he married her in the Nazarene Church near the train station in downtown El Paso.

Somehow, Minnie's mother had forgotten to tell her about the physical rigors that accompanied married life. After three weeks of drawing diagrams for his bewildered virgin bride, Bill finally consummated their union, to Minnie's everlasting horror and dismay. Less than a year later, Viv was born in Minnie's childhood bedroom, leaving her mother with less than an overwhelming desire to continue having sex. Nonetheless, some sex was slipped by her, resulting in another pregnancy, ectopic this time. After a radical hysterectomy, Minnie had, instead of additional children, a heart condition that would eventually snatch her struggling from this life at forty-eight.

Cora vaguely remembered Minnie, a big-breasted, cheerful woman, sensual somehow despite her widely known aversion to intercourse. Her final illness had provided Bill with a new wife, who took to her wifely duties with greater enthusiasm, and Bill seemed to enjoy this sexual respite before Alzheimer's began to spirit him away. But now, as his mind forgot the present, it brought back vivid recollections of his earlier life. He'd taken to making strange attempts to redraft the conjugal maps he'd drawn for his first wife. Current events slipped by him, like a grounder hit between his legs, heading straight for the fields beyond. Yet he could catch Minnie's enormous breasts as she stood in the bleachers cheering, could recapture the Rudiosas dancing slowly behind her as he tasted again that warm celebration beer. Somewhere back back back in the days of still summer heat, Grandpa Bill stood behind the plate, his eyes cast skyward like Viv's, his catcher's mitt warm and wet on the inside, waiting for the crack of bat on ball.

'Hawaii was great,' he said suddenly, snapping Cora out of her reverie. Cora and Bud glanced at each other. Viv still seemed lost in thought.

'Which island were you on?' asked Bud tentatively.

'Jim and Alma,' Bill said dreamily. 'Their island with a house.'

'How are Jim and Alma?' Bud asked politely.

'Dead, I think,' responded Bill.

'Maybe they're just not good writers,' Bud offered. But Bill failed to respond, having been rocked gently off to sleep.

They rolled along in their compartment, surrounded by slow-moving scenery, unreachable by telephone or television or any other electrical impulse Cora could think of offhand. There were several announcements about shoes having to be worn in the dining car, which seemed to be one of the biggest train imperatives. They were notified of the impending sunset, with the suggestion that each passenger make a wish.

Cora wished Esme all right. 'All right, all bright – first child I have tonight,' she sang to the baby. Viv wished her museum would successfully come to pass. Bud wished he would never fart in front of anyone again – especially a woman – and that he wouldn't lose any more hair.

Viv leaned toward her father in the deep pastel light. 'What do you wish for, Daddy?' Bill opened his eyes and searched his daughter's face for some clue as to who she was or what he was supposed to say. Then, after lengthy concentration, his face lit up. 'A bottle of warm Coke filled with the peanuts I picked up from the stands after a game.' He lay back with satisfaction as the sun continued to make its way down behind the mountains and the train rolled on. He had made at least two connected exchanges in the ebbing evening. Life was good.

'I'm going to see if there's any espionage going on,'

Bud announced, pulling aside the orange curtain at the door. 'Maybe a romance/espionage combo à la Eva Marie Saint.'

'That was *North by Northwest*,' Viv called after him. 'We're heading east.'

'Irrelevant,' Bud countered. 'I'm in an expansive mode.'

After he was gone, Viv looked keenly at her daughter. 'He's a very good boy, dear,' she commented dryly, uncrossing and recrossing her slim legs. 'Sweet, but strange. And I'll never understand why he doesn't trim that hair on his ears. Doesn't he want to be attractive to women?'

'Women get over it,' Cora said. 'He's funny. You can overlook little tufts of hair on someone's ears if they're smart and funny.'

Viv wrinkled her pert nose. 'I suppose so,' she conceded. 'In my day, of course, he'd have to be rich, too.'

'He makes good money. He makes the same as I do.' A burning sensation evidenced itself in Cora's center, and she moved a hand there to quell the heat.

Viv nodded. 'And you don't have little tufts of hair on your ears.'

'Yeah, but soon I'll have cellulite, skin tags, and stretch marks.'

'Speaking of which, I've been meaning to talk to you. I hope you realize that a vaginal birth is simply out of the question for you. You remember Elaine Calhoun, don't you?'

Cora didn't.

'Of course you do,' Viv continued without pause. 'Well, I warned her, but she didn't listen to me. Some other people had told her that labor wasn't that bad, so she went ahead, and' – Vivian paused here for dramatic effect and leaned forward – 'she bit her tongue in half.'

Viv leaned back with a satisfied expression on her lovely face. 'Needless to say, she had the next two babies cesarean.'

Cora frowned. 'But, I mean, her tongue – '

Viv waved her away with one of her pale, manicured hands. 'My point is not her tongue. I simply do not want you to have to go through what I did. What's the point nowadays? With all the technology they have available, why go through all that – why split yourself from stem to stern?'

Cora grimaced and held on to her abdomen for reassurance, for luck, wondering which orifice counted as stem and which stern.

'Agh, in my day they didn't have any of this technology they have now. If they had, I never would have lost those last two babies. I'll never forget as long as I live. We were in Italy, your father and I, and I got into bed that night and everything was fine. The baby was moving and very high up on me and I had difficulty breathing. So, I go to sleep and I wake up the next morning and I know – I mean, I just know – something is wrong. I say to your father, 'The baby is dead.' But no one believes me. I go to the bathroom and there's just the tiniest bit of this rust-colored discharge.'

Bud lurched through the doorway like an unexpressed vivid memory and perched on the edge of the bunk next to Cora. 'So everyone thinks I'm crazy, as usual,' Viv continued. 'The baby's fine, what am I talking about? And two months later, this perfect little baby slides out of me – dead.'

Bud looked at her, alarmed.

'I was just telling Cora to have a cesarean section,' Viv said pleasantly.

Cora sat silent, watchful, depressed.

'But . . . what was all that other stuff?' Bud said.

'The rust-colored watchamacallit and the . . . the dead
. . . baby?'

Viv waved him away and sat back. 'Oh, that. That will
never happen to Cora – I was just telling her about the
brother and sister she almost had. If that had happened
today, of course, it never would've happened.'

Viv had lost both children in the same way. Not
the rust-colored discharge and trip to Italy way, but
somewhere in the seventh month of her pregnancy
something had gone wrong and she had had to carry
to term and deliver a baby that . . . wasn't alive. (Cora
wouldn't even think the expression *dead baby*, one of the
most horrible combinations of words possible, followed
closely by *nice try*.)

Now that she was pregnant, Cora realized in a much
more tangible way how terrible this must have been –
not only to carry a child to term and then not have a
child, but how awful you'd feel and how awful everyone
would feel for you, their heads tilted to one side in
unfathomable pity, as though their hair was heavy on
one side. And then there'd be the weight you'd gained
and the little clothes you'd bought and the names you'd
picked out, even Little Stinky Hair.

Viv was telling Bud of the several previous children
Cora had lost. If there was a crisis, she was explaining
– a life-and-death crisis – and it came down to a choice
between saving Cora or the baby, she'd be forced to
choose Cora, of course. That way Viv would get to be
both hero and martyr in one fell swoop, Cora thought.
And, of course, there was the bonus of not having to
become a grandmother.

To Cora's recollection, she had never lost any children, and it seemed to her that it was not something
that generally slipped your mind. But her mother tended
to spin fanciful, dramatic scenarios whose accuracy was

not their strongest aspect. Heartfelt delusions. Delusions of grandma.

Bud closed the door of the compartment quietly behind Viv, who had finally finished her tales of delivery and salvation and had taken herself off to bed in her and Cora's compartment.

'So let me get something straight,' he said, turning back to Cora. 'That woman gave birth to you. You're sure.'

'Shhh,' said Cora, glancing at Bill, who was snoring gently, the covers pulled over his mouth. 'Don't say it like that,' she complained. 'Anyway, take a look at your own mom for a while. You could pick both of them out of a lineup for the same crime. Go see *Gypsy* again, then take a gander at the goose that bore you.'

Bud wrinkled his nose. 'She doesn't bore me,' he said reasonably. 'Though she does tend to tell stories twice.' He sat looking out the window. 'Doesn't this seem unbelievably real to you?' he wondered. 'But not in the usual way. It's horribly soothing, though, don't you think? The rollicking and the rolling and the heading slowly east? Maybe we should do a book about train therapy. What if I get off this train and am forever – what would the word be? Calmed. Instead of going somewhere fast, I end up somewhere slow. You know, I went to the bathroom down in the club car and the experience of relieving yourself with scenery rolling by is extraordinary. Maybe I should have a train car constructed in my apartment to keep myself calm and my colon clean.'

A small, rhythmic pulse evidenced itself in Cora's abdomen, as if the tiny fetus lying dormant there had just awakened and was knocking the softest of knocks. 'I have the hiccups,' she reported to Bud, fluffing up her fallen hair. 'Babies get hiccups, too, you know, Buddy. In the womb.'

'Really?' he said. 'Trippy. Do they do other things, like coughing or sneezing or, dare I ask – farting?'

Cora nodded solemnly. 'They do all of it,' she said gravely. 'Including pissing and defecating and vomiting and ordering things by phone. And it all comes out in a giant *whoosh* – a river of collected body emissions and mail-order items follow in a disorganized procession behind the tiniest of all possible human beings. Sometimes it takes hours to mop up the room – not to mention the mothers.'

Bud looked happy. Cora might tell him a story if he didn't push it. 'Tell me more about the catalog items and the farting,' he said delicately.

Cora looked stern for a fraction of a second. Then she said, 'Well, as you probably gleaned, they are interrelated.' Bud sat cross-legged next to the bed on the floor next to her. He hummed quietly, rocking back and forth.

'Have you ever noticed that all the baby catalogs operate twenty-four hours?' Bud didn't respond, simply continued rocking to the sound of her voice steering him away from his shallows to her unquiet shores.

'Well, they do that because late at night, when the mothers are sleeping, the fetuses start dialing the customer-service lines. The fetuses can only get toll-free numbers, of course,' she said softly, patting his rocking head whenever it swayed near her hand. 'And only by hiccuping and farting in a very high-pitched particular way that doesn't cause an undue amount of bubble. And a breeze blows the fetal noises through the open window in the main computer, which knows that all the mothers are The Wendy made heavy by various and sundry Lost Boys.'

Bud rocked faster. 'Various and sunday,' he murmured. 'Various and sundried.'

Cora continued. 'And the noises arrange themselves into orders and credit card numbers and addresses where everything is to be delivered. The delivery is very important,' she said ominously.

'Oh, Caesar,' Bud sighed rapturously. 'And do all the fetuses get delivered their deliveries?'

Cora nodded. 'They get delivered and they get their deliveries,' she told him tenderly. 'And that is why all the baby catalogs stay open round the clock – for the clock is round, and the babies are willing. And on the day that has been arranged, the deliveries deliver themselves down the chimneys of the Wendys and arrange themselves under the Lost Boys' trees. And that way every day is Christmas and every night is Christmas Eve with her apple to tempt Adam. And the babies are formed every which way round, all around the clock. Between a rock and a hard place, your heart's the hard place, your head's the rock. And that's why the Grinch stole Christmas.'

Bud nodded. 'It's all so hideously clear now,' he said, staring at the space before him, the cycle complete.

'Yes,' Cora said. She stood up, careful not to disturb the unperturbed Bud, and reached for her handbag. She dug around in it until she felt something hard and square. Gingerly she pulled out a small tape recorder. She sat down, lifted the recorder to her still-hiccuping midriff, and pressed the play button.

Cora had read somewhere that a study had been done on babies in vitro. Half of them had been played music and half had not. And the half that had were lulled instantly after they'd been born by the music they'd heard. Cora wanted Esme to get a jump on lullableness, so she was starting early. For some reason, she thought that the music in the tests had been Mozart, and that if one chord of the music was distorted, the babies went berserk. Cora always thought Mozart sounded like bees trapped in your head anyway. In a good way, but bees all the same. Not wanting to take any chances, she had opted for Puccini.

An assortment of strings swelled out of the tiny black box, followed by ancestral orchestral singing. Pavarotti serenaded Esme in elongated Italian. He oozed dark, creamy words, making cavernous caves out of regular old vowels, echoes glorious in his chamber.

'*Guarde le stelle*,' he crooned through Cora's skin. 'Look at the stars,' she said whispering the subtitles to her daughter, keeping time with her foot. The operatic constellation twinkled and soared, dragging the moments musically by.

'*Vincerò, vincerò, vinceeeeeeeerò*.' The music rose to a crescendo and fell back into sweet darkness. 'I will win,' translated the Wendy dutifully. The black box fell silent, Luciano rested, embryonic Esme slept.

Cora stirred herself, crossed to Bud, and kissed him on the head. 'See you in the A and M,' she said sweetly.

'Not if I see you worse.'

Dear Esme,

I feel very bad that I am not one of those people who can easily make silly noises and faces and throw infants up in the air. I can do these things, of course, just not with a lot of conviction or for very long. Conversely, however, I feel fairly confident about my hide-and-go-seek abilities and my Disneyland chops (not Disneyworld – Disneyland). I've often thought that I was a silly person – but I realize now that I meant silly in a very different way. Silly as in the wrong kind of serious, or badly dressed. You know the type. I also have a tendency to be irritable, which really takes your silliness apart. And restless – too restless to be the lullaby sort.

A friend of mine who lives in Wyoming told me that the rangers up there frequently take a couple of eagles' eggs out of their nests in order to tag them. They can do this without worry of upsetting the mother eagle, because, as everyone in Wyoming knows, eagles can't count. Imagine – the symbol of our country, found if not in the wild then on most of our currency, unable, unaccountably, to enumerate their young.

The requisites for child rearing aren't my strongest suit – they're not even my bathing suit – but I have at least that much number sense. I promise to point things out to you, both practical and poisonous, helpful and hilarious. I know the best rides at Knotts Berry Farm and the words to several songs that you might find yourself singing en route from crawling to staggering to standing to borrowing the car.

In fact, I can't imagine I'll be much of a mother to you before you begin labeling everything with language. I have never been much at nonverbal communication. Additionally, I don't have much of an attention span, and what I lack in patience I make up for in ambivalence and an inability to sleep. But I was hoping that if you fiercely require me, I might rise to some of your less towering expectations. Hopefully, by the time I am letting you down in any large way, they will have developed the disappointment patch.

Hope the birth canal thing isn't too nightmarish

a ride. And, of course, the subsequent months of spitting up. Forgive me, train me, push me to the wall (uterine or otherwise).

Love,
Mom Sequitur

Cora woke to the insistent gentle rocking of the train. She clocked the sun with one eye, rolled over, and returned to the womblike trance of train napping, interspersed with announcements of breakfast seatings and the endless imperatives of foot cover.

She had dreamed that the baby could speak fluently. She was sitting across from Cora and speaking in sentences, sentences that came to her and made perfect sense. Cora was shocked. She asked her how long she had been able to speak like this. 'From what date?' Cora asked urgently. 'Please tell me the date.' But she woke before the baby could pinpoint her onset of language, of paragraphs, of sense. Or, if her daughter told her the date, she lost it in the laborious transition into consciousness. When she'd shaken off her sleep, the baby was mute in her belly. She put the flat of her hands over the base of her abdomen and held her breath, searching for the lost date when she and the baby would finally speak.

When she reentered the world fully, her mother was there, brushing her light, wet hair.

Cora blinked and sat up on one elbow. 'Did I miss anything?'

'If you call Tucson something,' Viv remarked lazily, 'which would make you a bit of a huckster in my book.'

Cora pulled back her blanket, swinging her legs over the side of the bunk. 'Is Grandpa okay?'

Viv shrugged. 'He slept through the night,' she said

breez-ily. 'Which is more than I can say for your hairy friend. The porters said he was up half the night in the club car talking to a Branch Davidian. Sinbad brought Daddy a deck of cards, so he's been playing his own version of solitaire since breakfast.'

'I missed breakfast?' Cora said with alarm.

'I saved you a Danish and an orange juice,' said Viv, putting the fine-tuning on her train look. 'They're in the sink.'

Cora squinted out the window. They were in the desert now, making their way through an empty riverbed.

'I can't help thinking we're taking him home to die,' said Viv, gazing at the graffiti that squiggled its way along the banks. 'That we're taking him home with his body still warm.' She blinked and looked at the purse in her lap as though surprised to discover it there.

'But his mind is cooling, Mama,' Cora reminded her gently. 'And he needs to go where it's a little warmer to rally himself.'

Viv glanced at her daughter sharply. 'Sometimes I think your real father is Clifford Odets,' she said thoughtfully. 'He had a very particular way of expressing himself also. I did tell you I knew him, didn't I? He could have been your father, you know. You may not think so now, but men really liked your mother.' Viv sprayed perfume on each wrist and behind each ear and went to check on Bill.

They picked up speed as they sped on eastward, the train tracks warming. The baby nestled below in her private compartment, her destination months away, but nearing. The Amtrak of the umbilical sac would thin and threaten to break into being. Esme would have her first out-of-body experience. When push came to shove, she would appear through the smoke on the prepped and shaved platform.

Although, actually, Cora thought of birth as some sort of critical accident – a severe blow to the head and spine, rendering you unable to do even the simplest of tasks. Infancy was a period of extended convalescence in which you had temporarily lost the ability to move or speak. It would be years before you recovered even the most rudimentary vocabulary, before you discovered – in the slow evolution from crawling to standing to tottering toward something that had caught your eye – the inclination of your imperatives.

One's task as a parent, then, was to restore the infant invalid to its mobility and senses. To nurture it to some state of standing and sanity with hair and teeth and clothes and then strand it somewhere – swaying and singing, amassing endless entanglements, sweaters, and the occasional goofy little hat. And, oh, yes, the other thing – between the standing and the singing and the sweaters and the hat: being mad at you. Intermittently, between sweetness – very definitely mad at you.

They stopped in El Paso in the midafternoon. Bud checked in with their agent, who told them they'd had an offer to write an animated children's short and a series for Ruta Lee.

'Maybe we could write an animated series for Ruta Lee, who for some inexplicable reason wears short shorts and hangs out with lots of kids,' announced Bud gleefully, his voice echoing in the train station – an odd edifice three or four stories high, tragically absent of almost everything they had fantasized might be there. The air was hot and angry, and the station did not represent a respite of any sort. There were no soda machines, no snack bars, no magazine stands – nothing but a tall, hot building, amply tiled and

211

containing two phones. They had fifteen minutes to enjoy these dubious offerings, ten of which were spent in line waiting for the phone. But Bud seemed pleased about their offers, having been concerned that once they passed over the Texas border, their careers would effectively cease to be.

'Now that you're pregnant,' he said excitedly on their way back to the compartment, 'we're the perfect choice for perverse, animated children's shows. We can make up a character named Rod the Bear, who helps kids from broken homes by mangling the offending parent. Think of it – they'll make Rod the Bear slippers and plates and cigarettes and cheese. We'll be billionaires. Then won't Cliff be sorry he said I was too butch.'

Back on the train, Cora sat with her grandfather and watched the world pass by their rattling window, the late-day light blinking back the landscape. Somewhere deep in the crevices of his treacherous cranium, light refracted, too, on the store of living amassed there. Betrayed by his inability to assimilate the present in any way or order that might occupy him pleasantly, he waited for a recollection to overtake him and place him at its center, young and certain and true.

Looking at her grandfather now, Cora recalled a livelier person. Not so lively that she could have said that she ever saw him run. But she remembered an expression in his eyes like that of an eagle, lean and alert and likely to fly. He'd always been a man of few words, inclined to reserve much of his mental energy in favor of physical expenditure, which made it difficult even now to see how much of his mind was actually gone. As a child Cora had watched him fixing radios or fishing, deft and definite in his movements, his gaze glazed in concentration, absorbed in his activity – enslaved to something at its center. She had been a little afraid of him, found him formidable and impatient. She wanted so badly for him to notice that she was not a frivolous person. She had sat noiselessly in his periphery, hoping not to disappoint. Now he seemed lost to her in his illness, trying to fight his way out. As if anybody could get out of anything so mazelike and smelling of Vicks VapoRub.

Cora could feel Texas sprawling enormous around her as they pressed on, snakelike and sinuous, through the desert. Keeping an open mind in this country could be a dangerous thing, you didn't know what might flap through. A constellation of cows hung in a passing pasture. Mesa, panhandle, shanty, y'all come back now, hear? Catfish Friday night, with a local band. All that they made their slow, circuitous way through made its most desolate impression on her.

Bill moved his eyes to his granddaughter and set to work placing her in his confused life, the life he could only intermittently recall. Suddenly a grin lit up his weathered, leathery face. 'Hey, you!' he exclaimed with as much energy as he could muster, slapping his hand on his thigh.

Cora thought 'Hey, you!' was a terrific greeting to use if you had Alzheimer's. It pretty much covered the boards.

'How ya been doin', punkin?' Bill continued. 'When did you join the show?'

Cora grinned until her jaw hurt, scrambling for a reply. Did he literally mean a show? Or was it just a figure of speech? She nodded, stalling, finally forced herself to speak. 'Same as you, pretty much, Grandpa.' They were both nodding now. 'Same as you,' she repeated.

Bill scratched the side of his head with his liver-spotted hand. 'Well,' he began, then stopped, considering.

A pause ensued. Cora heard laughter in the corridor beyond. 'Good,' he concluded. He put his lips in the position customarily reserved for whistling, but no sound came out, just air.

Cora leaned forward. 'Are you looking forward to going home, Grandpa?'

His lips fell out of the O. He regarded Cora as if she were a stranger who had just wandered in. 'Hey, punkin, what's new?' he said again brightly.

'I was just asking about Whitewright, whether you were excited to go back there.'

He looked out the window somberly, then declared, 'I grew up in Whitewright.'

Cora sat back with a rush of relief. 'What's it like?' she asked in a louder voice, attempting to access his memory, which fluttered about his head butterflylike, while it retained life and movement.

'Oh, it was a horrible place. Just horrible. Me and Sis couldn't wait to get out. Daddy worked over yonder in the schoolhouse.' He pointed vaguely into the twilight just outside the window of the train. 'Well, one day Mom found out that Dad was fooling with one of the other teachers, so Mama packs up us kids and moves us to the little white house near the Methodist church on the corner. Didn't talk to him for nigh on two years.' He paused, examining the nail on his left forefinger, gray and disfigured. Cora waited and watched.

'That summer me and Joe Briggs used to go fishing down at Dead Mule River. We'd dig up these big fat worms in the banks and use 'em for bait. Find worms, go fishing.' He paused. 'Well, one day I moved too fast or somethin' and before I knew it the hook had gone plum through this here nail. See that?' He held up his crooked finger so Cora could examine it more closely.

214

Cora touched his hand. It was tough and dry. She held very still in case Esme was listening. Listening to the sound of her history, her wellspring, what stood behind her. The link to a simpler time, first names, fewer numbers, no motors, no big deals. Or perhaps this was just how Cora preferred to imagine it. After all, people died younger then, from the flu, abscessed teeth, no food. But whatever the times had been, her grandfather had felt them quicken around him, felt them whip to a frenzy, roll you over, pass you by. Her grandfather was giving her what was left of his memory. Not wisdom, but his life, which time was breaking up around him, like clouds.

Viv materialized. 'Anybody want a stick?' she said, brandishing a pack of Juicy Fruit.

'Nope,' said Bill in a tone of irritation, without interrupting his vigil at the window.

'Thanks, Mama, no,' said Cora. Through the dirty glass she could make out a sign announcing miniature baby goats and railroad ties for sale.

'Are we there yet?' said Bill to no one in particular.

Cora looked at him, his hands resting once more on his thighs. 'Not yet, Grandpa. Soon,' she replied. He nodded, organizing himself around this information.

They passed a sign proclaiming the 'city limits' of a place called Louella. 'A considerable exaggeration of the word *city*,' Viv remarked touchily. 'And perhaps a fine use of the word *limits*.'

Suddenly Bill pointed. 'If you keep on this road straight up, they got these real big watermelons. Maybe twenty-five miles from right here. Me and Howie Parker used to go there day before a game and get ourselves a bunch of 'em for the whole team. One day we brought 'em back and hot dog if we didn't know that they got Bobby Douglas to pinch hit for 'em. I mean he was an

Olympic winner. Well, so we play and I remember that day, it was mild – like seventy degrees – and Bobby hits this grounder right to me and I scoop it up and let fly and we nailed the sucker there and then.' He nodded, gripped by the memory – lost in it. Found himself someplace real.

'So what happened?' cried Cora, calling to Bill in a safer, more vivid past. Happy, happy. Bill looked stricken, folded his rumpled hands.

'Daddy,' said Viv, 'tell about the time you were robbed by Pancho Villa.'

A look of consternation crossed Bill's face, then passed. 'We were bush leaguers, semipro, goin' to Mexico by train to play there. Next thing you know, train stops in the middle of nowhere and . . . and . . .' He turned to the window again as if the memory lay out there.

'You said Pancho Villa was short,' prompted Viv. Listen, Esme, listen.

'No bigger 'n me. Yup,' Bill said, pleased. 'That's how it wha, wha, wha – went.' And then he lapsed back into silence, groping around in the black.

At dinner they sat in the dining car buttering rolls and stabbing their string beans with plain sterling forks. Thick cream-colored plates laden with slabs of steak were lofted overhead and dispensed to diners chug-a-lug (a train term).

'You know, this reminds me of a cartoon I saw in some magazine,' Viv said. 'Two people are sitting in the back of their Rolls-Royce, and one of them says to the other, "The champagne is warm and the caviar is too salty – will it never end?"'

They got into a lengthy dispute over the name of the gift shop in Viv's museum. Cora's suggestion was Tinsel Town Treasures. Viv was partial to Viv's Entertainment Gift Emporium. Cora saw that it would be a real stretch for her mother to keep her name out of the configuration. Bud's contribution was Buy This Stuff Now.

Viv narrowed her eyes at him. 'What about, you're too strange to suggest?'

Bud thought for a moment then shook his head. 'No. Too oblique. The public won't go for it.'

Cora listened to them bicker, suddenly feeling immensely grateful to have the sort of mother she had. She supposed her mother was surreal, but that was its own form of reality. It was dependable and colorful and had its own code of offbeat conduct. She came at you from an angle you frequently didn't know existed. She was an indomitable force, except when, by some brief freak accident, she was temporarily dominated. If becoming a grandmother made her uneasy, Cora could understand it. Viv had formed the greater bulk of her identity when she was somewhere in her twenties, not unlike most people. But she had barely revised it over time. She remained effervescent, girlish, bubbling with energy. Not the conventional adjectives for a grandmother. But then, Cora had never grasped the criteria for convention anyway. To the very best of her trampled recollection, her mother had never been earnest. Nor had she been coy, demure, or, God forbid, irresolute or retiring. And Cora would take that over conventional any day of the week.

Viv talked on, in her rhythmic Western way, sitting tall in her soothing saddle, and Cora rode along behind her, taking the ride she'd dearly loved to ride. She would make mistakes with Esme, she knew, but she would do her best to make sure that they were the sort she could make up in summer school. And the baby wouldn't know that Cora was supposed to be a better mother, at least for seven or eight years. Her squeaky clean slate would stare back at her satisfied. Not consistently, of course. There was that business of puberty and those terrible twos. But her daughter would always be her daughter, since even before she was yanked out yelling – a priority traveling at light speed toward being a person. There to care for, to keep track of the years.

After dinner Cora went back to her compartment to get a sweater and went in search of the observation car. Bud had promised to meet her there to gaze madly and moonily at the stars. The observation car was warm from all the observations that had been made there on the countless journeys the Sunset Limited had made as it carefully zigzagged its way back and forth between California and Texas, up the coast to Portland, and over the border to Canada, and then, of course, back again. She sat with her knees pulled up underneath her, her enormous pink and black woolen sweater wrapped closely around her. She put her hand up to the flat surface of the window and felt the ache of cold move into her fingers and the palm of her sweaty hand. She heard the automatic door slide open behind her and the clomp of heavy boots on the carpet making their determined way toward her.

Bud appeared at her side. 'Are we ready to have our talk, creature?'

Cora shifted in her seat in order to look up at his face, perched sturdily at the top of his furry neck and cocked inquisitively to one side. 'Did we have a talk scheduled for this point in our journey?' she asked, making room for him on the warm seat beside her.

'Juncture,' Bud corrected as he took his place to her

right and took her hand. 'We always talk at this juncture in our pilgrimage. If I remember rightly, we either talk or play cards.'

Cora nodded thoughtfully and put her head on his shoulder. He smelled of smoke and beer. Their reflections in the window beside them showed a sleepy couple traveling east to visit friends and family. 'You start,' said Cora, watching her mouth move on the face in the window. Her eyes traveled to Bud's as she waited for him to speak.

'What are we going to do with Ray's baby?' he asked the face beside his. 'I know we've discussed this, but I can't seem to recall the whole thing.'

'We're going to keep it, of course,' she said carefully, shifting her weight to curl herself deeper into her friend, like a small swirl of clumsy dense smoke. 'We're going to keep it and let him visit the baby – whenever he wishes, I guess – within some kind of reason. You know?' Bud wrapped his arm protectively around her and squeezed her. It was an uncharacteristically earnest gesture from him, and Cora felt something a little like alarm, a little like the train-whistle sound that soared into the nighttime, a long curved line of mournful.

'It's a big deal, huh?' she continued in quiet amazement. She felt unequal to the task of treating this decision and its long-term, three-term, permanent implications with the proper degree of awe. There just didn't seem to be any way around what she was about to do and already doing. With William, she had discovered that if you surround yourself with enough tragedy, it becomes another thing. The only thing that she could figure at this point was that if you surrounded yourself with enough pregnancy, it would ultimately become another thing. A mother thing.

Bud cleared his throat. 'It's just that you're making a decision that will alter a big part of his life.'

Cora turned her face up to his awkwardly. 'Don't get too out of character, okay? You might have a problem finding your way back in, and then what would I do?'

Bud smiled and leaned his head back on the seat, squinting up at the stars. 'You're totally sure that you can't be with him?' he asked, addressing the Big Dipper. Big Dipper, Little Halsey.

Cora sighed a sigh that seemed to drift up from baby Esme down below. 'Here's the thing,' she began, frowning. 'We could probably be together for a while, but my guess is that I'd burn him out pretty soon. So why not be together in whatever way we have to be to raise the baby between us, so that we're together in an apart way rather than apart in a together way – or whatever it is that I mean. We're already going to be together in a way, our genes all jumbled and confused in her from the start – '

Bud interrupted her, startled. 'Wait. You know that it's a girl?'

She nodded gravely. 'No other explanation would be acceptable.'

'Ah,' said Bud. 'I see.'

They were silent for a moment, facing forward in their seats as they hurtled helplessly on toward Whitewright.

'Look, I'd better be perfectly candid with you,' she began again, playing with a ring on her left hand. 'I know that what I am doing is the absolute right thing. With all its inherent complications, and maybe in some way because of them. But if I called him now and told him, I know that he'd feel obliged to marry me or something. And I don't want to put him – or me or the baby – in that position just because culturally it'll be considered the way to go. I don't want to make someone miserable just by doing what it is that I normally do – just by being who I am. We had a good enough relationship to help one life out and another in, like some freaky portal or cosmic black hole. In the end it doesn't matter if he makes too many drinks or feels unappreciated or whatever it is that he does and feels. What matters is that we're not really good together. But he's a great ameliorator – he's the Ameliorator, a superhero in that regard – and with the baby he won't feel cheated or unappreciated like he did with me. . . . What he is will be perfect for the baby – she'll enable him to fulfill his truest destiny. He will be a great and dedicated parent and I will toil meekly in his shadow by comparison. But I will toil all the same. I just need for you to help me figure out how to tell him so that he doesn't hear about the failure of him and me as a couple so much as what a success he will be as a dad.'

It was quiet when she finished speaking, and Cora noticed that Bud was nodding – had been nodding through most of what she had been saying, keeping time with the rhythm of how she wanted things to work out. The train made its way serpentlike through rock and stone above the Rio Grande. Shadows of prehistoric beasts arranged themselves over the landscape. Bud yawned mightily and stretched and crossed his black buckled boots at the ankle. Cora wound her way out from under his arm and turned and stared expectantly at her friend. 'Were you listening to me at all?' she asked him finally, when it seemed less and less likely that he would respond.

'I'm trying to think of what I would do. Which isn't entirely applicable in this case, I know.' He paused and narrowed his eyes. 'I think that our best plan of action, based on my general feelings as a lonely guy, is to call him at some point in the near future and tell him some version of what you just said. Of course, we'll have to rework it a little, 'cause it's way too pretentious and long-winded. And no way am I gonna let you alienate the guy, in case there's a glimmer of a chance he might give back that watch.'

Cora smirked. 'At least you have your priorities straight.'

Bud nodded with exaggerated gravity. 'And I know that even if you don't get the watch back from him – God forbid – you'll find me another one just like it. You'll feel that nothing less would really do, after I've taken you for your amnio and to all those absurd breathing classes and the rest of your coming ordeal.'

Cora had to stop herself from embracing him. Relationships, pets, and children. For her he would put his cynicism aside and help her to hatch the baby who was currently curled up inside.

Bud regarded her sternly. 'You realize, of course, that it's critical that we refrain from engaging in any conventional forms of sentiment. That way madness lies. Just concentrate on the watch and keep the breast-feeding in mind. And I'll help with the breathing and the pushing and the call.'

Bud walked Cora back to her compartment. They made their way down the corridors wordlessly, straddling the squeaking islands of metal that connected each car to the next in the sudden rush of cold wind from the darkness beyond. She remembered how she'd turned off each light as she'd gone to join Ray in the darkness beyond at the back of her house. Now it was Bud, her boon, her best companion who would stand at her side in the place where couples customarily gathered to learn to breathe and to breed.

'Good-night, Caesar,' he whispered as they reached her compartment.

'*Et tu Brute?*' she intoned softly, her mouth mumbling and soft to his cheek. 'Then let fall Caesar – let Caesar fall asleep.'

She opened the door and slid into the darkened room. She pulled her dress over her head as silently as possible, careful not to disturb her mother. Reaching into her suitcase for her oversize cotton nightgown, Cora smiled. Viv was sleeping in her daughter's berth. Berth and birth – she attempted to wrangle the words into a suitable pun, but nothing came.

She considered brushing her teeth, but using the perfectly plausible excuse that this action would most likely awaken her mother, decided against it. She stood watching Viv from the narrow space between the bed and the combination toilet/sink and, for the first time since she knew that she was pregnant, felt an overwhelming need to talk to her mother. If anyone had the information she required in order to have a successful gestation – even more, to know what to do with a child, whom to be, how to be it – her mother must. Even if she'd forgotten, Cora would help her to remember. Her mother would mother her into motherhood, would provide the spark that would ignite whatever flame one needed to emanate the warmth parents dispensed to their children.

Cora put her hand to her abdomen. She doubted that she had the right sort of warmth. How did you know what someone wanted and needed when they were unable to communicate at all? Maybe there was a gene for the neglect Ray had felt, and no matter what she did, the baby would feel it, too. She moved to the head of the bed, hesitated, then drew back the covers and slid in beside her mother. Viv stirred.

'Mama,' Cora whispered. 'It's me, Cora.'

'That's good, dear,' Viv countered. 'I was worried it might be Elijah. He was eying me at dinner, you know.' Her hand reached automatically to smooth her daughter's hair.

'Mama, I needed to ask you. Is there . . . I mean, can you remember anything that I might need to know that would help me to have a child?'

Viv smiled and rolled over onto her back. Cora was struck by how young and pretty her mother looked, like some freshly scrubbed country girl. With makeup, she was a beauty, from any angle. But now she looked like someone who ran barefoot through train cars, ignoring shoe imperatives and wishing on sunsets and stars. Her eyes glittered in the dark, filled with secrets she wanted to tell. But all she said was, 'You'll know just what to do, Cora. You're just like me – you hold it all inside until one day you have an ulcer. But you always know just what to do.'

Cora squirmed. 'But Mama – '

'Like with your friend William – you knew what to do with him – you told me so.'

'Yeah, but – '

'There is no real difference. When you love someone – when they're family – you do whatever you can to make them feel better, to do what's right for them 'cause they're that important to you. Like with Grandpa – we're taking him home, right? 'Cause that might be where he wants to go. It's not important in a way if he gets there – it's that we're taking him. And your being there for William, or for Bud when he's unhappy – it's all the same. That's the instinct you count on when you have a baby. That's really truly all.'

Cora frowned. 'That can't be totally all, Mama. If that were – '

Viv interrupted and sat up in bed. 'Honey, it'll change your life. You won't sleep a lot, you'll get vomited on, and you'll clean up a lot of shit. But I'm telling you, you'll know what to do. Now roll over and let me scratch your back so you can fall asleep.'

And fall asleep she did, listening to her mother sing a song she had sung to her as a child. It was about a little red pony that ran down roads and into barns. Neither the melody nor the lyrics were certain, but her mother sang that old pony all over the place – and no matter how long it wandered, the pony never grew into a horse.

Sometime during the night, they passed through Marfa's ghost lights, which had been sighted consistently since 1938. The cars creaked with the curves as the fivesome from the West wove their way dawnward, to home.

Cora dreamt that she was in Whitewright, and the oddest thing about it was that she had been there before. She understood it to be the place where she'd been raised, a place to which she would inevitably return. Her home was there – that is, her actual home, the house she lived in in L.A. On one side of the hallway her favorite Morandi painting hung crooked on the wall. It was the portrait where he had painted the spaces between her daughter, her mother, and herself.

There was a room just off the bedroom that had been William's – Cora hadn't realized it was there. She couldn't believe that she'd had this room all along – why, if she'd known it was there, think of all the things she would've done. She could've had more friends come stay with her, made another office or even a porch. But then she realized that it would make a perfect room for

225

her baby. Maybe if she'd known sooner that the room was there, she wouldn't have had to wait so long to have a child. Looking around, she realized that she'd have to get to work if the room was to be ready for little Esme Bing. She didn't remember when she'd chosen the name, but at least that was ready in case the room was not. Then she glanced out the window and saw the scenery rolling past and realized that she'd forgotten to get off the train. Which would make it doubly hard to get the interior decorating done. Still, she'd do the best she could.

Elijah awakened them before dawn. They were nearing San Antonio, and the end of their particular line.

Cora blinked in the musty darkness. For a moment she couldn't remember where she was. Her mother lay sleeping in the bed beside her. She rolled over onto her stomach and her whereabouts came snapping back into consciousness. She bunched her pillow into another shape, finding the cooler side, and curled herself back into as small a shape as possible, something cozy and rounder all the time. Listening to her mother's steady breathing, feeling the smooth, sure feel of metal wheel on metal track, she lay there as long as she could, doing her best to continue the family line. Starting at the top, with a man no longer master of his memory. Then her lovely, eccentric mother. Then herself, the soon-to-be mother, mistress of Fine/No Fine. And lastly, the incoming, ongoing Esme, just forming hands and making her first funny face. A little line of traveling relations, related by berth or about to be born. Accompanied by their wandering Jew minus some breast milk and an antique platinum mesh watch.

It was all just some ridiculous euphemism, she decided – the train, Whitewright, even her disheveled hair. Things did not always go as you planned, much less make a handy brand of the right kind of sense. But she was doing what human beings did. No one could deny her that. She considered carefully what she might have for breakfast, hoping that if she could successfully negotiate that selection, the rest would just naturally take its course.

Dear Ray,

I hope you aren't too surprised to hear from me. You have to understand that once you open a line of communication with me, that line may be interrupted, but it's never entirely closed. I don't mean to say that I plan to go on and on through infinity yapping at you. It's just that certain forms of connection refuse to disengage. And it turns out, in our particular configuration, that might be more true than usual.

I am writing to you from the birthplace of my mother's father, Bill (the baseball player, remember?). We were returning him like a cross between damaged goods and some sacred object we'd been harboring. We had some vague hope that the nearer he got to the place of his creation, the closer he'd get to who he once was. Not your basic wellspring of logic, plan-wise, but there you have it.

As it turns out, the main street of Whitewright is one block long. There is a karate school and a convenience store, both open, and a doughnut emporium, a newspaper, and a secondhand store, all closed. The hardware/car repair shop is open, but it no longer sells the barbecue it professes to out back. There is a spry little gift shop where I bought a doll (more about that in a minute).

227

The bottom line is, everywhere is home to someone – except, at this point, Bill, who longs for some memory he'll never recapture. He sat on the bench in front of the library, smoked a cigarette, and said, 'Are we there yet?' and 'I want to go home' – which is what he'd been saying all along.

Speaking of family, I'm proud – and a little inexperienced – to announce the inadvertent impending arrival of the child we appear to have made during our recent stressful albeit heroic circumstances. I just want to say right off the bat (any baseball references are included in honor of my grandfather, of course) that I'm not telling you this so that you'll feel obliged to marry me or support me for the next eighteen years. I want you to know because you're the father and you deserve a chance to be involved. I'm sorry we weren't and aren't about to configure ourselves into a more conventional constellation, but better we know that now, before she (I've decided she's a she) is old enough to wish it was back to how it was before it got so bad.

So although we couldn't make a relationship that worked, we've managed to fashion a human being. I hope she has your patience and my humor. I hope she lacks my laziness and your passive-aggressive charm. Her name will be Esme Bing – unless she's started defying me already and turns out to be a boy (in which case I thought I'd call him Lillian Ross). Either way, she'll have your last name, if that's okay with you. Let me know your imperatives, and please, work toward being glad. I am. Think of us as two people who managed not to throw the baby out with the bath water. Which, by the way, started out as a pretty swell bath.

See you in seven months.

Love,
Cora

One sweltering morning in July, Cora awakened in Viv's hotel in Vegas in a bramble of Braxton-Hicks and a high sense of alarm. She sat up in bed and gazed out at the Strip, still twinkling brightly in the early half-light. The skin across her abdomen tightened, causing her a sharp intake of breath. 'Uh-oh,' she groaned softly, waiting for the pain to pass through her and on to somebody else. She groped across the bedclothes and found Bud's ample tattooed arm. 'Buddy,' she said softly, shaking him. He stirred and rolled away, pulling the covers up around him, and stuck his pillow over his head. The pain came sharper. '*Now*, Buddy,' Cora said sternly. 'I've got Braxton-Hicks.' Bud snapped upright. 'Who's that?' he said, reaching for his scary black glasses. 'A Southern private eye?'

'We have to go to the hospital,' Cora panted. 'The baby's on her way.' Bud grabbed his towel, groping for the phone. 'Is it time, Caesar? Oh, Cora, what do I do?'

Despite the sweat on her brow, she nearly smiled. 'First off, don't start calling me Cora – not at this late date.'

'Breathe, Caesar,' he urged as he dialed the front desk. 'Do that breathing. Hello!' He was all but screaming into the phone. 'We need a . . . a . . . someone . . . we're having a baby here . . . send up help . . . call an ambulance . . . call Vivian Ness . . . hurry!' He slammed the phone back into its cradle. Cora moaned softly from the bed and Bud fell to her side.

231

She looked up at him and saw that he was about to blubber. 'Don't worry, Buddy. It'll be okay. Everything will be all right.'

He blinked weakly. 'I'm supposed to tell *you* that, Mumser.'

Cora winced and closed her eyes. 'Tell me, then. I'm listening.'

So Bud stroked her hair and told her. He really, really did.

Lillian Bing Beaudrilleaux made her way into the world at three thirty-five p.m. the next afternoon, to the accompaniment of *Hearts and Minds*, which Cora had been watching between contractions. She had been unable to get the association of the name Esme with nasal noises out of her mind and had decided against it at the last minute, using it instead as a joke in a bad movie she and Bud rewrote. Also, her book of baby names said that Esme means 'esteemed,' and Cora thought that sounded like an attribute better suited to an eminent oral surgeon or a Supreme Court justice than to an adorable child of hers. Bud had lobbied hard for Bunny or Buena, the nearest feminine approximations to his own name that he could find. This was the closest he had come to being a father, and he found it difficult to resist attempting to have his involvement permanently recorded in some way. In a desperate moment, he even tried Budwina.

But in the end, Cora had settled on Lillian, which would be Lily for short – which was close to Billy, after her grandfather and her dearly departed William. Bud, to his satisfaction, was named a legal guardian, along with Joan. In the event that both Cora and Ray were crushed in an elevator or went down in their respective planes, Lily Bing would divide her time between Joan's great and formidable good graces and Bud's colorful depressions and hairy ears and all the various and sundried things they had to offer. That is, unless Viv got her great white way.

Bud and Vivian were at Cora's side for the birth. Grandpa Bill sat in the waiting room, playing solitaire with less than a full deck. Cora had wondered how long her stoicism would hold out – whether it would simply leave her, like a hat in a hurricane. She watched the numbers on the monitors, which reminded her of the indicators over the doors of elevators. In this case, she figured, she was both the elevator and the floor. The pain crawled in, the kid came out.

Events seemed to be taking place above her. She was given an epidural, and Viv rubbed her feet, for which Cora was grateful even though she couldn't feel a thing. She slid under all the urgency as smooth as glass, feeling as if she were holding up the ceiling with her passivity. Bump, bump, bump, she fell, the cushioned fall toward birth.

When Cora first saw Lily, she was convinced something was wrong with her. Her ears didn't seem quite right, and her feet – her toes! There were too many toes! She had been expecting something wrong – how could it be that the baby was all right? She counted again. Ten fingers, ten toes. The ears turned out to be situated in the right place. She wasn't going to be punished after all. At least not in this way, not now.

Ray arrived soon after Lily's birth, per their agreed-upon arrangement. He seemed to be doing well and Cora found herself vaguely glad to see him. She hoped their civility would persist long enough to get their child through her teens, and made a note to herself to watch the lawyer jokes around her.

Everyone seemed to be thriving – Bud had written a television miniseries shot entirely in Viv's hotel. It was a critical success, panned only in the *Village Voice*, and although the ratings were lower than might've been hoped, he had made a lot of money and the show had put Viv's hotel on the map. Even the scary costume ride had come off better than Cora expected – it was almost hip, she'd decided, although by that point she was deep into her pregnancy and undoubtedly hormonally imbalanced.

Her grandfather had a new friend, who lived in the mirror in the hotel bathroom. No matter how hard he tried, though, Bill couldn't make him talk. It seemed that he was incurably shy. On the second day of Lily's life, Bill gazed down at her as though trying to place her in his past life. Finally he looked up at Cora. 'Is this some kind of trick?' he asked suspiciously. Cora tilted her head to one side. 'Looks like the guy in your bathroom mirror, doesn't she?' Bill's face lit up. 'You know, I do believe she does,' he said, smiling broadly. 'She does at that.'

As for the baby – well, the baby was beautiful. She looked a lot like Viv, although Cora watched her nose carefully – she thought it was beginning to fashion itself more toward Ray's shape of feature with each passing day. Joan told her she was imagining things and suggested that she finish her thank-you notes before the baby came of age.

Cora found herself following her mother around with the baby, coveting her nearness. As long as her mother was pleasantly ranting, all was not lost – just temporarily misplaced. Cora got vomited on and cleaned up endless amounts of shit, as Viv had predicted, but she didn't mind half as much as she'd feared she might. True, the baby trespassed on her limited territory of trouble-free sleep. Sometimes Lily sobbed inconsolably, leaving Cora to kiss her and rock her and ask her in frustration, 'What's the matter? What can I get you?' like a waiter with a background in psychology and an over-developed instinct for consolation.

Lily talked and moved her hands in her sleep, prompting Bud to call her Little Hand Ballet. Every so often a smile would light up her features like something flying across the face of the moon – something so small that when it passed, you wondered if it had ever been there at all. Maybe it had been a floater. Lily would walk late, but she would talk a blue streak – this Viv had predicted. Cora would teach her the location of her fine hair, which straggled in slowly and golden. She would point out her nose and elbows and boobs and eyes and toes and hooter and teeth. The baby tide had come in, leaving her barren beach of a body strewn with one perfect baby shell. Cora put her ear to it and heard her whole life roar.

Dear Esme,

I looked up child *in the* Oxford English Dictionary *and here's what I found:* childie – *meaning dear little child, as in* 'You needn't be so decided, childie,' *said her father (E. Coxon, 1881). Also,* All her fleet of spirits came swelling in, With child of Sail *(Chapman, 1606). And* Is the parent better than the child into whom he has cast his ripened being? *(Emerson).*

See? Who says you can't study for the parent finals: three trimesters and boom – dilation/graduation and home. How the time does fly. Her Children gone, The Mother Nightingale laments *(Dryden).*

I also found out that Morandi didn't so much paint the spaces between objects – he made the

spaces more important than the objects themselves.
It was all just space – negative space and positive
space, the No more important than the Yes. By the
time I found that out, though, Morandi had come
to sound to me like a dance people used to do –
a festive fad dance, done wearing big sleeves and
fruit on your head. Wouldn't you have loved to
live in the time when they did the Morandi, their
laughter filling the positive space like a sky full of
birds, the negative space so far away that the No
of it just couldn't be heard.

Love,
Mother Nightingale

Acknowledgments

*F*or Boris Yeltsin, who took my late-night calls when no one else in Russia would even speak to me.

For Meryl, who is either a true and loyal friend or the best damned actress in the world. For Chana, who stuck fast to my slippery slopes. For Gavin, who restored my faith in the basic goodness of man but has since admitted that he was kidding. For Arnie, whose easygoing manner and searingly optimistic outlook have enabled me to achieve protracted moments of abandonment and optimism. For David, who patiently awaited and facilitated my return from a troublesome and tangled place.

For Harvey, a prince among queens, truly the finest person to spend a Sunday in Poland with and an unexpectedly limber dancer. For Michi, my semi-Semitic holiday brand of Victorian shut-in, who every so often reminds me of what I'd forgotten to know, almost exactly as though it had come to me by my very own self. For Penny, my traveling companion and perennial partner in party-throwing, who is either one of my oldest and dearest friends or I've seen too many 'Laverne & Shirley' reruns. For Buck, in the hope that he will return the nude photos with the bag on my head.

For my mother, coveted family member, and her slant, secret language of sane. For my grandma, Maxene, who figures in this book as a kind of memory, and in this life as a force without equal and an end to equanimity of any kind. For May, temporary reconstructor of my deposed cozy round. For Bob, who rolled out the iambic pentameter and attempted to stroll me off the rhyming plank into the rhythmic sea.

For Gloria Crayton, without whom I would be more like myself than any respectable person would be able to stand. For Abe Gurko, my dedicated executive writing assistant (whatever the fuck that means), who helped me through a difficult, seemingly endless period of writing, pelting me with pens and colas and faxes and the same old music one more time. For Gloria Carugati, Miss Billie's boon companion and curator of a full spectrum of Play-Doh, and Catalina. For Bruce – into the breach, my boy, with all but the watch (more later). For Angelo, for making me look better than I would come to feel in quite some time. For Nina, who gave me monster notes – monsters that kept making sense.

For my Uncle Bill, Billie's namesake along with our very own President's. For my brother, Todd, who runs the hotel, even when he appears to be walking. For my father, who saved up an empassioned fit of fatherhood for when it was most appreciated and required, and for his wife, Betty, for making the ultimate sacrifice and sending me Ronald Colman's special player piano.

For my evil twin, Kevin, my bargain and guardian agent and better sort of self, the Ionesco of intermediaries, and Doc, who means so much more to me than Little Switzerland (words fail me, but I have found a few solemn songs of the hunt). For Becky, my editor, who got an A on the Beverly Hills Water Torture Test. For Lester, for being a cheery sort of alarmist and giving me a few weeks before letting panic set in. For Michael, for keeping me legal and for treating me as if I were normal when it wasn't generally considered precise or even hip to do so. For Mort, who saved the deal without making a Big Deal of it. For Little Nancy

Girl (for short), our fleet-fingered frolicking friend –
and a Mormon to boot. And, even, oddly, for Bryan –
for beginning the quick-crochet that became what we
know as Billie Catherine.

For the varied throng of physicians who tend to our
myriad, much-made-of needs: Dr. Beatriz Foster, Dr.
Eva Presslar, Dr. Neil Haas, and Dr. Joel Lebowitz
– you all know who you are, and at some point will
remind me exactly what it is that you do.

For Judy and Freddie, for populating Billie's week-
ends with Skee-Ball, reindeer, and loud kitty noises.
For Charlie and both Jims and Toni and even Peter,
who were greater than the sum of my parts and vice
versa. For Patti and Ruby, my fugitives from fire,
Ed, Mike N., John C., Connie, Romanelli, Charles
Bennett, Michael Lucas, Maria, Meg R., Tim Flack,
Paula, Chaik, Melissa, Mary, Bea, Mike and Bryn,
Robin and Marsha, Vincent, Hannah and Griffin, Bob
and Anjelìca, Freilino, Ted Pugh, Rose, the Scotts, the
Idles, Christie, Sandy, Barry, Demi and brood, Rino, the
Ostins, the maxi and mini Malles, the multi-Lucases,
the multi-multi-Spielbergs, the Fords, Betty B., Barbara,
Beverly, Jean Lo, my Dreyfuss, Laurence Fishburn,
Nora, Dan M., Linda M., Dani J., Alain, Shirley,
Mr. Nicholson, William S., Carolyn Reidy, J. D., La
Seldes, Meg W., and Leslee.

Scribner

The Best Awful

Carrie Fisher

Born into privilege and Hollywood royalty, Carrie
Fisher has been a movie star, a bestselling author,
and one of the hottest script doctors in Hollywood.
Her tumultuous life has been fodder for her
hilarious and often scathing novels: in POSTCARDS
FROM THE EDGE she turned her gimlet eye to
drug addiction and rehab, SURRENDER THE PINK
examined modern romance, and DELUSIONS OF
GRANDMA explored the rocky terrain of pregnancy
and motherhood.

In her latest book, Carrie moves into the territory
occupied by Sylvia Plath and Susanna Kaysen in
a darkly funny portrait of a woman who survives
a psychotic breakdown, a stay in 'the bin', and
survives to tell all.

ISBN 0-7434-7857-6
£6.99

**POCKET
BOOKS**

Little Earthquakes

Jennifer Weiner

This is the story of what comes after 'happily ever
after' as three young wives make the journey into
motherhood, and discover how it changes their sense
of themselves and their relationships with friends
and family.

There's Becky, a plump, sexy chef, with an
overworked husband, an adorable baby girl . . .
and the mother-in-law from hell. There's Kelly, an
over-worked event planner who charts her baby's
every move on a spreadsheet while hoping that her
husband will pull his life together, pull on some pants,
and find a job. And there's Ayinde, who is married to
Philadelphia's most prominent basketball star, until the
combination of new baby and infidelity threatens their
marriage.

By turns moving, funny, and inspiring, LITTLE
EARTHQUAKES is a great big delicious read from a
prodigiously talented author.

ISBN 0-7434-6893-7
£6.99

POCKET
BOOKS

Good in Bed

Jennifer Weiner

Cannie Shapiro never wanted to be famous. The
smart, sharp, plus-sized reporter was perfectly happy
writing about other people's lives for her local
newspaper. And for the past twenty-eight years,
things have been tripping along nicely for Cannie.
Sure, her mother has come charging out of the
closet, and her father has long since dropped out
of her world. But she loves her job, her friends, her
dog and her life. She loves her apartment and her
commodious, quilt-lined bed. She has made a tenuous
peace with her body and she even felt okay about
ending her relationship with her boyfriend Bruce. But
now this . . .

'Loving a larger woman is an act of courage in our
world,' Bruce has written in a national woman's
magazine. And Cannie – who never knew that Bruce
saw her as a larger woman, or thought that loving her
was an act of courage – is plunged into misery, and
the most amazing year of her life.

ISBN 0-7434-1528-0
£6.99

**POCKET
BOOKS**

The Dog Walker

Leslie Schnur

Refreshing and insightful, rich with humour
and brimming with life, this is the story of Nina
Shepard, dog walker extraordinaire. With the
keys to many strangers' apartments, Nina has the
access, the freedom, and the choice to cross a moral
boundary, and several foyers, and enter into other
people's lives.

And so she falls in love with Daniel, a man she
has never met but whom she thinks she knows
from snooping in his apartment when she picks up
his dog for walks. But both Nina and Daniel are
imposters, pretending to be what they are not. By
the time they learn who the other really is, after
mishaps and mistaken identities, deception and lost
dogs, it's too late. They've learned too much about
themselves and will never be the same again.

ISBN 0-7434-8950-0
£6.99

S c r i b n e r

This book and other Simon & Schuster titles are available from your bookshop or can be ordered direct from the publisher.

0 7434 7857 6	The Best Awful/Carrie Fisher	£6.99
0 7434 6893 7	Little Earthquakes/Jennifer Weiner	£6.99
0 7434 1528 0	Good in Bed/Jennifer Weiner	£6.99
0 7434 8950 0	The Dog Walker/Leslie Schnur	£6.99

Please send cheque or postal order for the value of the book, free postage and packing within the UK; OVERSEAS including Republic of Ireland £1 per book.

OR: Please debit this amount from my
VISA/ACCESS/MASTERCARD ....
CARD NO: ....
EXPIRY DATE ....
AMOUNT£...
NAME...
ADDRESS...
....
SIGNATURE ....

Send orders to: SIMON & SCHUSTER CASH SALES
PO Box 29, Douglas, Isle of Man, IM99 1BQ
Tel: 01624 836000, Fax: 01624 670923
www.bookpost.co.uk
Please allow 14 days for delivery. Prices and availability
subject to change without notice.